Running Back

by

JJ Greene

Bella
BOOKS

2014

Bella Books, Inc.
P.O. Box 10543
Tallahassee, FL 32302

Printed in the United States of America on acid-free paper.

First Bella Books Edition 2014

Editor: Cath Walker and Katherine V. Forrest
Cover Designer: Judith Fellows

ISBN: 978-1-59493-418-6

Other Bella Books by JJ Greene

First Down

Acknowledgments

Writing a novel was always somewhat of a crazy dream of mine. To be now releasing my second is a bit unbelievable. It's not a solitary task, and as such, I'd like to give a few quick shout outs: Thanks to my friends and first readers, Little Mel and Roomie. Thanks to Cami, for crafting the awesome little cartoon me in my bio. Thanks to my younger brother, Mike, for writing my bio. Thanks to all my crazy friends and family, for keeping life interesting. And finally, thanks to you, my readers, for making this dream possible.

About the Author

JJ Greene is an up and coming author as well as an enthusiastic Notre Dame Alumna and Fighting Irish football fan. Her debut novel *First Down* not only demonstrates her passions for sport, mystery and romance, but also is nominated for a Goldie Award for lesbian fiction by the Golden Crown Literary Society. As the second child of five, JJ mastered her craft as a storyteller by regaling her siblings with rich and memorable narratives. In addition to watching football, JJ engages in the active community of vibrant Boulder, Colorado.

CHAPTER ONE

"I can't believe you're really leaving all the glamour of the city to settle down in some boondock farm town!"

Both hands on the wheel of her beat-up Honda Civic as she talked over the Bluetooth connection, Kaya rolled her eyes at her best friend's whining. She knew the real reason Toni complained so much about her move was because she would miss her. She would certainly miss Toni just as much.

"For the thousandth time, I'm not even going that far away. And you know what the city did to me. You got the glamour, I got the grime." She couldn't suppress the sigh that escaped her lips, though even she wasn't sure if it was a sigh of relief at finally leaving or something else entirely.

"Oh please, my life is hardly glamourous," Toni scoffed.

Kaya chuckled. "Then stop using that to convince me to reconsider."

The line went silent for a few moments as she wound her way through the cornfields of western Indiana. "I'm less than a four-hour drive from you. You know I won't be able to keep away from the city entirely. I've always been a city girl. I just couldn't handle my job there anymore." *I couldn't handle my life there anymore.*

Toni sighed. "I know. I know you need this. But can you blame a girl for trying? You had better at least come back for a couple of Bears games this fall."

"Okay, now you're just driving me further away!" She actually enjoyed the games that Toni often treated her to, but not so much that she'd ever admit it to her friend. It was more fun to pretend she wasn't interested. "I guess someone needs to be there to save Rynn from your obsession, though."

"I am not obsessed! I'm just very dedicated." Toni's feigned indignation made Kaya smile. She stole a quick glance at the GPS on her dash, knowing that her turn was coming up soon.

"Like I said, someone needs to save Rynn. Anyway, hon, I've got to go. You know how easy it is to get lost in these…what did you call them? Boondock farm towns?"

"Indeed. You'll disappear into a cow pasture and no one will ever hear from you again."

"I think the greater threat in these parts is the fiendish corn. Or, maybe I'll get lured to certain doom by a crop circle. I'll let you know how things are once I get settled into my new place."

"Don't die."

Kaya laughed. "Rural living is hardly fatal. But I thank you for your concern. I'll miss you, too."

"Yeah, yeah. Take care of yourself, Hotshot. Love and hugs."

Kaya said her goodbyes and ended the call just in time to pass the faded *Welcome* sign to the right of the narrow country road. Despite her brave claims to Toni, Kaya was more than a little apprehensive about leaving the city for such a drastic change. Even though she knew this was home to more than forty-five thousand people, it still felt like a completely different world from the South Side of Chicago that she'd called home for the past ten years.

But that's exactly why I'm here. Isn't it?

* * *

Ricki slowed her pace to a jog as she rounded the track for her last lap. Despite the heat of the August days, the predawn air was still cool and comfortable. She loved these morning runs, some of the most peaceful moments of her day. Teaching and coaching high school were anything but peaceful, but she enjoyed her place in life.

The gridiron. She stopped at the west end zone of the field and worked through her stretches. A new school year. She usually felt a bit wistful about it. Her sanctuary had always been a football field. This football field.

She took a deep breath and watched the sun rise through the uprights. The golden rays cut through the orange haze and illuminated her haven. Light mirrored off the aluminum benches, adding a sparkling frame to the picture.

Ricki was ready for a new day. A new year. The football staff was meeting soon to continue their preparation for the coming season. Likewise, the faculty would complete their in-service today before welcoming the students back tomorrow. Time to get started.

She took one more look at the glorious sunrise before her and turned to the locker room. Just enough time for a shower.

CHAPTER TWO

Kaya took a deep breath and resisted the urge to drum her fingers on the pale green surface of the cafeteria table in front of her. Even though she knew it was silly, she had to admit she was anxious. First day of school jitters, just like when she was a new student, starting at another new school. She wasn't the student this time, but that didn't do much to calm her nerves.

Today was the in-service, when she would officially be introduced to her new colleagues and truly become a member of the faculty. That introduction should only last a moment or two, until topics turned to the other issues of the impending school year, but she would be happy when it was over nonetheless. In fact, she wasn't sure which first impression was more vital, meeting her co-workers or her students.

She looked up as a cluster of people entered the room, chatting happily. When they noticed her, though, the chatter quieted. Two of the women offered polite smiles, but they all proceeded to a different table without a word.

Definitely the co-workers. Students, I know how to handle. Co-workers, on the other hand... Polite but not friendly. Kaya couldn't help but wonder if the teachers here had some sort of social hierarchy that she would have to break into. God, she hoped not, but she couldn't deny her fear that this was an indication of what small-town life would be like.

The cafeteria was slowly filling up as teachers drifted in, usually in small groups. Eventually, a few settled themselves at Kaya's table, but after simple hellos and introductions, they resumed their conversations. Kaya tried to join in, but she was clearly an outsider.

She turned at the sound of raucous laughter behind her. Two more people walked in, apparently having just gotten to the punchline. The man tossed an arm over the shoulders of the woman beside him and they paused to peruse the room for available seats.

The woman's gaze passed over to the near side of the cafeteria and, for just a second, locked with Kaya's. *Damn.* Kaya had never seen eyes that crystalline, that ice blue. She felt her breath catch involuntarily as the newcomer's laughter shifted ever so slightly into a cocky grin.

"Ricky! Jamie!" Someone shouted from across the room, and the woman turned and nodded to the source of the call. Kaya watched the woman as she worked her way over and sat at one of the more boisterous tables.

Despite knowing her body's reaction was absolutely ridiculous, Kaya couldn't stop her sudden pulse pounding. She didn't normally respond this way to a pretty face. *More than pretty.* Despite herself, Kaya found she was no longer so worried about the new school year before her.

* * *

Ricki glanced back at the stranger sitting across the room as she and Jamie took their seats next to Ian and Mike. She would find out soon enough who she was, and in the meantime, Ricki went on with her normal routine. But still, there was something about the look in the other woman's beautiful hazel eyes.

"Isn't that right, Ricki?" She was jolted back to the conversation by Ian's question.

"I, uh...sorry, what was that?"

Ian just rolled his eyes. "I was telling them about your little stunt with Keenan yesterday at practice. Taught that boy a lesson, didn't you?"

"Oh," she chuckled. "I guess so."

Her fellow coach continued to regale the others with the story of how she had outrun one of hotheaded boys on the team yesterday. Ricki just sighed as she listened. Leave it to the men to miss the lesson she'd really tried to show Keenan yesterday. Humility in sports was not something that was easy to find.

Before Ian could finish his recap, Mr. Fisher walked in and cleared his throat, quietly demanding their attention. He was a short man who spoke softly even to the large room of assembled faculty. His head was topped with a shock of thick, pure white hair, and Ricki thought it looked like he'd gained weight over the summer. Her attention soon drifted, though, as the principal went through all the standard points to start a new school year. She didn't realize she'd been staring across the room until Jamie nudged her and whispered, "New teacher caught your eye?"

Ricki quickly turned away, shooting Jamie a scathing glance before turning her attention back to Mr. Fisher. Internally, she denied that had been where her mind had wandered. She had just been daydreaming, that's all. Then, Mr. Fisher finally said something that caught her attention. "And now, before we break out into our departmental meetings, it is my pleasure to introduce to you our three new faculty members this year. Ladies, if you would join me here?"

Three women, all seated near the front of the cafeteria, rose and walked up to stand near Mr. Fisher. With some surprise, Ricki realized she hadn't even noticed the other two who now stood between the principal and the one who had caught Ricki's eye when she had first entered the room.

The faculty's attention held on their three new members. While Mr. Fisher introduced them each in turn, Ricki allowed herself to study the last in line. She didn't quite look like her companions, or many of the other teachers in the room for that matter. Her loose, pale blue blouse and dark navy slacks were just a cut above the typical attire. The clothing accentuated her curves, but in a subtle way that didn't take away from her appearance of calm, cool confidence.

"Lastly, we have Miss Kaya Walsh, our new physics teacher. Miss Walsh hails from Chicago, where she spent the past few years working in one of the South Side public schools."

As they had done with the other new teachers, everyone studied Miss Walsh while her background was briefly outlined. Then, to Ricki's surprise, Kaya's eyes met her own. The slightest smile graced her lips, and suddenly Ricki needed to look away. Unexpectedly short of air, she took a deep breath before glancing back up as Mr. Fisher finished his introductions. It appeared Kaya's attention was now on the principal, where Ricki knew hers should be as well.

"Let's show these wonderful women a nice, warm, Glenwood High welcome!"

Ricki joined in the friendly applause, wondering at the unfamiliar feeling running through her.

CHAPTER THREE

As always, the first week of school flew by. On Wednesday the following week, Kaya prepared for one of her first challenges as a new teacher in a school—announcing the first test. She wrapped up the lesson two minutes before the bell would signal the end of class and grinned at the eager eyes looking up at her. Well, perhaps not all so eager as she might have hoped, but not bad for a high school classroom.

"This wraps up chapters one and two. So who wants to hazard a guess as to what that means?"

"We movin' to chapter seven?"

Kaya smiled at the smartass student in the back of the room, now bumping fists with his buddy. She appreciated students with a sense of humor and encouraged them to participate. That didn't mean they got a free pass.

"*We're*. And close. But now the class can thank you for an extra question on the test Friday."

As expected, the room filled with groans. Among the complaints, a girl's voice rang out. "But Miss Walsh, it's only the second week of school! You can't give us a test already!"

She walked across the room toward the student but only responded with a smile and a shrug. Another boy whined, "You're already killing us moving this fast! Two chapters in a week? Can't we at least push the test back to Monday?"

She chuckled and shook her head, "You know as well as I do that this has all been review. You're all ready for the test, and then we can really dive in on new material."

The smartass from the back piped up again. "But Miss Walsh, we got a game Friday night, and coach has us practicing extra on Thursday. When we supposed to study?" A few other boys scattered along the back nodded their agreement.

Kaya sighed. It hadn't taken her long to realize that football reigned supreme at this school. She didn't really mind, having spent years dealing with Toni's fondness for the game, but priorities had to be established. "Study after practice. I'm sure your coaches understand that you have schoolwork."

"But Teach! Coach says we gotta focus on what important!"

Obviously not grammar. Kaya suppressed another sigh. "We are, Mr. Keenan." The boy next to him opened his mouth to protest further. "But Coach said—"

She cut him off. "What qualifies your coach to determine what is important?"

At this, both boys seemed confused for a moment. Then Keenan simply stated, "Coach knows."

Kaya had started to walk back to the front of the room, ready to end the debate, but turned at the tone in his voice. He had that typical teenage smirk that basically said "Well, duh," but that hadn't been all she had heard. There was something else, something bordering on reverence in the way he'd last spoken.

"Knows what, Mr. Keenan?" she asked, genuinely interested in his response.

"Coach knows what it's like to win." When Kaya said nothing, he went on. "Surely you heard of Coach McGlinn. Ricky McGlinn, *the* running back, y'all?" He slipped into an imitation of some kind, but Kaya couldn't place the reference. Suddenly very serious, Keenan continued his explanation. "Ricky McGlinn is the best running back in school history! Led Glenwood to a *state title*, like, a long time ago. The only state title we ever had. I know you're new and all, but don't you know anything about us?" Murmurs of assent filled the room.

Kaya was surprised that his words stung a bit. *Us?* An "us" that she was clearly not part of. She glanced around the classroom, aware that the students were all watching this exchange, waiting for her response. "You're right, Mr. Keenan, I am new. As such I'm still learning." She looked around the room again, now addressing all the students. "Tell you what, you help me learn the ropes at my new home here at Glenwood, and I will come cheer you guys on this Friday."

She saw a few smiles of approval. Students often respected teachers who cared about them beyond the classroom doors. Keenan, however, looked at her skeptically. "Does this mean no test?"

She laughed. "Nice try, but the test is still on." The bell announcing the end of their class was almost drowned out by the groans. "Bring your questions and we'll review tomorrow," Kaya shouted her last instruction to the class as they shuffled toward the door.

* * *

"Yo, Ricki!"

She turned from her computer screen and waved her greeting to the tall, lanky man who approached. He spun a chair around to straddle the back and slumped down into it, leaning his arms against the worn wood. "Have you had a chance to watch that film on the Rangers for this week?"

She nodded, pointing to a spreadsheet on the screen. "Sure, Ian, I've got everything broken down. We're ready for them."

Ian looked over her shoulder, and she could feel his bulk looming over her. He was the classic high school football coach: tall, broad, perhaps a little overly muscular. His slightly balding blond hair betrayed his age, but he still retained the energy of a young athlete. He said, "Why do I get the feeling that's not really why you're in here?"

She rolled her eyes. "Because you know me too well. I did break down the film, but you know I've got other things going on right now. I spent way too much effort writing grant proposals and petitioning for this new system to not have it up and running as fast as possible."

Ian looked at her as if she'd grown a third eye. "During football season? Come on, Ricki, can't this stuff wait till the spring?"

She just looked at him blankly for a moment, before turning back to her computer without even dignifying him with a response.

He sighed, apparently recognizing he'd just put himself in the doghouse.

"Oh, Ricki, you know I don't mean it. Hell, if you concentrated this much on football, I'd be out of my job as the head coach. Maybe I should be grateful you get so into this computer crap."

She turned back to him, trying to summon patience. She did know he didn't mean it, even if sometimes *he* seemed to forget that. He heckled her for her passion as a math teacher, but she threw it right back at him for "only" being a coach and phys ed guy. Ian was a good man, and despite his tough jock attitude, she knew he respected academics. He always backed her up, demanding the best from their boys both on the field and in the classroom. She also knew his flattery was just that. She had no desire to be head coach, and they were both happy with the staff they had. "Anything else I can help you with, Ian?"

He rose from his chair, knowing he'd just been dismissed. "Naw. I'll see you later on the practice field."

Ricki's full attention was back on her computer before he'd even left the room.

CHAPTER FOUR

"Excuse me." Kaya waited a long moment for the secretary to look up. "Hi—" she glanced at the nameplate in front of her, "Trish. I'm just wondering if you can tell me where I might find the football offices. I'm looking for Coach McGlinn."

The woman popped her gum in response, studying Kaya as if the new teacher were from Mars. She might be a bit lost in this school, but still, she didn't really appreciate the patronizing look. "Football offices are downstairs by the locker rooms." The secretary paused, twirling her blond hair and looking as if she expected Kaya to need her to draw a map. Not interested in that type of assistance, Kaya said her thanks and started to leave the front office. "But you'd probably do better looking in the math lab. Coach McGlinn tends to hang out over there instead."

Kaya turned back. "The math lab?"

Pop. "Yeah, it's over—"

"By the physics department. I know," Kaya interrupted. "I was just a little surprised to hear the football coach would be there."

Pop. "Yeah, that one's almost always in the math lab, unless they're all over on the football field."

Again, Kaya nodded her thanks and headed toward the door. She'd been thinking about the episode in her junior physics class all afternoon. Keenan had made a good point that she needed to be more engaged in the school, but that didn't mean she was going to let a football coach skew her students' priorities. She'd seen that type of coach before, laughing at the real purpose of school and thinking academics were merely background noise to distract from sports. She might be new around here, but she was not going to be a pushover. The boys clearly respected their coach, and she would have to make it clear to all of them that football would not affect the expectations in her classroom.

She walked down the faded speckled tiles toward the math and sciences wing, which had recently become her home. The mathematics lab was only two doors down from her own classroom, but she hadn't been in there beyond the brief tour given to her as a new faculty member. Apparently the school had just updated many of the computers and had big plans for the facility as a result of a significant state grant.

Kaya knocked at the half-closed door as she crossed the threshold, alerting the figure seated across the room. When that person turned, Kaya was startled to come face-to-face with the gorgeous teacher who had caught her eye that first day. Just as it had then, her heart was suddenly racing. She hadn't seen tall, dark and handsome since that staff meeting, but then the past ten days had been hectic.

For a moment, it felt as if she were locked in a trance with this stranger, but then the woman spoke. "Hello. Can I help you with something?"

Kaya started, having temporarily forgotten why she'd come to the math lab. "Oh, yes." She glanced around and realized that there was no one else in the room. "Actually, maybe not. I was looking for Richard McGlinn and was told I might find him here."

She was surprised to be met with laughter. Not wanting to be the butt of some unknown joke, Kaya had to tamp down the impulse to take offense.

"I'm not laughing at you," the woman stated. "It's just, you won't find a Richard McGlinn in this school. Or this town, that I know of."

Confused by this contradictory information, Kaya wondered for a moment if she was being made fun of. Unsure of herself in a way she hadn't been in quite some time, she simply turned to leave.

"Wait!" The woman was laughing again. "There's no Richard, but I might be able to help you out anyway."

Kaya regarded the other woman warily when she rose from her computer station and crossed the room. Holding out a hand, she grinned, the same cocky grin Kaya had seen the first time their eyes met. "Allow me to introduce myself. Ricki McGlinn, math teacher extraordinaire. At your service."

What? This is Ricky McGlinn? But not Ricky...Ricki. She'd been looking for a football coach, probably gruff and grizzled. Not a laughing, toned, stunning...*Woah, stunning? Slow down there, Hotshot.* She simply wasn't looking for a woman, regardless of that woman's attributes.

Kaya shook Ricki's hand, studying her, breathing in a scent of fresh-cut grass and autumn leaves.

"Confused? It's okay. You'll get used to me. What can I do for you?"

Ricki released her hand and gestured to a couple of computer chairs. Kaya was still trying to process it all and was thrown off further by the odd feeling of her hand being strangely cold, as if she'd just taken off her favorite mitten on a winter's night. She watched as Ricki pulled one of the chairs around, threw her leg over the seat to straddle the chair back and looked up at her with an expectant expression.

Kaya shook herself back to reality. *Okay, so Ricki McGlinn is not who I anticipated. Doesn't change why I came here.* She took the seat next to Ricki and introduced herself. She was still having a hard time gelling this woman with the image of a football coach, let alone a player. Maybe she was missing something. She studied Ricki again, still skeptical. "You're the football coach?"

Ricki nodded. Then she elaborated. "Not the head coach. Just running backs, receivers and general team agility. But yes, I'm a football coach."

Kaya shook her head. It was silly, but she'd psyched herself up to stare down a brute of a man. The mental transition was taking her longer than she might have expected. "Okay then, Coach. I'm afraid I have a concern to raise with you. I've got a few of your players in my junior physics class, and they seem to be under the impression that football is more important than their classwork."

Kaya paused, trying to read the coach's response. Where she expected an aggressive defense or denial, or even the "well, duh" look young Keenan had given her, she was met merely with narrowed eyes and a studying expression.

Kaya went on. "Coach, I'm new here. I don't know how things normally run, but I'm here to teach. Academics are my priority, and that isn't going to change for your football players. They've got a test Friday, and it won't be rescheduled for the benefit of extracurriculars."

Still, Ricki remained silent, and Kaya felt her pulse quicken out of rising anger, any trace of attraction forgotten. Ricki wasn't ignoring her, but merely listening wasn't good enough. Kaya would be taken seriously. Kaya spoke through gritted teeth. "Your thoughts, Coach?"

"Which students?"

Kaya leaned back in her chair. Once again, Ricki was not what she expected, and she wasn't even sure how to read the coach's terse response. She named Keenan and the two other football players who'd been so resistant in her class.

Ricki simply nodded.

"Thanks for bringing this to my attention. I'll look into it." With that, she turned back to her computer.

Kaya was stunned at having been so blatantly dismissed. Her anger flared again, but she realized Ricki hadn't really given her anything to complain about. She hadn't denied or resisted the accusation. She'd said she would look into it. Wasn't that all that

Kaya could ask for? She rose from her chair and left without another word.

* * *

"Keenan, Stanford, Dillon! Over here!" Ricki called to the boys as the rest of the team circled up to finish their cooldown stretches after practice. She'd been surprised when that new teacher had shown up questioning her academic integrity. Had it not been obvious in a dozen different ways that Kaya was new in town, that alone would have told Ricki. Well, the only way to make someone see who you really were was to show them. She would not insult Kaya with platitudes or promises of reform. Especially when no reform was required.

"Yes, Coach?" The three jogged quickly over and stood at attention in front of her.

"How are classes going so far?"

Stanford shot a confused glance at Dillon, then Keenan answered for all of them. "Just fine, Coach. Why?"

"I understand you have a physics test on Friday." Ricki watched as they exchanged looks of surprise and just a little bit of guilt. "Yes, Coach."

Ricki studied them for a moment. They knew her policy, and she suspected they knew what was coming. "Dillon, what are you?"

Josh Dillon looked at her blankly. "A football player?"

Ricki sighed. "Is that an answer or a question, Dillon?"

The boy cleared his throat and answered with more conviction. "I'm a football player, Coach!"

"Yes, but that's not all. What else are you?" This time, Dillon had no answer and his brow furrowed uncertainly.

She turned to the next one. "Stanford, what are you?"

Stanford merely shrugged. If he knew what she was looking for, he wasn't going to say it. Instead, Keenan spoke up. "We're student-athletes, Coach."

Ricki nodded. "That's right. Student-athletes. And what part of that comes first?"

All three of the players stared at their feet and muttered, "Student."

Ricki waited a moment for the boys to raise their eyes to her again. She had no intention of humiliating them, but she would get her message across. "Do you mind explaining to me, then, why Miss Walsh was under the impression that we do things any differently on this team?"

At this, Keenan caught a spark of indignation. "She's giving us a test on Friday! It's only the second week of school and she don't even care we got a game that night!"

"Grammar, Keenan. She *doesn't* care. And I don't expect her to. You know school comes first on this team. I expect all three of you to score nothing less than an A on that test."

At their shocked protests, she silenced them with a simple look. "Go home and study tonight. If you're having trouble with the concepts, come to my office an hour before practice tomorrow and we'll review together." They grumbled a bit more before Ricki continued, "And I want you to apologize to Miss Walsh for disrupting her class today."

"But Coach!"

"No 'buts,' Keenan. If you want to be a leader on this team, you better learn to be a leader off the field as well. If you screw up, you apologize. If you can't do that, then you can't play for me."

Keenan's jaw worked and Ricki could see that he was torn between respecting his coach and asserting his independence. After a moment, his gaze dropped again. "Yes, Coach."

Ricki nudged his chin, silently commanding him to keep his head up. She gave them all a stern look, making her expectations clear. They nodded their understanding and headed off to join their teammates.

"Oh, and boys?" They paused. "If I ever hear of you pulling that stunt again, especially with a new teacher, you'll be running sprints till your legs fall off."

They looked at each other, knowing full well that Ricki meant it, and escaped as quickly as they could to the locker room.

CHAPTER FIVE

Kaya stared somewhat absently over her class as they took their test. Despite their protestations, she expected them all to do well on what was just a review test. Thinking back to the events of Wednesday, Kaya found herself again frustrated from her encounter with the coach of few words.

No. I'm not going there. I don't care. She did care about her students, and she didn't know if Ricki had taken her concerns seriously or blown her off.

The students scribbled busily on their papers, a few glancing nervously at the clock while they worked. As time wound down, they drifted forward and tossed their tests on Kaya's desk. The bell sounded and Kaya started browsing through the papers as they shuffled out of the classroom. At a small cough in front of her, she looked up to find Keenan standing there, flanked by Dillon and Stanford.

"Yes?"

Keenan cleared his throat as if he were preparing a speech. "Miss Walsh, we just wanted to apologize for disrupting class and whining about the test the other day."

Kaya carefully kept her surprise from showing on her face, instead nodding to the obviously unhappy boys itching to get out of her classroom. "I appreciate that, gentlemen."

Keenan nodded, and either Dillon or Stanford grunted their agreement, before the boys hurried out to the hallway.

Kaya doubted that they acted of their own accord, which meant that Ricki was behind their apology. Kaya smiled. Apparently Ricki had been listening. Then the smile faded as it occurred to her that she'd really made a fool of herself, basically accusing Ricki of being a dumb jock.

Good job, Hotshot.

* * *

Ricki walked back out onto the field late Friday night, wanting to breathe in the thrill of the game one more time before heading home. She loved football season, and starting the year off with a solid victory against their crosstown rival had everyone in a good mood. The players and other coaches had packed up and headed home, but, as was her habit, Ricki lingered on the deserted field.

She drifted out onto the turf, still lit by the massive stadium lights. The area had a completely different feel now, less than an hour removed from the game. A familiar peace settled on Ricki's soul. She closed her eyes, giving her other senses the freedom to absorb her surroundings. The smell of the grass and the quiet of the night calmed her in a way little else ever had.

Ricki was pulled from her reverie by the sound of footsteps approaching on the track behind her. Ricki drew a deep, regretful breath before turning to meet her guest.

"Hello." Kaya smiled shyly from the edge of the track some twenty feet away. "I hope I'm not disturbing you."

Ricki shook her head and greeted Kaya with a smile. She'd wondered when she might hear from the fiery new teacher again. She walked over to her, silently saying goodnight to her sanctuary on the field and leaned on the chain-link fence between them.

Kaya drew a breath and spoke. "Congratulations, first of all. I understand tonight's win was a pretty big one."

Ricki met her studying look. "Thanks."

Kaya nodded, and a comfortable quiet fell between them. Then Kaya sighed. "I also wanted to apologize to you."

Ricki hadn't expected an apology, but then, she wasn't exactly surprised either.

Kaya chewed her lip for a moment, evidently accepting that a smile would be Ricki's only reply. "I jumped to conclusions before I'd even met you, and that was foolish of me. I appreciate you talking to your boys. They stayed after class to say sorry for the other day. I'm guessing that wasn't their idea."

Ricki nodded. "I'm glad to hear they did the right thing."

Kaya smiled. Ricki realized that she probably could have made this easier for her by shrugging it off or saying not to worry about it. Perhaps she'd been mentoring high school kids for too long because she felt content to let Kaya own her actions. She had more respect for a person who could look her in the eye and admit a mistake.

They lingered a moment longer and Ricki wondered if there was something else. She turned and started to drift toward the gate. Kaya matched her stride on the other side of the fence. Then she stopped abruptly and asked, "Can I make it up to you with a drink? I don't really know where the popular hangouts are around here, but I'd appreciate it if you could show me."

Ricki looked at her, surprised by the offer. Then she realized how much she wanted to say yes, and just what a dangerous impulse that could be.

At her hesitation, Kaya quickly backtracked. "I mean, if you have to get going, I completely understand. I know you've had a busy day."

Ricki shook her head and followed her gut. "No, it'd be my pleasure. I don't know where the popular hangouts are, either, but the Alumni Grill is one of my personal favorites."

CHAPTER SIX

The next day, Kaya smiled at the name that popped up on her caller ID for the incoming call, and answered.

"You left me three weeks ago and I don't hear a single word? I was beginning to think you'd been swallowed by the *Children of the Corn*."

Kaya sighed and stretched her legs out along the sofa. "Toni, you know that's Nebraska, not Indiana."

"Close enough. My point remains. I suppose you've been too busy to call your best friend?

Kaya rolled her eyes. "Actually, things really have been hectic here, but I'm sure if I try to tell you that, you'll just trump me with tales of NFL insanity."

Toni laughed. "Well, my life doesn't seem to afford me any dull days. I'm not calling to talk about my life, though. Tell me what's going on. How are you?"

Kaya filled her in on the events of the past few weeks. It always amazed Kaya that Toni really cared about her humble life as a teacher. Even through all the drama of her Teach For

America years and extended stay in South Side Chicago Public Schools, Toni had been her pressure valve, keeping her sane through the craziness of everyday life.

"You sound good, hon. I'm glad to hear things there are going a bit better than here. Even though I miss having you around," Toni said.

Kaya sighed. "Thanks. Any chance you'll be down in this neck of the woods for a Colts game this season?"

"It's possible. I did pick up another player in Indianapolis this offseason, so a weekend trip may be merited. And I think Rynn might appreciate a road trip. I won't have access to all the luxuries that you enjoy up here at Soldier Field, though."

As a sports agent with clients throughout the NFL, Toni often provided a view into professional football that Kaya knew she'd never have seen otherwise.

"Toni, you know I'm more interested in hanging with you than I am in your fancy box seats. I'm not above using you for tickets, though. Think you could swing a four-pack?"

"Four? Will you be bringing a date?"

At the hint of curiosity in Toni's voice, Kaya knew she'd made a mistake. Now that she'd opened the door, Toni would not let her get away without spilling details. The problem was, there really weren't any details to spill. Kaya couldn't deny that Ricki had been on her mind all weekend, and she was sure Ricki would love going to a football game.

Her mind flashed back to their Friday night together. It had taken some prodding, but after a while Kaya had gotten Ricki to talk a bit more. Just a bit, though. Despite her efforts, Ricki had still managed to keep most of the conversation focused on Kaya. The best part was that Kaya's anecdotes had made Ricki laugh several times.

"Hello? Kaya?"

"Yeah?"

"Where did you go? I asked if you've met someone and you completely checked out." Kaya didn't realize she'd stopped listening.

"Nowhere. I'm right here. Just got distracted for a moment."

"I should say so. Now, who is she? Details!"

Kaya settled back a little deeper into the couch and tried to gather her thoughts. "That's just it, Toni. There are no details. This woman is an enigma."

"Sounds interesting, but let's start with a name."

"Interesting doesn't begin to describe Ricki. I haven't felt this way about anyone in…well, I don't even know how I feel. I can't read her—she keeps everything under lock and key. I don't think she's straight, but I don't know if that's wishful thinking or reality. Normally I can tell if my attraction is mutual, but with her? I don't know. Toni, I think I might be losing my touch."

Toni chuckled. "I don't think so. Could be your touch is just experiencing something new."

Kaya ran her fingers through her hair, frustrated and yet not unhappy. "Is this what you felt like when you first met Rynn?"

The line was quiet for a moment. "Well, well. Kaya, I never thought I'd see the day. Are you ready for your first U-Haul?"

Kaya hid her face in her hand. "You caught me. And after I book the truck, I'm going to start looking at wedding invitations." Now that Toni had pointed it out, she felt completely ridiculous. She'd been acting like one of the love-struck teenagers who pined and waxed poetic during her classes. *Good God. What is wrong with me?* Kaya hadn't felt this off balance in years. Perhaps not since high school and her first major crush on Jada Morissey.

Toni's laughter faded on the line. "In all seriousness though, are you okay, Kaya? I've never heard you like this."

Kaya sighed. "Of course. I'm fine. You're right. This is silly, really. I've only just met her. We went out for drinks once and it's driving me up the wall that I can't read her. I guess I just need to go for a second date. Or maybe still a first."

"I'm sure you'll figure things out. She sounds intriguing. You should invite her to a game. I'll see what I can do about tickets. Does she like football?"

Kaya laughed. "Yeah, you could say that."

They talked for a while longer, and it was soothing just to chat with her oldest friend. Surely she was overreacting when it came to the confusion she felt over Ricki.

* * *

Monday morning was already warming up and the sun had yet to rise. Early September had brought with it a heat wave, and today looked like it was going to be another sweltering late summer day. Ricki took a deep breath of the predawn air, searching for the peace that had eluded her for days now. She hadn't been sleeping well and had almost been tempted to skip her run yesterday morning. Today, however, she was eager to feel the escape her morning ritual usually brought. Concentrating on keeping her breathing long, slow, deep, Ricki tightened her laces one more time and loped into a light jog around the track.

The golden sunshine blinked over the horizon and slashed its rays through the lingering mist. Ricki hadn't felt the need to outrun this particular demon for some time, and she wondered why Bre had decided to start haunting her dreams again. Ricki never completely forgot about her, but in recent years, the memories had taken up residence toward the back of her mind.

This week though, Bre had been at the forefront again. The confusion, the fear, the pain. Ricki didn't want to think too hard about why. She knew, though. She knew the return of these dark feelings wasn't random. She knew who had triggered them. And she knew how to prevent the nightmares from coming back full force.

Even still, fear and pain were not the emotions that dominated when Kaya crossed her mind. Thinking of her almost soothed the ache of remembering Bre, but Ricki couldn't let her thoughts go there. Instead, she forced her focus away from women altogether and grounded herself in the rhythm of her pace around the track. Kaya might turn out to be a good friend. Ricki deserved nothing more.

Each morning that week, she ran progressively farther, but by lunch on Friday, she had to admit her usual tactic wasn't working. With a sigh of frustration she tossed her sandwich onto the desk by her computer and leaned back in her chair.

She'd been unable to concentrate on her work all morning. The afternoon would be better, she knew, since she had classes all four periods. But with only two in the morning, she was usually able to use the time to make progress setting up new systems in the math lab.

Today she'd made absolutely no progress, and she'd told her senior Applied Math kids that they would be starting a programming workshop the following week. She had to get the setup finished before Monday. Rubbing her fingers roughly across her eyes, Ricki surrendered to the need for a different approach.

Time for Plan B. As a running back, she knew what the next step was. She taught this lesson to her boys every year. If you can't run around the tackler, run right through him and drive it hard for an extra yard or two. She would never be able to do anything about all the things left unsaid between her and Bre, but maybe it was time she talked to Kaya again. Besides, it had been a while since she'd eaten a hot lunch in the cafeteria.

Walking down to the large basement dining area, Ricki tried to figure out why Kaya had triggered so many memories. It wasn't looks or voice or anything physical that Ricki could place. In fact, Kaya couldn't be more opposite from Bre's soft warmth. Bre was a comforting glow, complete with gentle blond curls and dancing green eyes, while Kaya apparently had a fiery demeanor to match her blazing auburn hair and the energy that shone in her eyes. If her obvious passion the first time they'd spoken hadn't been enough to show Ricki that Kaya was all hunger and action, hearing her paint the details of her life last Friday night certainly had.

Ricki had to admit she hadn't laughed that much in a long time. Maybe that's all this was really about. Just a breath of fresh air, a new face in the monotonous crowd that comprised her everyday life. A life that hadn't changed much at all in the years she'd been teaching back at her own alma mater. But farm town life never changed very quickly. Nothing around here moved at the pace of the auburn-haired city girl.

Rounding the corner to the teachers' lounge next to the cafeteria, Ricki was captured by the very hazel eyes that had just been dancing through her mind. Kaya cracked a big smile the moment she saw Ricki walk in.

"I was beginning to think they didn't give the math teachers time off for lunch," Kaya teased.

Ricki grinned and shrugged, settling into the chair next to her. After taking a glance at the half-eaten pizza on Kaya's plate, she wasn't so sure that a hot lunch was the best idea after all. But the company felt right.

Kaya gestured at the teachers sitting with her and explained that they had just been talking about tonight's gridiron opponent. "I'm being tutored on all the finer points of Glenwood's rivalry with West End. They tell me your boys should put on a good show."

Ricki smiled. "We've been working hard all week. Hopefully things will play out in our favor." Football. It was nice to have something neutral in the conversation, some safe footing. Ricki could tell from the curious expressions on the faces of Duncan and Louis, the other two teachers, that they were a bit surprised to see her down in the lunchroom. It didn't matter though, and really, she doubted that anyone cared where she ate her lunch. She just didn't make many appearances in the staff room unless she was with Ian, Jamie or Mike. But even without her fellow coaches, she could still count on football to be a familiar backdrop.

"So which points have you learned so far?"

Kaya chuckled. "Ah, let's see..." With Louis's occasional help, she proceeded to work her way through various statistics and trivia tidbits about the upcoming game. Ricki didn't hear anything she didn't already well know, but for some reason it made her grin to listen to Kaya going through it all. The times she fumbled a stat, inevitably to the exasperated groans of at least one other teacher, were the moments that Ricki found herself most amused. It was only when Duncan rose from his chair to clean up from lunch that Ricki realized the period had flown by.

It was the first time all week that the passing time hadn't felt like cold molasses on a crisp autumn day. Ricki found herself somewhat reluctant to leave the lunch table. "So, will I see you at the game tonight?"

Kaya nodded, pushing back in her chair. "I promised my sophomores bonus points if they could diagram the projectile motion of the first touchdown pass we score tonight. I guess I should be there to make sure they tell me the truth on Monday."

Ricki grinned, and Kaya continued with a conspiratorial wink, "You know, even though running backs are your specialty, I understand you work with the receivers, too. Maybe you could throw in something a little special for them."

"Send 'em long? I might be able to manage that."

Kaya's eyes flashed with laughter. "Good. Because if you keep your boys grounded tonight, my kids might be a bit disappointed."

"We wouldn't want that," she replied.

Rising from her folding chair and bending to pick up an abandoned fork on the floor, Kaya was surprised to find that Ricki had grabbed her lunch tray with the forgotten pizza and cleared her place for her. "Chivalrous," she murmured.

Ricki fought down a blush, not entirely sure where the impulse to help Kaya had even come from. With a shrug, she simply replied, "My mama raised me right."

"Well, then, I should thank her sometime."

Ricki glanced away for a moment, carefully concealing any reaction. She doubted she would ever introduce Kaya to her mom. Looking back to her now, she was surprised to find Kaya watching her intently. Not many people seemed to notice when she felt uncomfortable, but she appeared to.

Kaya didn't pry for more information about her family, apparently opting instead for an invitation. "Can I persuade you to join me for a drink after the game again?"

Ricki hesitated. How could something feel dangerous and right at the same time? But she had enjoyed lunch and she wanted to talk with Kaya again, so she agreed with a curt nod. After all, one beer couldn't hurt anything.

CHAPTER SEVEN

Kaya loitered near the gate of the stadium, waiting for Ricki. The Alumni had been so much fun the week before, and Kaya had been looking forward to a repeat. Breathing in the sweet evening air, she lingered on the edge of the crowd, keeping an eye on the home team locker room.

Students and parents still filled the walkways outside the stadium fence, with no one in any apparent hurry to leave. Perhaps because the good guys had pulled out a thrilling victory. Perhaps just because it was a beautiful late summer night. Most of the bystanders wore the green and gold of Glenwood, but here and there Kaya saw a few more somber fans sporting the red and blue of West End. She turned from her people-watching to look again for Ricki, and when she saw the coach crossing the field, she couldn't help smiling.

Their eyes met and Ricki returned her grin, but held up a hand as if asking her to wait there. Ricki met an older man waiting a little way down the sideline and greeted him with a hug and a kiss on his cheek.

Then Kaya heard a shout behind her. Not ten feet away, a group of boys from the rival schools were locked in a fight, trying to beat each other's brains out in the clumsy way only high school boys can. Kaya immediately slipped into teacher mode and stepped through the circle of onlookers that had formed instantly.

"Hey! Come on, break it up." She grabbed one of the boys she recognized from her junior class. She forced herself between them, her main goal simply to separate them, only to have Josh Dillon's fist connect squarely with her face. She stumbled back a step. *Seriously? This is what I get?* Cupping a hand to her cheek, she felt someone else pull the boys apart. Apparently, the idea that he'd just hit a teacher was enough to take the fight out of Dillon, because he was now blundering through a panicked apology and practically begging for mercy as Ricki held back the boy from the other school.

"Dillon! On the bleachers, now!" Ricki commanded her player automatically, and the boy meekly obeyed. The other was still struggling to escape, but a man sporting a red and blue jacket arrived and helped her. They exchanged a few quiet words that Kaya couldn't make out, and then Ricki was at her side, gently moving her hand away from her cheek to check the injury.

"Didn't anyone ever teach you to guard your face in a fight?"

Despite the throb that was growing stronger by the breath, Kaya laughed. "I must have missed that lesson in phys ed." At the strong, warm touch of Ricki's hand, Kaya instantly forgot the pain, focusing instead on the blue eyes looking at her with concern. "What's the diagnosis, Doc?"

Ricki smiled, her thumb stroking carefully across Kaya's cheekbone. "You might have a nice shiner in the morning, but I think you'll survive. Nothing a beer can't fix."

"Can't I get anything stronger?" Kaya asked.

"We might be able to do that. Ian and Mike want to join us. I hope you don't mind."

Ricki dropped her hand from Kaya's cheek, and instantly the throbbing returned. Kaya reached up herself, touching the tender spot where Ricki's fingers had just been, and drew a slow breath.

"Fine, as long as I can tell the guys I won the fight."

Ricki chuckled. "Sure. Let me go take care of Dillon and then I'll drive you over to the pub."

Kaya watched while she talked quietly to the boy, who was visibly upset and, Kaya now saw, sporting a split lip and a probable black eye of his own.

A short while later at the bar, Kaya explained to them what had happened after the game, and their laughter over the whole incident helped her to see how funny it really was. Of course, it would be funnier once her cheek stopped aching.

It seemed fights between rivals weren't uncommon. Ian laughed and clapped Ricki on the back. "Oh, come on! Like you never got into a fight during your playing days!" She rolled her eyes but didn't deny his claims.

"Really? Ricki was a fighter?" Kaya asked innocently, earning a glare from Ricki. She'd been amazed when they'd first gone out the week before to learn that Ricki had actually played in high school. Kaya had never met a woman or girl who had actually played competitive tackle football. It was the ultimate man's sport. After the surprise of looking for a coach and meeting Ricki, she should have expected a complex individual, but the quiet woman next to her was proving hard to crack. Fortunately, the guys seemed happy to aid her in that regard.

"Are you kidding me? She was obnoxious!" Ian hooted again. "Cocky sonofabitch never shut up. She backed it up on the field though, or else her own team probably woulda beat the shit out of her."

Kaya smiled sweetly, "Surely you boys would never hit a girl?"

"A girl? Ha!" Mike laughed. "I had the misfortune of playing against her back in the day. This girl knew how to lay a guy out on the field. In fact, I seem to remember her going after the opposing team's toughest defender early, just to prove a point."

"Hoo, yeah, I 'member that! Any idiot what tried to treat her different 'cuz she was a girl got knocked on his ass real quick." Ian laughed again as he told her the stories of their youth.

Ricki just sat quietly, shaking her head at their antics. Kaya was amused by her patience at her friends' boisterous chatter. When the waitress finally returned with an ice pack, Ricki grabbed it, wrapped it in a napkin to blunt the cold and leaned in close. As she nursed Kaya's swollen cheek, Ricki muttered, "Don't believe everything you hear. These guys are all talk."

Kaya, who had been laughing right along with Ian and Mike as they rambled on, now found herself suddenly short of breath. She hadn't expected Ricki to take care of her, and even though she was perfectly capable of holding an ice pack to her own face, she didn't want Ricki to move away. The ice sent spears of cold through her face, but all Kaya could think was *Damn, she's hot.* Having Ricki so close felt...good.

Ian's booming laughter reminded Kaya to keep things light. "So then, who was it you picked a fight with back in the day? Was the rivalry with West End still the top?"

Ricki leaned back, shifting away from Kaya just slightly, "No, when we played, West End wasn't as strong, and we'd had a good team for a few years. That wasn't much of a game then."

"Much of a game? Jeez, you've gotten soft in your old age," Ian teased her. "Glenwood trounced West End about sixty to nothing Ricki's senior year. Nah, it was Montgomery we hated."

He laughed, but Kaya caught something dark flash in Ricki's eyes. Instinctively, she knew not to say anything, but as Ian continued, Kaya barely looked at him, watching instead for some indication of Ricki's thoughts.

"Montgomery's about an hour's drive away, but when the state high school athletics association reorganized the districts about ten years ago, they got lumped in with the northern schools. We only run into them in the state playoffs now. Ricki had this personal rivalry going with the tailback from Montgomery, though. The two of them were easily the best running backs this state had seen in years. Haven't seen anyone like 'em since, either."

Mike jumped in, "Oh, you're talking about what's-his-name...Carroll. Billy Dean Carroll or something."

"Bobby Dean." Ian and Ricki corrected him simultaneously, but Kaya was the only one who heard Ricki whisper the name.

Ian went on. "Man, what an asshole. He faded out in college. Don't even know really what happened to him. But I swear, in high school I thought you two were seriously gonna kill each other."

Ricki forced a smile and only shrugged. Kaya knew something was wrong, but if Ian noticed, it wasn't enough to stop his jovial recap of the good old days.

* * *

"Well, now you've heard all about my exploits as a player." Ricki walked with Kaya through the parking lot of the Alumni, slowly drifting over to Kaya's car. Above them, a clear sky shone with countless sparkling stars.

Kaya nodded. "Yes. I now know the sordid details of the all-star running back who led Glenwood to the only state title in school history."

She didn't respond, so Kaya pushed further. "What's the real story?"

Ricki knew Kaya would ask her that. She saw the careful way Kaya had been watching her all night. Some part of her screamed to keep quiet, to shrug it all off as no big deal. But a bigger part didn't want to do that. Not anymore, and not with Kaya. "To this day, no one gives the rest of the team much credit. I think I was to blame for some of that." She shrugged, gazing up at the darkness overhead. "I was your typical, hotheaded, arrogant athlete. I would saunter down the school hallway like I owned it, and I'd talk up myself any chance I got. Today, I know that 'There's no I in team,' but back then, 'I' was all I thought about."

When the guys had been telling their rambling stories over their drinks, they had spoken with the grudging respect that men often give the tough guy. She had certainly been portrayed as a pain-in-the-ass and worse, a description she knew was accurate back then.

Ricki continued, "People have since offered justifications for me. 'Being a girl in a boy's world, of course I had to overplay my toughness,' they've said. Maybe that was part of it, maybe not.

But either way, it's no excuse. When we won the title, I hogged the glory even more. I bragged about my stats, how I single-handedly crushed Montgomery. In reality, it was a close game, and if our defense hadn't been able to contain their offense, we wouldn't have stood a chance. Bobby Dean Carroll was a hell of a running back in his own right. Our rivalry was a raging inferno on and off the field.

"We may have won the title, but all through that season I played with a major chip on my shoulder. My teammates and rivals alike were getting recruited by universities nationwide, but no one—not one single college rep, even Division Three—contacted me. No one could even imagine a girl playing in college, despite the fact that I had my way with every high school defense I faced. It made me angry." She shook her head.

"The sweet thrill of victory after the state title soothed some of that, but Bobby Dean made sure I was well aware that *he* was the top-rated running back in the state on all the recruiting boards. Every chance he got, he and his friends would remind me of his scholarship offers and opportunities."

She sighed, and Kaya spoke quietly, "I can't even imagine going through that in high school. To be the best and simultaneously ignored? That must have sucked."

Ricki nodded.

"You don't sound angry about it anymore, though," Kaya ventured.

"No." Ricki swallowed around the knot in her throat. "Without any hope of a future in football, I stayed close to home for college, going just two hours south to Indiana University. It turned out he was so busy bragging, Bobby Dean never mentioned the fact that he wasn't the brightest crayon in the box. His academics kept him from going anywhere with much football tradition, and without my knowing it, he ended up accepting a scholarship at IU.

"Kids pick colleges for all sorts of strange reasons. Had I known Bobby Dean was going to play at IU, I probably would have gone somewhere else. Anywhere else. I suspect he chose IU just so he could continue to rub it in my face that he was still suiting up and I was now in the stands. It was stupid and petty, but we hated each other. Eventually I moved on, but when his college career didn't really go anywhere and I still had my state title, Bobby Dean's jealousy only grew."

This last sentence was barely a whisper, and then Ricki fell silent for a few minutes. She could feel Kaya watching her, probably searching for her eyes, but Ricki had barely looked at her since they'd reached the parking lot. She couldn't meet Kaya's eyes just now. "God, I was so angry back then," she said. "We both were. I'm not proud of it. I learned the hard way that ego and anger only gut you from the inside out. Kill the things that matter most."

They stood in the quiet dark for a few minutes before Ricki finally turned to face Kaya. "How's your cheek?" She reached forward to brush her fingers against Kaya's bruise, but thought better of it and dropped her hand.

The small, sad smile that curled at the corner of Kaya's mouth signaled she understood that Ricki had shared enough for one night. "I'll be okay. Maybe I'll devise some physics lesson around this to torture Dillon."

She grinned and Ricki did her best to return the smile, her heart heavy with the story she wasn't yet ready to tell.

They stood together a moment longer. Ricki realized she didn't want to part company but she couldn't think of a reason to stay either.

Kaya seemed to feel the same. "Thank you for tonight," she whispered.

Ricki nodded. "My pleasure. Sleep well."

CHAPTER EIGHT

In what had become their Friday night routine, Kaya waited in the stands after the game for Ricki to finish things up in the locker room. It was the first weekend in October and Kaya could just barely see her breath on the cool night air. Sitting on the cold bench, she couldn't help thinking about how quickly she'd felt welcomed by this school and this town, despite her initial misgivings on the first day of school. She knew more parents, and even some grandparents, of her students after one month here than she had after years in the South Side. Everyone came out on Friday nights to cheer on the boys, and a victory was the highlight of the weekend for the whole town.

Kaya's personal highlight always came a little later in the evening. She really enjoyed going out with Ricki after the game. Their conversations were light and funny, and although Kaya still did most of the talking, Ricki was beginning to chip in more each week. She had developed friendships with several of the other teachers, two of whom regularly joined Kaya and Ricki at the Alumni after the games, but it was obvious that Ricki was her closest friend here at Glenwood.

That she was a friend, though, was a point of some consternation for Kaya. She regularly talked with Toni to keep things in perspective, but Kaya couldn't deny that she wanted more with Ricki. She had never been one to shy away from going after what she wanted, but Ricki was something different altogether. *Evasive.* That was the best word Kaya could think of to describe her. She knew the attraction was mutual. She could read it in Ricki's ice cool eyes. But for some reason, Ricki was dodging her.

If that was some kind of warning sign, Kaya didn't feel inclined to heed it. Instead, she had been toying with the idea of calling Ricki out on it. Push the issue just enough to get an answer, one way or the other. However, Kaya wasn't certain that she would like the answer, and their fledgling friendship was too important to her to risk losing. *Then again, high risk, high reward.* Kaya sighed into the chilled night. She hadn't been this turned around over a girl for a long time.

She was saved from having to figure it all out tonight by the welcome sight of Ricki crossing the field. Rising from the bleachers, Kaya drifted down the stadium steps to meet her. "Tough one, tonight."

Ricki shrugged, the disappointment evident in her features. "It's rough on the boys when we lose a close one, but they'll bounce back for Fairfield next week."

Kaya looped her arm through Ricki's, one of the little affectionate moves that she couldn't resist when they were together. She could feel Ricki stiffen, but that she didn't break the contact reinforced Kaya's suspicion that her attraction was shared. "Is it rough just on the boys? You work hard for this team, too."

She sighed. "Yeah, but it's not the same. I had my glory days. I love what I do now, but years of experience allow me a certain emotional distance from the wins and losses."

"Really? I've seen you pretty fired up after a win."

That big, cocky grin that Kaya adored cracked across Ricki's strong features. "Well, sure. Who doesn't love to win? Okay, maybe I've just gotten better at distancing myself from the losses. I know it's not the end of the world now."

Kaya smiled. "So, are you ready for your Alumni burger?

She had started teasing Ricki about ordering the same thing every time they went out, but she insisted that the Alumni had one hell of a bacon cheddar burger. "Nothing wrong with sticking to what I know. You'll pick a favorite sooner or later."

"I might have to. We've been doing this for what, six weeks? I'm afraid the Alumni is running out of variety."

"Hey now, just because we're small-town doesn't mean we don't know how to live it up. I'm sure there are at least eighteen different ways of serving beef on that menu."

Kaya laughed. "And I hear the pulled pork isn't bad either."

* * *

It was getting harder and harder for Ricki to say goodnight to Kaya without leaning in for the kiss she knew Kaya wanted. She couldn't deny that she wanted it too, but she also wouldn't do that to Kaya. Kaya deserved better.

Slipping her key into the lock of her front door, Ricki turned once more to wave goodnight. She knew Kaya wouldn't drive away until she was safely in her house, and that protective instinct warmed Ricki somewhere deep in her core. Not that she was ever unsafe in this town, but still, it was sweet of her to wait.

Ricki crossed her living room in darkness, knowing the house so well she didn't need light to find her way to the kitchen in the back. Out of habit, she filled herself a glass of water from the tap and stared out the big bay window into the moonlit yard. That moonlight had caught in Kaya's eyes before they'd said their goodbyes, making them sparkle. Kaya was so full of energy, so outgoing and unafraid. Ricki couldn't help but look forward to their time together, even though the fear never left its hiding place in her heart. She knew she should probably avoid Kaya, should probably discourage her interest, but she found she simply couldn't.

Kaya made her laugh and comforted the hurting places inside her, even if she didn't know she was doing it. Her smile, her touch soothed the still-raw wounds that Ricki was unable to share with her. Ricki smiled to herself, thinking back to their time in the bar and grill tonight, and the way Kaya caught her hand when she got excited about the story she was sharing. Ricki enjoyed just sitting back and listening as Kaya made the most mundane events seem like hilarious comedy skits or dramatic life-changing affairs. Everything was important to Kaya, and Kaya made Ricki feel as if that even included her own broken soul.

Finishing her glass of water, Ricki sighed and headed up to her bedroom. Flicking on the small lamp on her nightstand, she readied for bed. The nightmares that had plagued her for the first few weeks of the school year had given way to more tolerable dreams, but the cold solitude of her bed still kept the peacefulness of sleep just out of her reach.

* * *

Kaya was restless. Sleep eluded her. After an hour tossing and turning, she got up and went instead out onto the balcony of her apartment. After ten years in the city, she was still amazed at how bright and clear the stars shone out here. *They still don't compare to the sparkle in Ricki's eyes.* God, she needed to stop doing that. She needed to get Ricki out of her mind, but she didn't know how. They weren't even dating and Kaya was trapped in some honeymooners' Bermuda Triangle.

She'd wanted to kiss Ricki goodnight before she'd hopped from her car that night, and for a moment, she thought that Ricki might just meet her halfway. Instead, Ricki simply left her with a whispered "Sleep tight." Now that was exactly what she couldn't do.

Kaya sighed. She listened to the crickets—*crickets!*—as she tried for the second time that night to decide what she should do. Things couldn't go on like this. She had to know if there was something between them, or if it was only her imagination. Staring up at the midnight sky, she felt a calm seep in with her new resolve. With a smile, she thought that this would be a perfect time for a sign, maybe a shooting star to confirm she'd made the right call.

But that kind of thing only happens in fiction.

CHAPTER NINE

It wasn't until Tuesday that Kaya saw Ricki again. When the coach hadn't come to the cafeteria for lunch for two days, Kaya had decided to look for her at the end of the school day. Knocking softly on the door of the math lab, she waited for Ricki to look up from her work. "Am I interrupting?"

"Mmm? No, just give me a minute."

Kaya crossed the room and took the seat next to Ricki, waiting until she finished what she was doing. "Sorry. Inputting grades. I just want to get this test entered."

"No problem." Kaya took a deep breath, studying Ricki's strong profile. She let her gaze drift over her body, tight and trim, and then up to her eyes. Eyes that were now completely focused on her. Just a look, and Kaya felt her insides turning to jelly. *All right, Hotshot. Go big or go home.* "Missed you at lunch the past few days."

Ricki just nodded, her eyes flickering down to the desktop for just a moment.

Kaya went on. "I like seeing you, Ricki." She waited a moment, wishing Ricki would say something, but at the same time not really expecting her to.

"A friend of mine got tickets for the Colts game this Sunday. I was wondering…will you be my date?" Kaya watched for Ricki's reaction, her own head lowered slightly, almost warily, waiting for the disappointment she feared was coming.

Ricki's eyes shifted to some unseen point across the room. Her jaw worked for a moment, but she didn't speak right away. Finally, a single word. "Date?"

Kaya arched her brow. Not an outright refusal. Maybe there was a possibility here. "Yes, Ricki, my date."

Kaya watched the emotions play across Ricki's face. A month ago, she would have thought that Ricki wasn't reacting at all, her response was so subtle. But Kaya had come to recognize the flashes in her eyes, the slowing of her breathing. *What is she so afraid of?* Kaya saw the refusal in her eyes before it reached her lips. "Ky—"

"Ricki, please. It's just a football game."

She fell silent again, and Kaya practically held her breath. Then, she nodded her assent.

Kaya couldn't suppress her wide grin. She hadn't really expected her to accept, and the joy that flooded her system with that slight nod made her whole body lighten with excitement. "Fantastic. It's Sunday at four thirty. I'll drive. We'll work details out later."

She bounced up from her chair, energy rushing through her. On some level, she felt like she should make her escape before Ricki had a chance to change her mind. Impulsively, she leaned down and gave Ricki a tight hug before practically skipping from the room. Turning back to smile, she murmured "Thank you," and slipped through the door.

* * *

Ricki sat in silence, staring after her. Kaya's excitement, her enthusiasm, was contagious. And Ricki did love the Colts. They had been her team since they'd fled Baltimore before she was even old enough to put on pads for the first time. But she knew that wasn't why her heart was pounding and she couldn't quite catch her breath. It felt as if she'd just run ten miles.

From the moment Kaya had asked, she'd wanted to give in to the searching she saw in her eyes. Wanted to accept, to see where Kaya might take her, but she knew it would be selfish. Then Kaya had said "Please."

Her resolve had never crumbled so fast before.

The scent of mango and coconut that accompanied their brief hug lingered, and Ricki felt a buried tension leach from her bones. She allowed herself a moment's peace before turning back to her computer. Her smile only lasted a moment though before the familiar apprehension seeped back. She'd accepted Kaya's invitation despite knowing it was wrong. She'd failed to rein in her own selfish needs. She could not make that mistake again. Not ever. But now what was she going to do?

CHAPTER TEN

"You were right. She really is the tall, dark and handsome type." Toni grinned at Kaya as they waited for their beers. They'd left Ricki and Rynn together in the stands to go grab another round of drinks and snacks. "Mysterious and quiet," she added. She tucked a loose strand of her long, nearly black hair back behind her ear, and Kaya could feel her curious gaze. Toni had the kind of deep brown eyes that had always made Kaya comfortable opening up. Still, she wasn't sure she knew what to say.

She stuck to a safe topic and said, "You've managed to get her talking a bit about football. I think that's more than I heard her say the first three weeks we were hanging out."

Kaya was pleased that Ricki was apparently having a good time, although she seemed to want to keep the conversation light. Almost superficial. Their car ride over had been uneventful, yet something felt off. It was as if Ricki was suddenly uncomfortable around her. That sinking sensation left Kaya unusually unable to carry the conversation, and Ricki had not filled the silence.

Kaya told Toni just about everything, but for some reason, she hesitated to discuss the unsettled feeling she'd had since picking up Ricki earlier that afternoon. "Is that all you do?"

Kaya had gotten lost in her thoughts for a moment. "What?"

Toni picked up the tray of beers and stepped away from the counter, and Kaya felt the weight of her scrutiny. "I asked if that's all you do. Hang out?"

"Oh." Kaya sighed. "Yeah, it is. I was kind of hoping that today might spur something…more."

Kaya paused, knowing if she didn't shut up now, Toni would draw her insecurities right out.

"But?"

Too late.

"What makes you think there's a 'but'?" She was only delaying the inevitable, but Kaya hoped for enough time to gather her own thoughts before Toni had her spilling everything.

"Oh, please. I know you better than that. You haven't been able to shut up about this woman for almost two months, and now you're finally on your first official date and you look like someone stole your kitten."

"I do not!" *Do I?* Kaya dropped her gaze, unable to look Toni in the eye. Could that be why Ricki seemed uncomfortable? Maybe she'd read tension in Kaya and wasn't sure what to do. But she knew instinctively that Ricki's distance was due to something else. If it were something she'd done, they could talk about it. If not…she wasn't sure what to do.

Toni just arched a brow, waiting for Kaya to really start talking. But Kaya wasn't ready. "They'll miss us if we don't get back," she said softly.

To Kaya's relief, Toni knew better than to push her too far. "All right."

They walked wordlessly back to their seats to watch the rest of the game.

* * *

All week, Ricki had replayed the feelings that had coursed through her with Kaya's invitation. Now she laughed as she listened to Rynn talk about life with her football-fanatic partner. To look at the two of them, she wouldn't have guessed that Toni was the sports fiend. Ricki felt an instant bond with Rynn, like teammates she'd had in the past. It seemed they both had experience being one of the guys. Rynn was about Ricki's height and just as strong, her short dirty blond hair often falling into her face with an air of casual cockiness.

"Really, I just come to these things to keep Toni happy." Rynn smiled, glancing out over the field, although Ricki suspected she didn't really care about the game. Despite the tough-cop appearance, it turned out Rynn had a major soft spot. The look on her face said she would do anything to keep Toni happy, and she still couldn't believe that she was lucky enough for "anything" to be going to NFL games.

Ricki grinned, a bittersweet reaction to hide her inner turmoil. She'd not spent any time around other lesbians since college. She knew who she was—she wasn't trying to deny anything. But she'd distanced herself from it all nonetheless. She'd accepted a life alone and she was content with it. That is, until Kaya had crashed in on her school and her world. Listening to Rynn and Toni, she wondered for the first time what she might have missed. Suddenly Bre's battered face flashed in her mind.

Ricki shuddered at the memory and stared out onto the field, no longer seeing the game. She saw Bre, but she also saw Kaya with Bre's injuries. The real-life memory of Kaya's black eye paled in comparison to Ricki's nightmares. That was why she should be alone. So no one else got hurt. Because of her.

Rynn hadn't noticed her sudden anguish—it was beginning to seem like Kaya was the only one who ever really saw her—and she continued talking as if nothing were different. "But that's what we do, isn't it? Keep them happy? Because God knows I'd be lost without Toni."

Ricki turned to Rynn and saw a knowing glint in her eye. "What? No, Kaya and I aren't—"

"Did you two survive without us?" Toni squeezed her way down the tight aisle, Kaya right behind her.

"Funny you should ask, sweetheart, Ricki and I were just talking about that." They couldn't have been gone more than twenty minutes, but Toni greeted Rynn with a quick kiss just the same.

Ricki looked to Kaya, and when their eyes met she knew immediately Kaya could see what Rynn hadn't. She turned away, not wanting the peace that Kaya would no doubt offer. Sure enough, she slipped into the seat next to her and leaned in close to whisper, "Hey. Are you all right?"

Ricki couldn't find her voice, but she forced a smile and nodded. Kaya reached over and took Ricki's hand in hers. Ricki wanted to lean into Kaya's embrace and accept the solace she knew Kaya would never hold back. Kaya was so kind, but that kindness couldn't soothe the torment that haunted Ricki. Even if she could, to use her like that just wasn't fair.

Ricki concentrated on the field, but she could feel Kaya pressed close, watching her. She needed the warmth of her body and didn't resist. Kaya spoke again, her voice low and barely audible over the low roar of the football stadium. "I'm here, okay, baby?"

Ricki didn't answer, and Kaya leaned back. Ricki shivered from the lost contact. With a gentleness and understanding that Ricki knew she didn't deserve, Kaya ran her fingers down Ricki's arm. "Will you tell me? Later?"

Ricki couldn't look at her. Her throat was closed and she swallowed, trying to recover any semblance of control. She took a deep breath. She hadn't been blindsided by waking images like that in years, or by the nightmares she'd learned to ignore.

Ricki closed her eyes, centered herself, breathed. After a moment, she regained her composure, but she didn't want to meet Kaya's probing gaze. "It's nothing. Just a bad memory."

Kaya nodded, and after a moment more turned her attention back to the field. This was hardly the time for an emotional conversation, and they both knew that. Ricki wasn't sure any time would ever be tolerable to explain her demons. For now, she could hide behind football as she always had.

What relief was possible, Kaya had given. Ricki wanted to flee, but there was no way to escape. Kaya had not released her hand.

* * *

Kaya had been driving in silence for over an hour, Ricki staring out the windshield beside her. The dark highway flashed by them, the pulse of the reflective centerline counting off their progress. Kaya still didn't know what to say. She couldn't bring herself to try small talk, although they'd managed to return to that for the last quarter of the game. Ricki had feigned laughter and occasionally joined in the chatter, but her eyes were ice, and not in the alluring, crystalline way that made Kaya's heart skip. This ice was cold, frozen with pain.

Toni knew Kaya well enough to see that something was wrong, but she didn't seem to see anything different in Ricki. Before they'd parted, Toni had pulled Kaya aside. "What did I miss?" Kaya had been unable to answer, not comprehending how Toni didn't know. *How can they not see her anguish?* Kaya really didn't understand how Ricki hid it so well from everyone else, and yet she remembered her frustration when they'd first met over not being able to read her.

"I don't know. I'll call you." She'd hugged her friends before leading Ricki back to her car.

A few hours ago, she would have linked arms with her as they walked, but now she felt as if there were an ironclad wall between them. Something had happened when Toni and she had gone to the concession stand, but Ricki wasn't talking about it. Not at the game and not during the drive.

Nearing Ricki's house, Kaya broke the silence. "Is this it?" she said, her voice so low it was practically a whisper. "You really aren't going to talk to me?" She kept her eyes trained on the road ahead, but she could sense Ricki stiffening.

When Ricki still didn't speak, Kaya went on. "Have I read everything wrong? Do you not trust me?"

Ricki finally responded. "Kaya, that's not it at all."

Kaya pulled up to the curb in front of Ricki's house and turned, searching for Ricki's eyes. "Then what is it?"

Ricki wouldn't meet her gaze. Instead she turned away to look out the window at the shadows around her house. "Ky, I don't want to pull you into my shit. Just…just let it go, okay?" Without waiting for an answer, Ricki bolted from the car.

Kaya sat dumbfounded for a few seconds, before jumping out after her. *I can't just let her walk away like this.* "Ricki, wait!"

To her relief, Ricki slowed on the walkway, allowing her to catch up. "Hey, what's going on?"

Still, Ricki kept her eyes averted, but Kaya caught the shimmer of tears tracking down her face in the moonlight. "Ricki, you know I care about you, right? Whatever you're dealing with, you don't have to do it alone."

Kaya reached out a tentative hand, touching Ricki gently on the shoulder. She was afraid that Ricki would run again, and she had no idea how to prevent that. "Ricki?"

Ricki swiped at her tears, a hint of temper flashing in her movements. She turned then, sharply and with forced resolve. "Kaya. Please. I'm poison, and I can't give you what you want. Just let it go."

She tried to step away, but Kaya moved after her. "How do you even know what it is that I want?"

"Because you're a good person. And you haven't made any secret of the fact that you're attracted to me. I don't know why—I'm messed up. You deserve better, and I don't want to be the reason anyone else gets hurt."

Kaya was shocked, and she didn't rein in her temper. "No, maybe I don't hide my feelings, but I'm not alone in my attraction. Am I, Ricki?"

Ricki turned partly away, her gaze dropping to the ground. Sorrow, confusion, guilt—even in the shadows Kaya could see the emotions run across her face. None of them good. "Am I?" Kaya repeated.

Ricki spun back and pulled Kaya into a crushing kiss. Stunned, it took Kaya a second to respond, but the heat and passion of Ricki's mouth flooded her and seeped deep into her body. She met Ricki's kiss then, allowing herself to really feel her desire and need for the first time. But as suddenly as it started, their kiss ended when Ricki staggered back. "God. I'm sorry. I shouldn't—"

"No, don't do that to me. Don't tell me you regret that," Kaya pleaded, reaching again for her.

Ricki shook her head, backing away with panic in her eyes. "I'm sorry, Ky."

And then she was gone, leaving Kaya dazed on the front walk.

CHAPTER ELEVEN

Ricki didn't know how long she had been sitting at her kitchen table. She didn't care how long ago the ice in her water glass had melted. She didn't need to be asleep for her nightmares to cripple her. She didn't have to close her eyes to see the images of her past flash across the darkened room.

"Ricki! Ricki, it's Bre. She's—she's in the hospital. She's unconscious, in a coma, and they don't know how bad it is. She's been beaten up—they found her in an alley. The cops think it was a random mugging. Ricki? Can you hear me?"

It wasn't. It wasn't a mugging, and it definitely wasn't random. It was Ricki's fault, despite what everyone else said. If she'd just been able to control herself, control her desires, then maybe Bre would have been okay. Maybe she wouldn't have gone back to him.

"Bobby Dean Carroll, you are charged with aggravated assault, battery and manslaughter. How do you plead?"

Staring into the dark, scenes from the past flickered in front of her, but then out of nowhere they would be interrupted by a more recent memory. Kaya's eyes sparkling as she laughed at a joke. Kaya's concern when she saw the turmoil Ricki tried so hard to hide. But Kaya's smile morphed to Bre's, and then Bre's face was shattered and bruised.

Ricki was back sitting by her hospital bed. Talking quietly to the still figure lying there. *"Bre? Bre, can you hear me? I need you to come back. I need you to be okay. I don't know how I can keep going without you."*

Dawn broke through the window, finally stirring Ricki from her torment. The tears that had streamed down her cheeks had long since dried, leaving her face feeling crusty and raw. Her eyes burned from exhaustion and anguish. She couldn't face the day. She couldn't face her life. She definitely couldn't face Kaya, and she didn't doubt that Kaya would look for her at school.

Ricki rose from the table and made a brief phone call. The school would have to make do with a substitute for a day or two. Ricki shuffled up to her bed, stripped and crawled under the cold covers. It would be the first morning in years she didn't greet the dawn with a run, and she didn't care.

The two faces that had haunted her night floated again into her vision. Both were smiling, both had joy and life dancing in their eyes. But only one would ever again live that joy. Ricki wished she could leave Kaya out of this. She wanted to spare Kaya her nightmares. But she couldn't get her out of her mind.

She hid her face in her pillow and whispered into the fading darkness, "God, Bre, I need your help. I'm in over my head, and I'm not strong enough. What should I do?" With that murmured prayer, Ricki escaped into the oblivion of sleep.

* * *

Kaya wasn't surprised that Ricki didn't join her for lunch. She was surprised, however, when Ricki was neither in the math lab nor on the football practice field later that day, and when the same was true again the next day. Tuesday afternoon, she sat in the stands and watched the boys run through their drills for a little while, uncertain what to do. It had been obvious Sunday night that Ricki was really hurting. But it was equally obvious that she didn't want Kaya involved. *Should I force the issue?* Kaya didn't know if she should go looking for Ricki more than she already had, or accept that Ricki wasn't going to let her help.

She watched the boys pound each other into the dirt for a bit longer. *An interesting game...*

These young men each take a brutal beating, but they can't succeed alone. So why, after all she'd done with team effort and group dynamic, did Ricki want to be alone? Kaya could hear Ricki's words from Sunday night. *I'm poison. You deserve better.* Kaya realized then that Ricki didn't want to be alone; she'd just given up hope that there was an alternative. What had happened to her that she was so lost in her suffering? And what could Kaya do to help her heal?

Ricki was running from any support that she had to offer, but Kaya hoped she wouldn't run forever. Rising from her seat in the stands, she came to a decision. *Ricki knows words don't mean much. That's why she says so little. I'll just have to show her that she's not alone.*

CHAPTER TWELVE

Ricki didn't want to get up. She didn't want to get out of bed. But she knew she had to keep going. Life didn't stop just because you wanted it to. She had learned that lesson once before. So on Wednesday morning, she forced herself to return to her routine. She got up half an hour before dawn, choked down a flavorless breakfast and laced on her running shoes. While she normally jogged the half mile from her house to the school track, going at all was a big enough step for today and she walked numbly along the dimly lit path.

Her time in isolation the past few days had served little purpose in figuring out what she should do, but it had helped to dull the pain. She'd been there before, so overwhelmed with grief that she wanted to give up, but this time was different. This time, the fear was as crippling as the loss. It didn't matter how many years had passed since Bre died, Ricki knew she would never get over it. She would never forgive herself, but she'd learned to live with it. She hadn't anticipated the agony of caring about someone again.

Kaya had managed to pry her way through her barriers. Now that she was in, Ricki wanted nothing more than to get her back out, to save Kaya from her despair. Maybe it didn't matter now, though. Maybe after Sunday night, Kaya would be too angry with her to even give her another glance.

Maybe that was for the best.

The October mornings were getting cooler, so Ricki worked through a few extra stretches before taking off along the track. Her body felt heavy, physically weighed down with the emotional baggage she was carrying. She'd run two miles before she realized she wasn't alone. There was someone sitting in the stands, nursing a steaming cup of coffee in the glow of dawn.

Ricki slowed her pace as she approached, curious despite everything else that burdened her mind. She was still a quarter-lap away when she recognized Kaya's auburn hair and piercing eyes. Ricki stopped, not wanting to get any nearer. Kaya didn't approach, just stayed where she was, watching.

She didn't know how long Kaya had been there, and now knowing she was, Ricki didn't dare move toward her. She could feel her heart pounding, her chest rising and falling from heavy breathing, but she didn't know if that was a result of her run or her unexpected visitor. Their eyes held for a few moments, the space between them meaningless. Then Kaya just shrugged, as if to say *I'm here*.

Ricki turned and walked away.

* * *

Kaya didn't much feel like lingering around the school at the end of the day. It was odd being there, where nothing had changed and yet everything felt different. Before the Colts game, Ricki had joined her for lunch two or three times a week, but that was usually all they saw of each other inside the walls of Glenwood. Now, they weren't sharing even that. In total, the loss was less than two hours' contact over the course of a week. How could such a small amount of time affect so much?

She thought back to her visit to the track earlier that morning and the way Ricki had walked away from her. She knew it wasn't going to be easy. *That's okay. It doesn't change anything.*

Unable to stay at the school any longer, she grabbed her shoulder bag and tossed in the tests and homework assignments to grade at home. Stepping out into the hallway and locking her classroom door, she headed down the corridor for the faculty lot. There was always something about a school after the students had gone home that made Kaya feel unsettled. The echo of lone footsteps off the concrete block walls, the flash of a reflection on the green metal lockers. For better or for worse, everyone remembered high school. These walls were so often a cage to students, but as a teacher, it had been awhile since Kaya had felt that way too. Now, with things so confused between her and Ricki, that sensation was back in full force. She sighed to herself, trying to escape the reverie as much as the frustration.

She paused at the sound of footsteps behind her. "Miss Walsh! Miss Walsh, can I steal a minute of your time?"

Kaya turned to find Mr. Fisher bustling toward her down the hall, breathing heavily. She refrained from cringing at his insistence on using the title "Miss." She suspected the use of "Ms." had probably never crossed his *traditional* mind. The plump man fit the image of patrician educator, if overweight. He had small spectacles resting on his round nose, and he pushed the glasses up as he raised his eyes to meet Kaya's. "Miss Walsh, I see that I'm just catching you on your way out."

Kaya just smiled and nodded.

"I wanted to follow up with you on how things are going. You've been with us two months. Is everything well?"

"Yes, Mr. Fisher. Things are going quite well. I do believe I'm starting to fit in here with the Glenwood community." She was unsure whether he wanted to sit down and have a job review or if he was just making small talk on his way to some other topic, so she settled into a more comfortable stance and waited for some indication either way.

They talked on for a few minutes, and he noted her attendance at the football games and other extracurricular student events. "They appreciate that, you know. The students. Coach Farley mentioned that you've been at quite a few of our girls' soccer games."

"Yes. I do try to support my students beyond the classroom. I suppose it's a habit I picked up in the city where some of those kids don't really have anyone there for them." *I also didn't want anyone to notice that I spend more time at football games watching the coach than the players.* She wasn't surprised the soccer coach had noticed her attendance. She was rapidly learning people in small-towns had a way of keeping tabs on each other.

"That's excellent. We love to see our teachers getting involved." There was a slight shift in his tone, and Kaya felt a foreboding. "As you know, Homecoming is in two weeks."

He paused, and Kaya resisted the urge to grimace. She knew now where this was going.

"I'm sure you've heard, there's a dance for the students on Saturday night. It's…tradition…" —he all but dripped the word in patronization— "for our newer teachers to chaperone the event. I was wondering if you might be available?"

Although phrased as a request, Mr. Fisher's inquiry was an expectation, and Kaya knew it.

As much as she wasn't in the mood to deal with something like that right now, she didn't have any good reason to refuse. Normally, it was even the sort of thing she liked doing. "Of course. I'd love to help."

Mr. Fisher smiled. "Excellent. There will be a memo with details a few days before the dance. I do appreciate you volunteering." He turned and hurried off down the hallway.

Kaya sighed. Oh well, if nothing else, maybe being stuck watching teenagers push the limits of acceptable public affection would help distract her from Ricki.

CHAPTER THIRTEEN

It didn't make any sense. Yes, running had always been a safe haven but shouldn't that escape be cut off now because Kaya was intruding? No, intruding was the wrong word. She was just…there. She never approached, never said a word. Just sat in the stands every morning and watched her run lap after lap. She should want Kaya gone, should try to get back to her old life. Regain her hold on reality. But Ricki didn't want to talk to her. Not yet. And particularly not to tell her to leave.

All right, maybe she liked it. It was selfish, she knew, but she liked that Kaya was there. They hadn't actually made eye contact since that first morning, but Ricki sensed her. She was just a spot in her peripheral vision, but she was ever-present. Somehow, even with Kaya there, her morning run had once again become the most calming part of her day. More than that, if she were honest with herself, Ricki had to admit that having Kaya there somehow soothed her raw nerves even more than a mere run used to.

At first, Kaya's presence had shaken her. She'd even considered finding somewhere else to run. But that thought stirred a deep sense of loss, so she just went on with her routine. After that, there had been a morning or two when Ricki had arrived first, and she felt unsettled until her silent companion took her place in the bleachers.

Ricki tried not to think about what that meant. Kaya was the cause of her nightmares returning, not the solution. Wasn't she? Ricki knew it wasn't her fault, but it was still better for both of them to stay apart. So why then did that notion cause her deep regret?

* * *

"I don't know, Toni. I'm beginning to think I'm out of my mind." As she spoke by phone with her friend, Kaya absently picked at a loose thread on the blanket she'd thrown over her lap. "What am I doing?"

"I don't know either, hon. But it's what you think is right. So nothing has changed at all?"

Kaya felt bad that she was tying up Toni's evening, keeping her stuck on the phone yet again, but she needed someone to talk to about all this.

"No. She hasn't spoken to me in two weeks. She's not quite avoiding me outright, but it's like I just blend into her landscape." Kaya thought again about her visit earlier that morning. Ricki was already running when she got there, and she hadn't stopped or altered her rhythm. As far as she could tell, Ricki had never even looked at her. She knew Ricki knew she was there, as she had been every morning since…since what? Since their fight? Did it even count as a fight? Ricki had just run away, and despite every logical synapse telling her she should let her go, Kaya found she just couldn't.

"Have I turned into a creepy stalker?" she asked Toni.

Toni laughed. "No, I don't think so. At least not yet."

"Do you think I'm doing the right thing?"

Toni was quiet for a second. "It sure seems like Ricki needs someone to talk to. Why shouldn't it be you? I guess all you can do is continue to let her know you're there for her."

"Yeah."

"You know, I think what surprises me most is you're actually getting up in the mornings to do this. As I recall, you used to hate any part of the day that came before noon." Toni tried to lighten the mood, teasing Kaya about her terrible sleeping habits when they lived together in college. Any story with Toni that began with "Remember that time you…" was probably good for at least a smile. Although Kaya was hardly as bad as Toni was now making it seem. Surely, she'd only slept through one or two morning exams in their four years. And the random girl racing disheveled across campus, still in her pajamas, wasn't all that uncommon on exam days. Possibly not the neon rainbow, tiger-striped pajamas that Kaya had sported back then, but still.

The memory did make Kaya laugh, but it wasn't enough to break her out of her melancholy. "A lot has changed since college, Toni. That whole real world thing happened."

Toni was silent, and Kaya knew her friend heard her sadness. When she did speak again, it seemed she decided to give up trying to change the topic. "Perhaps. Or perhaps it's something else that has you getting up before dawn."

"What are you suggesting?" Kaya didn't want to admit her feelings to herself, and she certainly didn't want Toni to analyze her.

"Nothing, hon, but maybe you should take a closer look at why you're doing what you're doing."

Kaya swallowed, her throat suddenly feeling tight. "I'm doing it because Ricki needs a friend, and I care about her. Isn't that a good enough reason?"

"Of course it is, but is it your only one?"

Kaya didn't answer. She couldn't. She didn't want to think about how quickly and how strongly she'd felt more than just friendship for Ricki. It was just an attraction, a crush. Nothing more.

"I think it's time I let you get back to your life," Kaya mumbled into the phone.

"Rynn doesn't mind waiting. She knows you've needed someone to talk to lately, and she cares about you, too."

"I said life, not wife," Kaya muttered.

Toni chuckled, the phone equivalent of a shrug. "Is there a difference?"

Kaya rolled her eyes. "Oh, please, you're going to make me gag. Good night. I'll talk to you in a few days."

"Okay. Take care of yourself, Kaya."

Kaya set her cell phone down on the coffee table and thought about their farewell. *I can take care of myself just fine. It's not me I'm worried about.*

CHAPTER FOURTEEN

The cafeteria tables had been folded and lined up against the far wall. A local DJ had arranged his equipment right in front of where the students would normally line up to get their food. The dance committee had decked the room out with crepe paper streamers and balloons in the school colors. Kaya hovered around the wall farthest from the speakers, musing on how little school dances changed from one place or one decade to the next.

The music was about all that was different. Kaya was fairly certain that her school dances hadn't featured quite so much censored profanity. Or maybe it had and she just hadn't noticed it back then. The bass pumped so loudly that she could feel it as much as hear it, and the students crowded into the cafeteria bumped and ground to the beat. *Did I really dance like that in high school?* It wasn't a far cry from the seething sexuality she saw at clubs when she went out, which was pretty rare these days.

The good thing about this event was that it was over at eleven, whereas if she'd gone out to a club, things only got started around then. It wasn't so much that she didn't stay up late anymore, she just wasn't in the mood for that sort of evening out. A laugh over a beer sounded much better. Like the times at the Alumni she used to have with Ricki.

Come on, Kaya, don't do this to yourself again. Think about something else. Anything else.

* * *

Ricki had given up trying not to think about Kaya. It didn't work, so why bother? In fact, she'd accepted that Kaya wasn't going away. That simple truth had somehow become a great comfort to her. What to do about it though was a completely different conundrum. She watched Kaya across the room, sure that she didn't even know she was there. Ricki had already paid her dues when she'd been a new teacher, but she didn't mind chaperoning the homecoming dance, if for no other reason than to make sure her players stayed in line.

"Are you going to stand and stare all night, or are you actually going to go talk to her?" Ricki jumped at the sound of a voice in her ear. Ian had leaned close and shouted over the blast of the DJ's music. Like her, he attended these events to keep an eye on their players.

"What?"

"I said, are you—" he started.

"No, I heard what you said. I'm just trying to figure out what you're talking about."

Ian quirked a brow and grinned at her. "Oh, come on, you think I don't see you staring at her? What's the deal with you two, anyway? You were hanging out all the time and then, what? You broke up?"

Ricki nearly choked in surprise. "What? No!" She had never talked about her sexuality with Ian, never discussed her past. And she hadn't dated since…since before.

He just looked at her, amused. "Ricki, just 'cause you never told me doesn't mean I don't know. It's cool. I'm guessing she's interested, too. Hell, I tried to talk to her a few weeks ago, and I swear she didn't know I was alive. Doesn't do much for a man's confidence. But I think you'd have better luck. I just don't get this game you're playing. Are you gonna go over there or not?"

Ricki stared at her friend. He made it sound so easy. So obvious. "You think I should?"

Ian laughed. "I've never known you to be shy."

"But what if she—"

"Don't get ahead of yourself. It's just talking to a pretty girl. You're acting like the students rocking out on this dance floor." Ian lifted his arms and did a dance, a little hip-thrusting mockery of the scene before them. Ricki couldn't help but laugh.

Stifling her amusement, she glanced out at the partying students. Surely she had more going for her than that. "Maybe you're right."

"Maybe?" Ian scoffed, and stopped dancing to instead feign indignation. "I'm always right and you know it."

"Yeah, whatever. Thanks, man."

Ian strutted away, but Ricki didn't move. She would talk to Kaya, but Kaya deserved a conversation somewhere where they could hear themselves think.

CHAPTER FIFTEEN

Waking up so early after being at the high school so late was not easy, but Kaya knew Ricki didn't even take Sundays off from her runs. Now though, she was beginning to worry. She'd been at the track for twenty minutes and Ricki hadn't shown up yet. For weeks, she had watched Ricki run every day. Kaya could see her own breath on the brisk morning air as she waited and wondered where Ricki might be. Did she change her routine as the dawn got later? Kaya hadn't really thought about that before, but she supposed Ricki would have to. After all, in another few weeks, it would still be dark when they were expected to arrive at the school for work.

It was silly, but Kaya wondered if Ricki would somehow inform her of her change in routine. *But why should she? She never invited me to be here.* How long should she wait today? Should she go looking for Ricki elsewhere? Should she just give up on this fool's errand and leave Ricki in peace?

She took another sip of her coffee and grimaced. Frappuccino was one thing, but coffee that was supposed to be hot and wasn't simply tasted awful.

"What are you doing here?"

Kaya jumped at the sudden voice behind her and spun around. There was Ricki, sitting two rows back leaning forward with her elbows on her knees.

"Jesus! You scared me." Kaya closed her eyes for a second, trying to calm her pounding heart. She had been certain she was alone.

She met Ricki's intense stare. As they studied each other, Kaya wasn't sure what to say. She hadn't anticipated this at all. "What?"

"I asked what you're doing here."

"I…Well, I was waiting for you."

"Why?" Ricki's voice was quiet, flat, but her eyes belied hostility. *Is she holding back a smile?*

"You know why. It was the best way I could think of to let you know I was here for you." Kaya finally twisted on the bleachers, facing Ricki fully. She drew her knees to her chest and wrapped her arms around them, alleviating some of the morning chill.

"But why? Why would you *want* to be here for me?"

Kaya heard the question, but Ricki's tone was more speculative than inquiring. Almost like she knew the answer and just couldn't believe it. Ricki dropped her gaze, turning briefly inward in her thoughts. Hearing and seeing that, Kaya decided not to answer.

After a moment, Ricki looked up again. "I haven't exactly been…nice. To you."

Kaya quirked a brow. "Nice? No, I don't suppose avoiding me like the plague really classifies as nice."

Ricki took a deep, frustrated breath and Kaya thought that perhaps she hadn't expected to be called out on her behavior. "No. It doesn't. So that goes back to my question. Why are you here?"

Kaya considered her. *Why am I here? Because something about you stirs something deep in my soul that I just can't ignore.* But she couldn't say that. That was crazy. "You're alone. You're dealing with something alone. I want you to know you don't have to."

Kaya could see questions in Ricki's expression but found it difficult to read what she was really thinking. This whole situation was bizarre but something compelled Kaya to return here each morning. Now finally, Ricki was in front of her and talking. Although she seemed at a loss for words at the moment. After a prolonged silence, Ricki just nodded. "Thank you."

Kaya moved up a row so that she was now on the bench right below Ricki. She tilted her head and tried to catch Ricki's eyes. Ricki hesitantly met her gaze.

Kaya reached up and rested a hand on Ricki's knee. "You don't have to be alone anymore."

Ricki swallowed and Kaya could see her fighting tears. Ever strong though, she apparently refused to break down here. Instead, she broke eye contact and looked out onto the field. Kaya knew it was her sanctuary and felt honored to be here with her.

She gave Ricki's knee a light squeeze. "Will you tell me? What it is that haunts you?"

Ricki turned back to her, seemingly startled by her word choice, but if she was going to talk, it wasn't to be now. "I haven't run yet."

Kaya laughed. "Are you serious?" But she didn't wait for an answer, instead shrugging, "Then I can wait."

Ricki grinned. "You don't want to run with me?"

Kaya shook her head vehemently. "Hell, no. I like to watch." She winked playfully. "As long as you promise to stop running *from* me, I'll be fine right here."

Ricki sighed. "You wouldn't let me run from you. Why, I'm still not sure." She leaned forward and caught both of Kaya's hands in her own, staring deep into Kaya's eyes. "But I'm grateful."

Kaya hoped for a second that she might be rewarded with a kiss, but Ricki jumped to her feet instead. "I'll make it a quick run. Just three miles today."

Kaya just shook her head. "You're insane. But go ahead."

* * *

"Do you want to come back to my place? I'll make you breakfast after I grab a quick shower." Ricki paced in front of Kaya, cooling down from her run but hardly out of breath. The morning was chilly, but she had shed her outer layers and now wore only a snug muscle shirt and baggy shorts that fell to her knees.

"And then we'll talk?"

Kaya watched her intently, and Ricki knew they needed to clear the air. Pretending their silence of the past few weeks hadn't happened would only reinforce the wall that had sprung up between them. She knew the wall was her doing, but maybe she didn't need it there. Maybe it would be okay to bring at least a part of it down.

She sighed and shrugged on a sweatshirt to protect herself from the morning chill. She knew she had to talk, but she still wasn't sure she was ready to face her nightmares. Or to share them. But then, Kaya had earned that much. "Yes. Then we'll talk."

Kaya smiled, a simple expression that warmed Ricki's heart and chased away a few of the shadows. "In that case, what are you cooking for me?"

Turning to lead her back along the path to her house, Ricki chuckled. "Bacon and eggs?"

Kaya matched Ricki's step, walking next to her closely enough to touch, but not crossing that boundary. "I've always been more of a fruit and waffles girl."

Ricki was surprised by the urge she felt to take Kaya's hand. It was an intimacy that she didn't deserve and she kept her feelings to herself. "I suppose I could make that happen. Although my fresh fruit selection might be pretty limited."

"That's okay. We'll compromise. Bacon and waffles."

"Deal."

Leaving Kaya's car at the school, they walked together in comfortable silence back to Ricki's house. The day was still young, and the morning light flickering through the brilliantly colored autumn trees lent a sense of peace to the path. Ricki bypassed the front entrance, instead leading Kaya around to the back and skipping up the steps to a deck patio door.

In the kitchen she flipped on some lights and started the coffee. "Do you mind making yourself at home while I go clean up?"

Kaya took a seat at the kitchen table. "That's fine. You want me to start cooking?"

"No, that's okay. I'll be back in just a few minutes."

* * *

Ricki smiled and ducked down a hallway, leaving Kaya alone to take in her surroundings. The house felt comfortable. The kitchen was clean, with just a few lonely dishes left to dry in a rack by the sink. The soft orange color gave the room a warm feeling, and it reminded Kaya briefly of summers spent in the country in her grandmother's farmhouse kitchen. That had been one of the most constant aspects of her childhood, until it wasn't. *Now, where did that thought come from?* She hadn't thought of those summers in years, not since her grandparents had sold the farm to be closer to their children in the city.

Lost in her own memories, Kaya didn't realize how quickly time passed until Ricki walked back into the room, her wet hair still sparkling with moisture from her shower. "You look happy," she observed.

Kaya shrugged. "Good memory. Your kitchen reminds me of something from when I was a kid."

Ricki's eyes flickered, a darkness flashing across them. "Memories. I'm glad you're thinking about good ones."

Kaya rose and crossed the room to her. "You have bad memories?" She reached forward tentatively, her fingers brushing against Ricki's arm, folded across her chest in an unconsciously self-protecting pose. Ricki sighed in resignation. She didn't shy away from Kaya's touch, but seemed to get lost in the past, gathering her thoughts. Finally, she stepped away, moving into the kitchen and pulling open the fridge.

"You know, I was a cocky pain-in-the-ass when I was younger."

Kaya was surprised. She'd heard that before, but it wasn't the sort of introduction she'd expected today. "I don't get that from you, now." She followed Ricki and leaned against a counter to listen.

"I talked a lot, but mostly because I had the walk to back it up." She paused, her jaw working as she tried to relay the shame in her past. As if on autopilot, she pulled ingredients for their waffles out of various cabinets and prepared the food as she talked. "You remember what I said I was like back then? About how I was so...so angry about being passed over in football?" Kaya nodded. "Well, I was an ass about it, and it took meeting Bre to teach me some manners."

At the mention of a new figure from her past, Kaya caught the unmistakable anguish in her voice. She worked on their breakfast in silence a while before continuing.

"From the moment she stepped into our dorm room, I knew my life would never be the same. We became best friends overnight and without even trying, she washed away all the frustration, anger and rejection I'd dealt with up to then. She was the sweetest, most gentle person I'd ever met, but at the same time, she had a wicked sense of humor. She used to make me laugh so hard, I'd have tears streaming down my face, and all with just a few clever words. Bre was quiet, never a wasted word. When she said something, it counted. Within weeks, I'd completely forgotten about the bitterness I'd arrived at college with. Life around Bre was good. I was happier than I could ever remember being."

Kaya picked up the plates that Ricki had piled high with food and led them over to the simple wood table. They ate quietly, Kaya giving Ricki as much time as she wanted to gather her thoughts and settle her feelings. Distracted or not, Ricki had managed to put together a delicious breakfast, and the addition of pure maple syrup perfected the meal. Knowing that Ricki was emotionally fragile, Kaya watched to make sure she ate but needn't have worried. Ricki was half finished with her food before she slowed at all, but then she mostly just moved the remaining food around her plate. Kaya took that as her cue to steer them back to Ricki's past.

"So was Bre your girlfriend?" she asked gently.

"No."

Kaya quirked a brow before she could stop herself. She'd been sure that was where the story was going.

Ricki smiled, the lingering bittersweet expression that Kaya had seen several times while they talked. "No," she repeated. "We never dated. Although I was madly in love with her." Ricki paused, shrugged. "She was straight."

"Ah." Kaya nodded.

"She'd arrived at IU from out of state, still involved with her high school sweetheart, and while that didn't last, she was rarely without a man in her life. She was gorgeous, a petite blond with a sparkling personality. Guys lined up to ask her out, and the ones she did date never knew how lucky they had it. I knew I didn't have a chance, but I was happy just being on the edges of her radiance. I could have been happy for the rest of my life just being her best friend. And no matter what guy was the flavor of the month, at night she still came home to me."

Ricki chuckled. "I know saying it that way makes it sound like there was something between us, and in my head, in my dreams, there was. Even in reality, we were inseparable, though just as friends. I accepted that she just didn't see me that way and had a fair bit of success in my dating life, too. IU is a good school for gay kids. Was then, still is. I learned a lot about myself, my tastes, my attractions. But Bre always owned my heart. I never got all that serious with any of the girls I dated, probably because they could always tell pretty quickly that I wasn't truly invested in it. So the ones who wanted more than physical good times didn't linger. And I was okay with that."

Kaya considered this. "You make it sound as if you were a player."

Ricki shrugged. "I was. Bre mellowed me, but I was still cocky, still loud. A lot of girls liked that, liked my confidence. Bre would tease me about it, about how I was just another one of the guys. I used to respond that I wasn't just any guy, I was the alpha male. That always made her laugh, no matter how many times I used that line."

Kaya smiled, hearing the playfulness even in the memory of their banter. Ricki spoke with such a tenderness, even now, so many years removed from her college days. The depth of feeling that Ricki now revealed uninhibitedly only deepened Kaya's regard for her.

"She was a good person, in the way that few people are truly good. She was pre-med, with a psychology double-major, hoping to specialize in sports medicine. When I learned that, any hope I'd had of not falling hard for her went right out the window. For three years, we lived in the dorm together, laughed together, even chatted sports together. Junior year, she earned an internship with the athletic trainer's office, and I used to love it when she'd come home and regale me with stories of the locker room antics our teams got into. It brought back wonderful memories of my own days on the team, and she understood better than anyone what they meant to me.

"Life was perfect, smooth sailing, until she came home one night during the spring of that year and asked me if I wanted to go on a double date with her and this new guy she'd started seeing. It was something we'd done on occasion whenever we were both seeing someone, and at the time, I was content in a relationship with..."

She paused, puzzled. "God, I feel awful, but I can't even remember her name now. What does that say about me?" She glanced at Kaya, an apology in her eyes.

Kaya simply offered her a soft smile. "It says you were in love with someone else. I don't think you should be ashamed of that."

Ricki shook her head. "You're too kind." She sighed and gathered her thoughts before continuing. "Anyway, not really thinking much of it, I agreed and we made plans to catch dinner and a movie that Friday night."

Ricki rose from her chair and moved over to refill her coffee. After filling Kaya's mug as well, she drifted over to the doorway and stared out into the bright, sunny sky. It was turning into a beautiful fall day, warmer than they'd had in a while with any lingering morning mist long since burned off.

Joining her from behind, Kaya asked quietly. "It was Bobby Dean, wasn't it? The guy that Bre started dating."

Ricki turned to her, a look of surprise flashing briefly in her eyes. Maybe she hadn't expected her to remember the name from a conversation nearly two months ago, but how could Kaya not have pieced it together when there was such hurt attached to those tales the other coaches recounted?

Ricki nodded sadly, but didn't continue immediately. Instead, she gestured to the Adirondack chairs out on the deck. "Want to enjoy this weather?"

Kaya smiled. "Sounds nice."

The fleece jacket that she'd worn to the track that morning proved to be too heavy in the brilliant sunshine, and Kaya shrugged out of it. Ricki, in jeans and a plain white T-shirt, eyes closed and the healing warmth of the sun shining on her face, looked more relaxed than Kaya had seen her in quite a while. They basked for a few minutes in the hot rays, Kaya once again content to let Ricki tell her story at whatever pace she needed.

"I don't think either of them knew the other's connection to me." She began her story again, her eyes still closed. "They'd met during spring football practices and had been flirting and talking for a few weeks before Bre agreed to a date. She may not have known that we had history, but the second Bobby Dean and I saw each other again, Bre knew something was up. I was so completely floored, I couldn't say anything. Bobby Dean, he just stood there dumbly, that cross of a smirk and a snarl I remembered so well dripping across his face. Bre actually dragged me aside, demanding to know what the hell was going on. She shook me out of my immediate shock and I was able to briefly explain our history. She laughed, incredulous. 'An old high school rival? You've got to be kidding me.' She punched me in the arm, told me to behave myself because Bobby Dean was a sweetie and we went back to the table.

"In all the years we had known each other, of all the times it seemed we could read each other's thoughts, connected beyond words..." Ricki's voice cracked, and Kaya looked over at her with concern. "That was the first time she didn't understand me. I remember the lump in my gut, the memories of anger and an inexplicable hint of fear that I couldn't justify clouding my thoughts. Maybe I should have listened to my instincts, but what could I have done? I had no say in who Bre dated, and even if I had, I couldn't justify my discomfort. Even in my own head, it sounded ridiculous."

She shrugged, whether to herself or because she knew Kaya was watching her, Kaya didn't know. "While Bre had a great night, I never quite regained my footing. It was worse still because she didn't seem to notice. She had always been so sensitive to my moods. Bobby Dean was the picture of suave and genteel. It was a side of him I'd never seen, and I tried to convince myself that the snarl on his face at our reunion had been in my head. My date—Sonja, that was her name—Sonja kept trying to steal my attention, but I couldn't take my focus off Bre and Bobby Dean. I guess that's why I never heard from her again."

Ricki's story was interrupted then by the buzzing of a ringtone. When Kaya scrambled to dig her phone from her pocket and started to hit the *Ignore* button, Ricki stopped her. "Go ahead and answer it."

"No, I don't want to inter—" Kaya started, but Ricki cut her off. "Please. I need a minute to gather my thoughts for this next part."

Nodding, Kaya shifted her thumb over to the *Answer* button and accepted the call, never taking her eyes from Ricki. "Hello?"

"Hey, there. How's my favorite stalker doing this morning?" Kaya resisted the urge to roll her eyes at Toni's tease.

"Funny you should mention that. Guess who I just had breakfast with."

Ricki looked at her with interest, and Kaya just mouthed *Toni*. Nodding, Ricki rose from her chair and crossed the deck.

"Oh really? Now, did you actually eat with her, or just sit in the booth next to her making googly eyes?"

"Googly eyes? Did you really just say that?" This time, she couldn't stop the eye roll. "Never mind. I know you're strange."

Toni laughed. "Thanks, hon, I love you, too."

"And yes, I actually ate with her. In fact, she cooked for me."

"Woah! How did this happen?"

While she chatted quietly with Toni for a moment, Kaya watched Ricki. She was leaning against a wooden railing edging the deck, and although Ricki's back was to her, Kaya could see the tension—and the sadness—in her posture. "I'm honestly not really sure. I'll let you know when I find out though. For now, I've got to get going."

Kaya slipped her phone back into her pocket. She watched Ricki, who was simply staring into the distance, before moving silently to join her. Sliding up next to her, Kaya tentatively brushed her fingers down Ricki's upper arm. She felt Ricki stiffen at her touch, but she didn't remove her hand. "Sorry about that."

Not turning to look at Kaya, Ricki asked softly, "You went to college with Toni?"

Kaya studied her, knowing the crack in her voice had nothing to do with her and Toni. "Yes. Boston University. We lived in the same dorm as freshmen, and then shared a house together with a few other friends the final three years."

Ricki nodded. "We'd been living in the dorms, but our senior year, Bre and I shared a house. We had a third roommate, but she wasn't often there." Ricki shrugged. "Maybe it was better that way. Something changed over the summer, something I couldn't define or explain. At first, I thought living in a house instead of a dorm room together somehow affected our closeness. I don't think that had anything to do with it anymore."

She paused, perhaps needing a moment to bring these elements of the story together. Kaya wondered if, on a subconscious level, she was avoiding the pain that was undoubtedly looming. She didn't speak though, giving Ricki as much time as she needed.

In the silence, Kaya traced her fingers softly along Ricki's arm again, hoping Ricki found the gentle touch both comforting and strengthening. When her tears finally spilled over, silently tracking down her face, she tried to turn away but Kaya pulled her back. Gently but firmly, she turned Ricki to face her and lifted her chin so that their eyes could meet. She cradled Ricki's jaw in her palms, and with the soft pads of her thumbs, she wiped the tears away. They stood together, wordless, and Ricki closed her eyes and let Kaya soothe her.

She slipped one arm around Ricki's waist and guided Ricki's head to her shoulder, holding her tenderly as she sobbed into the crook of her neck. Kaya rubbed her fingers along the back of Ricki's neck and pressed a kiss into her short hair. Mostly, she just held her. Held her in a way that invited her to release whatever she'd carried alone for years.

Finally, Ricki's sobs quieted. She stayed where she was, slowly regaining the breath she needed to go on. Still tucked in Kaya's embrace, she began in a voice so choked that Kaya could barely hear her, as close as they were. "I knew I was losing her, but I wasn't sure why. I knew she was still seeing Bobby Dean, that he'd apparently changed. Occasionally, I'd still catch that smug glare, particularly when he was in a place where he could physically demonstrate that Bre was with him. His hand on her thigh or his arm around her shoulders. But he stopped trash talking, stopped egging me on. It was like he'd stopped competing with me, sure that he had finally won. He had the one thing that I wanted most and could never have."

"And he knew it."

She stopped, and Kaya could practically see the anger and fear and the memory of helplessness choking her. It was a few seconds before she could continue.

"I felt like part of me was being flayed open, a new wound every time I had to see them together. But I couldn't look away—I couldn't walk away. She meant too much. So I hung out with them, with Bobby Dean's gang. For the most part I stopped dating, letting myself drown in my misery. I thought it couldn't get any worse."

Ricki leaned back in Kaya's embrace and let out a deep sigh. Staring over Kaya's shoulder into some memory, she went on. "My only pleasure in all of this was that Bobby Dean and the rest of IU's team was having an awful football season. They were never known for being the top of the Big Ten, at least not in football, but that year was particularly ugly. And college guys being just that, some of them heckled Bobby Dean. His frustration and annoyance were among the few things that made me smile that fall. Coming from the other guys, though, there wasn't much he could do but snarl and bear it.

"That was the routine until a weekend in late October—not unlike this one—with beautiful weather and plenty of football. The team lost—brutally—at the hands of Penn State. The backbreaking play was Bobby Dean fumbling the ball in the red zone, and IU never got back into it. We were all out for pizza together later that night, and one of the guys in the restaurant, a guy I didn't really even know but must have grown up here in Indiana, made a crack about how maybe Bobby should give his roster spot up to someone who could really run the ball. Someone like *me*."

Kaya's heart quickened. *That can't be good.*

Ricki met Kaya's gaze, her own ice-blue eyes begging her to understand what a crack like that meant. "I froze. Here was some stranger, mentioning my playing days and our old rivalry. I looked at him and saw the old hatred but a thousand times darker and more powerful, more sinister than ever before. My blood ran cold. But just like that it was gone, and he was joking his way past the heckling. I turned toward Bre, who was in her obligatory seat by his side, and saw for the first time something other than tender infatuation when she looked at him. I saw fear. And I didn't understand."

Ricki broke away from Kaya's embrace and turned. Kaya let her go, but not before she saw the change to crushing anguish in her features. Ricki's entire body language shifted Kaya couldn't stop herself from offering a gentle touch, tracing her fingers down Ricki's back, a gentle rub of reassurance. The thin, plain white T-shirt might have been a steel vest between them. They were inches apart, but Ricki couldn't be further from her, lost in her memories.

"A week later, at the house, I knocked and entered her room, looking to borrow a pair of socks. How silly is it, that I remember that? She'd just gotten out of the shower and was still wrapped in her towel."

She paused, swallowing back tears. "Her entire left shoulder was black and purple, like she'd been slammed violently into something, maybe a wall. Maybe that's exactly what happened. I don't know. When I asked, she just said it was nothing. She'd fallen. No big deal. But she couldn't meet my eyes when she told me that."

Ricki couldn't continue any further. Her throat seemed to close up, her body trying to keep what she was feeling in—or maybe out—Kaya wasn't sure. She took a few minutes and a few more dry swallows, trying to gather herself enough to finish.

"I began to notice a pattern. She looked thinner, started wearing long sleeves. Even so I'd notice bruises. I tried to talk to Bre about it, but she shut me out. That hurt. That made me angry. I knew Bobby Dean was abusing her, but nothing I said made any difference. I was close to confronting him—God knows how that might have ended—when…"

She shook her head. Kaya could sense there was more, some final piece that she was trying to get out. "Something happened one night and he lost it. He beat her so badly, she…she never woke up. Never regained consciousness. Stayed in a coma for two weeks before we lost her." Her voice dropped. "Before *I* lost her."

Kaya had known where the story was going, but hearing the anguish in Ricki's voice and being unable to do anything to help her was worse than she could have imagined. She reached for Ricki again, and Ricki let herself be guided back into her arms, burying her face at Kaya's neck.

"I'm so sorry, baby." *What else can I say?* Nothing seemed adequate—nothing could be. Ricki's eyes were dry now but her misery was unmistakable. Kaya just held her, gently rubbing solace in small circles on her back.

After a few minutes, Ricki stepped back. She kept her eyes down, swiping at her cheek for tears that weren't there. She studied her fingers for a moment as if confused. "I guess, after a while, tears just don't express enough anymore," she whispered.

Kaya didn't want to break their contact, keeping her hands loosely around Ricki's shoulders. She waited for Ricki to let her know what she needed, ready to give anything she had. She herself had had crushes on girls who didn't return her feelings, but to truly be in love and have no hope? And then, even worse, to have your love ripped from you so violently? Kaya couldn't imagine that horror and she hated that Ricki knew it intimately.

Finally, Ricki sighed and finished. "Bobby Dean beat her to death. He didn't even try to deny it. During the trial, he just sat staring at me with this smug grin on his face, as if he believed he'd finally beaten me. I guess he had. I'd give a thousand football titles to have her still be here—alive, safe, and well."

She shook her head. "He managed a plea bargain, manslaughter. Five years in prison, that's it. Five years. But he never was smart when it came to picking friends. He was shanked in prison, died three months into his sentence."

Ricki looked up. "Is it terrible that when the anger gets to me, I feel like he didn't suffer enough for what he did? Is it awful that I want worse for him?"

Kaya shook her head. "No. No, baby, that's natural. I feel that way, and I never knew him. Never knew either of them."

Ricki managed a small smile. "You would have liked her. But then, everyone loved Bre. She was just one of those people who somehow quietly touched every single person she met. She was too good for all of us."

Kaya thought about her words, about the history she'd just been told. For Ricki to share that showed an enormous trust placed in her, and she wanted nothing more than to deserve it. *What would I want, if our positions were reversed?*

"Will you tell me about her?"

CHAPTER SIXTEEN

Nature photos faded from one to the next on the screen saver, reminding Ricki of the work she should be doing. She was aware of the computer, aware of the assignment that she was supposed to have graded for her last class of the day, but she didn't turn from staring out the window. She had not been able to get much work done all morning, but, surprisingly, she didn't feel as if that were a bad thing. She'd been thinking about Bre, about Kaya, about everything she'd shared the day before.

It was the first time she'd ever been able to think about these things and feel at peace. Was that all a result of opening up to Kaya? Was her full night of dreamless sleep simply a side effect of sharing her burdens? She didn't know, but she knew she had Kaya to thank in one way or another.

The bell sounded for lunchtime. Kaya would most likely be down in the faculty lunchroom, and Ricki wanted to see her. But at the same time, she didn't want to socialize with the other teachers. Not so soon after such an emotionally raw day. Her typical solitary lunch held great appeal.

But still, there was Kaya.

The computer screen cleared, and a green pipe again began its darting course across the black field. Yes, there was Kaya, but there were also papers to grade. She nudged the mouse and pulled up the lab reports that the students had submitted the week before. She was only two paragraphs in when a soft knock sounded at her door.

"Hey," Kaya greeted her softly, stepping into the room. "You mind if I join you?"

Kaya was carrying a tray from the cafeteria, and when she set it down, Ricki saw two meals there. "I figured you might not want to be in a crowd, but that doesn't mean you shouldn't eat." Kaya glanced at the food. "Sorry I can't do better than nuggets and noodles."

Ricki smiled. "No, this is great." She poked at a limp lump of chicken. "One of my favorites."

Kaya's expression was skeptical and Ricki confessed, "Okay, maybe not."

They ate in silence, and she noted the ease she felt with Kaya's presence. Her mind drifted back to their conversation from yesterday. Somehow, Kaya had known, known exactly what she needed even when Ricki herself hadn't. After all the revelations Kaya had listened to, drawing out recollections that she hadn't had in years, always leading her back to the good times. Kaya had gotten her to tell of things that filled her with a warmth that she hadn't known was possible. She'd made her *laugh*. Bre and Ricki had gotten into some crazy situations, and somehow Ricki had forgotten the laughter they'd shared. For the first time since she'd lost Bre, remembering wasn't painful.

"Are you okay?" Kaya asked quietly, breaking into Ricki's thoughts, but not in an unwelcome way. "After yesterday?"

Ricki smiled. Yes. She was. She nodded.

Kaya seemed to accept her silence, though watching her carefully. Ricki felt her scrutiny but didn't mind it.

Then Kaya reached across the desk between them and took her hand. Ricki didn't pull away, and she spoke softly, "Thank you."

Ricki had followed the movement of Kaya's hand, simultaneously somehow both unnerved and calmed by her touch. But at Kaya's whispered words, she looked up, meeting her hazel eyes.

"For what? I'm the one who should be thanking you."

Kaya held her eyes for a moment, before dropping her gaze to their joined hands. "I know it can't have been easy for you, to share all of that with me yesterday. I'm honored. Bre meant so much to you, and you trusted me with her memory."

Ricki swallowed around the lump in her throat. "You listened. You pulled me out in a way I never imagined. No, it's you who deserves thanks."

Kaya looked up again and smiled. "Well, perhaps we're at an impasse, then."

"No." Ricki scrunched her brow, and feeling playful in a way she hadn't in a long time. "No impasse. You just need to see that I'm right."

Kaya laughed. "I guess, this time, I could let you win."

Ricki grinned. "You've been at this school long enough now, didn't anyone tell you I'm a proven winner?"

Kaya rolled her eyes, but her smile mirrored what Ricki felt. She liked that their hands were still linked as well. They talked a few minutes about mundane things, and she was comforted by the effortless conversation. When the bell sounded, Kaya stood and grabbed their tray. "Come over for dinner tonight."

Ricki hesitated, giving Kaya enough time to add some convincing. "I owe you a meal after yesterday. You gave me breakfast and lunch. Nothing major, I'll just throw something simple together." She turned away, not giving Ricki the chance to say no.

"I'll see you later," Kaya called behind her as she disappeared out the door.

* * *

Kaya sat back and watched Ricki swallow another bite of steak. She was pleased that Ricki was enjoying her meal, and didn't mind the compliments that she'd received several times already that evening. As she cut the last piece, Ricki looked up at her. "You said you were just going to make something simple. This is delicious."

Kaya smiled. "Grilling is simple, and after ten years in Chicago, I'm going to enjoy this weather and the ability to cook out on my balcony as long as possible."

Ricki chewed thoughtfully for a second. "What was it like, living in the city?"

She shrugged. "I like it here better."

"That doesn't answer my question," Ricki pointed out, setting her fork aside.

"No, it doesn't."

Kaya felt Ricki's studying gaze on her, knew she must realize how unusual it was for her to show any reluctance in conversation.

"Was it that bad?"

Kaya sighed. "Not at first."

Ricki nodded, but didn't push.

Kaya looked up and met Ricki's eyes. *So easy to read.* And right now, she read concern and uncertainty. *She bared her soul for me yesterday, and I pick now to clam up about my past? Good job, Hotshot.*

"It just got to me, after a while. Teaching in the South Side is so different from anything at Glenwood. Here, I not only have students who let me know them, I get to know their parents, families, neighbors even. You know that saying, 'It takes a village to raise a child'?" Ricki nodded. "Well, it seems small-town life actually provides that. Not so, where I used to be."

Ricki appeared thoughtful for a moment. "Small-town life isn't all honey and roses, though. I'm sure there must be things you miss about the city."

"Some things, yes."

When she didn't expand on that at all, Ricki guessed. "I'm sure you had more social opportunities in Chicago. As thrilling as the Alumni can be on a Friday night, it can't compare to the big city bars and clubs."

Kaya laughed. "No, that's true." She drew in a breath, "But I, for one, love our nights out at the Alumni." She caught Ricki's eye. "Better company than what I was used to."

Ricki grinned. "I'll tell Toni you said so."

Kaya rolled her eyes. "Go ahead. She'll dispute that till the day she dies, but honestly, since she met Rynn, I lost my wingman. And maybe I'm just getting older, but the clubs stopped being quite as much fun as they used to be. I wasn't looking for easy hookups or one-night stands anymore." Kaya caught Ricki's uncomfortable shift at that, so she turned the topic back. "And by the time I finished dealing with all the issues at school, most weekends I just needed the downtime to recover my sanity."

"What was so different about teaching there? I mean other than the parents' involvement," Ricki asked.

"That was the biggest thing. It might not sound like that big a deal, but I can't tell you how many nights I'd be on the phone for hours, trying to get these parents to care that their kids were flunking out. Or the number of times I'd get cussed out or hung up on, people telling me it was my job to teach, so I should quit whining to them and do my fucking job. What kind of parents take that approach to their child's education?"

She leaned back in her chair. Ricki took the opportunity to refill their wine. She continued, "I finished up college ready to tackle the world. I was going to change things, make a difference in children's lives. But that system, the South Side public schools, chewed me up and spit me out without blinking. My naivety was shattered, but I was stubborn, for better or worse."

Ricki quirked her brow at that and succeeded in getting Kaya to chuckle. "Yeah, yeah. You've already learned that I'm stubborn."

"I'd say it's for better, though."

Kaya lost her train of thought, watching as Ricki brought her wineglass to her lips. *Focus.* She mentally shook herself and went on with her story. "My dreams went from changing the world to making a difference for even just one kid. That approach got me through ten years, but in the end, I couldn't take it anymore. If I didn't leave, I would lose myself to the system I had been fighting against my entire career. I wasn't strong enough to keep swimming against that current and I don't know how it's ever going to get any better. I don't have those answers."

She sipped her merlot. "Toni was sad to see me go, but she understood. I had to leave, or give up teaching. I considered staying in Chicago and switching careers, but that idea felt all wrong. Even just the noise of the city was wearing me down. I think some part of me was itching to move on for other reasons. I'd never stayed in one place that long before. As a child, I was a military brat and used to a new school every couple of years. Having some sense of permanence was nice, but I felt like I wasn't in the right place to truly settle down. When I heard about the opening here, it sounded like a godsend. I applied, and Fisher hired me after just one short interview. I suppose the rest is history. I haven't looked back."

"Really?"

It was just one word, but Kaya heard more. "Why is that so hard to believe? You must like it here, or else you wouldn't have come back after college."

Ricki nodded, pensive. "Yes. I do like it here, but I have family here, history here, and I've never really known anything else. Bloomington is the biggest city I've ever lived in, and that's not a tenth the size of metro Chicago. And you've lived in Boston, too."

"Yes." *But this isn't about me, is it?* Kaya watched Ricki mulling over something, certain she knew where her mind was. There was only one place—one person—that put that look in Ricki's eyes. The question was whether or not Ricki wanted to talk.

Kaya decided to go for it. She'd never been good at subtlety, and Ricki might as well learn the real her. "Was Bre from a city?"

Ricki looked up and met Kaya's eyes. There, Kaya saw resigned acceptance rather than surprise, which itself surprised Kaya. She knew Ricki wasn't used to being read, but the sad smile said that maybe Ricki was okay with Kaya knowing.

"No. She was a farm town girl like me, but she had big city dreams. She was sure life would be so much better there. It didn't even matter which city, although what farm girl doesn't fantasize about New York? The best dreams were the ones that included me, with the two of us sharing a closet-sized flat in the glamourous Big Apple."

Kaya heard the echoes of Toni's tease when she first moved away from Chicago. She had enjoyed living in the city. In Boston, too, but there were things about this small town she'd stumbled into that made leaving the city worth it. Although the appeal for a young girl like Bre who'd never known that kind of life? It was undeniable.

"Did you ever think about going..." Kaya paused, uncertain how to end her question.

"Without her?" Ricki finished. Kaya nodded.

"No. The city was Bre's dream. For a long time, I imagined I really would go with her, but after...I managed to finish school, stumbling through that last semester in a daze. I graduated and had no idea where to go, what to do. So I came home. Drifted aimlessly around town, eventually started running at the track at Glenwood. I bumped into Ian, who'd just finished his first year coaching. We'd played together—I think he told you that in one of his crazy stories—and he'd landed a job as coach of just about all the boys' sports at Glenwood. I think the only one he didn't touch was soccer, but that's a different story. We caught up, and he got me a position as an assistant coach for football that fall. My head and heart were still in pieces, but somehow I put together a passable job and slowly cleared the fog from my life. When one of the math teachers took maternity leave, they gave me the extended sub position, and that morphed into a full-time gig."

She stopped and smiled. Kaya couldn't believe how much things had changed. Ricki hadn't talked this much in the entire few months they'd known each other, and now conversation came easily for both of them. She matched Ricki's smile and Ricki shrugged as if acknowledging the change. "I guess that's the long way of saying I ran home after college and never left. Never wanted to."

Ricki set her wineglass aside. "I know it's nothing like your past. More subdued, I suppose, but small-town life can do that to you."

"It might not be what I've known, but I think I could get used to it nonetheless."

* * *

Kaya rose from the table. "Should I open another bottle?" She asked as she gathered their dishes and crossed the apartment to the kitchen.

"No, I think I'm good for the evening." Ricki stood up from the table as well, but didn't move far. "Thank you though."

She nodded and set the dishes near the sink. Moving back over to her, Kaya gestured around the room. "Couch or balcony? It's chilly out, but you can see the stars."

Ricki smiled. She'd seen the sparkle in Kaya's eye at the suggestion. Ricki wasn't blind, and Kaya wasn't subtle. Stars were far more romantic than a couch, especially since casual friends usually sat at opposite ends. And while "casual friends" wasn't really accurate, the night sky was a far better backdrop for ensuring that. But was Ricki ready for more than friends?

She considered the offer and the implication. Kaya simply waited, holding Ricki's gaze. The warmth that infused Ricki within that gentle look told her what she needed to know.

"Stars."

That was all the permission that Kaya needed. She took Ricki's hand and led her outside. "This is one of things that cities can't hold a candle to," she murmured, her face turned up to the sight above them.

Ricki nodded and followed her lead. "They are beautiful." The two of them stood in silence, just close enough to touch, letting the peace of the evening flow around them. The night sounds and smells offered a perfect complement to the sky above. Ricki watched the sunrise almost every morning, but she didn't often stop to admire the other end of the day. It seemed this was just one more thing that Kaya drew out of her. How she did it, Ricki wasn't sure. She somehow knew when to talk—and she loved to talk—and just when to listen. Ricki couldn't remember the last time she'd felt so at home with her own thoughts. It surprised her that they weren't quite as haunting today as they had been the times they'd sneaked up on her over the years. It seemed almost unreasonable to attribute all of that to Kaya's simple, patient presence, and yet Ricki knew it was because of her. She hesitated still, knowing that Kaya didn't yet know the whole story and afraid of what she would say, how she would feel, if she did. But Kaya knew more than anyone else.

Ricki was shaken from her reflections when Kaya shivered beside her. "Cold?"

Kaya turned just enough to give her a teasing look. "No, I'm melting. I'm just trying to throw you off so you can't sense my real weakness."

Ricki grinned. "Smartass. And here I was thinking about wrapping my arms around you to keep you warm."

Kaya's grin disappeared, though she tried to hide whatever blend of nerves and hope she was feeling. Ricki was secretly pleased to have thrown her off, even just this little bit. "But if you're too warm as is, I wouldn't want to exacerbate the situation." Ricki turned so that they were facing each other and raised her hand to brush Kaya's arm in a loose embrace. Teasing—God, when was the last time she had teased?

* * *

"Remember how I said I was melting? I'm not lying anymore." Kaya didn't move, was almost afraid to move. *If she doesn't kiss me, I'm going to combust.* But she was powerless to do anything. She knew this had to be Ricki's lead.

The fingers that had been grazing her arm shifted higher, gently cupping Kaya's jaw. Ricki met her eyes and smiled. If Kaya could have forced a word out, it would have been *Please,* but Ricki thankfully didn't seem interested in making Kaya beg. When their lips met, Kaya had to remind herself to stay standing. This kiss was soft, so soft. Gentle yet strong in a way that was so distinctly Ricki. Kaya had tasted the sweetness the first time they had kissed, but the emotion that charged their sudden and brief explosion couldn't have been more different than this connection.

When Ricki pulled back, Kaya kept her eyes closed a second more, memorizing the moment. Opening them, she met Ricki's blue eyes, somehow ever vibrant even in the night shadows. "Time to leave?"

Ricki simply nodded, and Kaya accepted that their night was over. In truth, it had turned out better than she had hoped. She sighed, not wanting to let go but knowing it was time. After lingering in Ricki's arms a little longer, she crossed back into the apartment and through to the front door.

"Thank you." Kaya whispered, leaning in for a quick goodbye kiss.

"I'm pretty sure that's my line." Ricki smiled and gave Kaya's hand a gentle squeeze.

"Good night." With that quiet farewell, Ricki turned and headed down the apartment steps. *Indeed, it is.* Kaya grinned, watching Ricki disappear down the starlit sidewalk.

CHAPTER SEVENTEEN

Ricki beat Kaya to the stadium the next morning, and as she rounded the track and neared her, their dance shifted. For the first time since Kaya had started joining her in the morning, Ricki looked up, met her eyes and smiled as she ran past.

She held her smile as she rounded the next corner. She wasn't actually sure if Kaya was going to come today, since they...since they what? Since they kissed? Yes, that changed things, but how much? And was Ricki ready for those changes?

She wasn't sure, but she had at least eight more laps to figure something out. She had been using running to clear her head or sort her thoughts for years. The rhythm of her feet, the steadiness of her breathing, the cool dawn air—everything about this was calming. Six laps later, though, she still didn't know what to do. Or if anything needed done at all. She wanted to explore things with Kaya, but she'd been alone for so long.

Ricki ended her run and walked one last lap for a cool down. Circling back to the home stands, she found that Kaya had moved down from her seat and was standing at the edge of the track, waiting for her.

"Good morning." Kaya stepped closer, not quite closing the gap between them, as if she could sense Ricki's uncertainty. Ricki looked at her, her breathing still just a shade heavier than normal.

"Mornin'." Ricki hitched her chin toward the locker rooms. "Walk with me?" Kaya nodded and fell into step beside her. After they'd gone halfway, simply taking in the early quiet, Ricki spoke. "Are we dating?"

Kaya chuckled and stopped walking. "Is that your way of asking me out?"

Ricki turned to her but then shyly glanced away. "Should I? It seems like we skipped that step, but that leaves me unsure how far we skipped."

She was surprised by her own nerves. This was not a great time to feel like a teenager again, waiting for Kaya to say something, but still she was unable to actually look up for a response. Then she felt Kaya's touch, felt her hand brush a loose lock of hair back from her brow. The simple contact was enough to shake away some of her anxiety and she raised her head. She pulled back from Kaya's touch, but grinned. "I'm gross. No touching."

"I'm not afraid of a little sweat. I want you to look at me." Ricki hesitated, glancing back at the stadium behind them, before bringing her gaze back to meet her hazel eyes. When Kaya spoke, Ricki gave her full attention. "What do you want, Ricki?"

Always so direct. Ricki looked away again, nerves returned, before finding Kaya's eyes once more. "I don't know. But I want to find out." Neither of them spoke for a moment, until Ricki asked, "Can we take it slowly?"

Kaya smiled and nodded, and Ricki grinned in return. "In that case, Ky, will you go out with me?"

Kaya pursed her lips and looked away as if she were considering it. Ricki laughed and stepped back. "Oh, man, if this is how you're going to be, maybe I should take it back," but Kaya grabbed her arm and pulled her closer. "Yes. You know I will." She leaned in and stole a quick kiss. "Now, go get cleaned up. I'll see you for lunch?"

"Okay. Because nothing's as romantic as a high school cafeteria."

Kaya responded, "The cafeteria is for food. Romance comes later." She winked, turned, and walked toward the school.

CHAPTER EIGHTEEN

"It's open." Her hands full with the food she was prepping, Ricki hollered to the front of the house at the sound of the doorbell and hoped Kaya heard her. When no other sound came, she muttered a curse under her breath and turned to wash the breading off so she wouldn't make a bigger mess than she already had.

"No, don't stop on my account." Ricki spun around and was met by an amused Kaya leaning on the doorframe of the kitchen. "I know you cooked me breakfast, but somehow the sight of you being all domestic is still surprising."

Ricki furrowed her brow, unsure whether to be offended or flattered. "Hello."

Kaya chuckled. "It's a good thing. You're a surprising person, Ricki."

"Thanks, then. I'll just be another minute with this, if you want to grab a seat in the living room." Ricki gestured to the pork chops in front of her, half of them breaded and the other half awaiting her attention.

Instead of following instructions, Kaya pushed away from her perch and pulled out a chair at the kitchen table and settled into it.

They chatted easily. Ricki laughed as Kaya shared stories of the antics her students had pulled in Chicago and how different the students were at Glenwood. "Not that they don't get into their fair share of mischief, mind you, but it seems more innocent here somehow."

Ricki slid a tray into the oven and walked over Kaya with a skeptical look. "Innocent? I thought city girls weren't supposed to be naïve. You should hear the things my boys talk about during football practice when they forget I'm a woman."

She watched as Kaya ran her eyes up and down her body before responding. "I'm not sure how anyone could forget that." She smiled at the appreciative glint in Kaya's expression. "If I had to guess, it's not that hard when I'm yelling at them to get their asses moving and making them run till they can barely stand."

"Mmm. A take-charge kind of girl. And here I thought you were so quiet and reserved." Kaya tentatively reached out and caught the hem of Ricki's T-shirt. "I had big plans for cracking that stoic exterior. Who knew all it took was a little slacking?"

Ricki stopped Kaya's roaming hand, but leaned down when Kaya tugged her forward. "Big plans, eh?"

"Yes. Starting with a proper greeting." They shared a long kiss before Ricki straightened up and pulled Kaya to her feet as well. Taking her hand, she led her into the living room.

"You, sit. Over there. Dessert isn't supposed to come until after dinner."

Kaya pretended to pout, but finally did as she was told and sat on the couch. Ricki deliberately sat at the other end and saw some disappointment flicker on Kaya's face. She was torn, wanting to be closer to Kaya and also needing to keep things cool. She pulled one leg up and hugged her knee to her body. She hadn't been this tempted to get lost making out with a girl in a long time, and part of her brain realized that the speed of adult relationships was an unknown to her. They had only been seeing each other for two weeks, yet the connection was so much deeper than any of her college dating experiences.

Despite her disappointment, Kaya apparently couldn't pass up the opportunity to tease Ricki. "Have I been banished? The cold end of the couch, so cruel."

Ricki smiled. "Not you. Me. Your end is where the heat is."

"Shameless flattery will only get you so far."

Ricki just shrugged. "Until then, though, I think I'll have plenty of material."

* * *

Kaya smiled. "Just like I said, shameless." *She's smooth. So much for shy and stoic.* When she caught her own gaze dropping back to Ricki's full lips, she realized she badly needed to change the topic before she jumped Ricki's bones. "How does a nice girl like you get started in such a violent sport as football?"

Ricki chuckled, undoubtedly knowing full well why Kaya had abruptly switched to sports. "My Paps." She said the two words as if they were all the explanation that was needed, but Kaya had learned to just wait and the rest would come. Sure enough, Ricki went on. "My father took off shortly after I was born. I don't even remember the man, but it seems having a newborn was too much of a crimp in his freeloading lifestyle. My grandparents helped my mom to raise me, especially since my mom often had to work two jobs to support us. When my grandma died—cancer—that left Paps as the only one around with this adorable, innocent little girl all day while Mom was at work." Ricki paused long enough to playfully slap Kaya's knee at the mocking disbelief she showed at her description. "Do you want to hear the story, or not?"

Kaya grinned. "Yes, dear."

Ricki left her hand on Kaya's knee and continued her history. "Paps didn't know the first thing about raising a little girl. My mom is an only child, and Grandma did all the child-rearing. To hear Mom tell it, there were many occasions that she would come home from work to find me and Paps under the hood of the car or painting the house. Since I liked that better than dolls, she didn't try to stop it. At least not until Paps threw some shoulder pads on me and sent me out to get tackled by the boys in the Pop Warner youth football leagues. Mom about had a fit when she heard what he'd done, but it was too late. I'd had my first taste of the game, and there was no stopping me after that. At first, I ran to avoid getting hit, but as I got older, I found that running through the tackles and knocking the cocky boys on their asses was just as much fun."

Kaya reached over and covered the hand on her knee with her own. "I can see that. You putting those big, tough boys in their places."

Ricki chuckled. "It was fun. And I was fast. It didn't hurt that I was bigger than most girls my age. Once my teammates began to respect me for what I could contribute, getting called a tomboy—or worse—didn't sting so much. When I realized I was gay, things just made sense."

"That's really great, what your Paps did. It seems like a lot of men of his generation would have preferred you to stick to your skirts and dolls."

"Skirts never happened and dolls were best decapitated." They both laughed at that.

"Are you still so close? You've mentioned before that you have family here."

For the first time that evening, Ricki's smile faltered. "Uh, yeah. Yes, he and my mom still live here. Just down the street, actually. It's part of the reason I bought this place when it went up for sale a few years back, to be close to them and still have my own space."

Ricki didn't look like she wanted to say anything more, and Kaya studied her, feeling out whether to ask. However, the oven timer picked that moment to beep, and Ricki hopped up to go tend to their dinner.

Kaya followed her into the kitchen, tucking the exchange away in the back of her mind. She might have to ask Ricki more about this later, but for now it seemed best to let it go. *Saved by the bell.*

CHAPTER NINETEEN

"God, can you believe another season is over already?" Ian, loud as ever, turned and slapped Ricki on the back. From her place on the other side of the table, Kaya just smiled and shook her head.

"It always flies, even when we get to play a few extra." Ricki grinned.

"And it's a treat to play on a Saturday afternoon. I love everything about playoffs. Too bad we couldn't win just three more," Jamie added between french fries.

Kaya caught Ricki's eye, silently asking her a question. *Three?* She didn't want to sound foolish in front of her fellow staff. Fortunately, Ricki understood. "Three more is a state title. I think our boys had a great year as it is, taking the sectional and giving those thugs from Indianapolis a good fight today."

Kaya smiled. *Thanks, baby.*

"Yeah, I'm proud of our boys, too. Just a big dreamer, I guess. I can't help it if I want a state title to match yours," Jamie defended himself.

Ricki just rolled her eyes, but Kaya caught the forced grin and understood that her times as a player weren't the glory days for her that everyone else thought. She stretched her foot under the table to nudge Ricki's. She was thanked silently with a soft smile, but Ricki quickly refocused on Ian, who was now raucously recapping his favorite drive from the earlier game. "...and then *pow!* Keenan popped that guy so hard he knocked him into next week! Ha!" His excitement was contagious, and they continued chatting about the game. Kaya let her mind drift a bit, not quite as into the sport as her dinner companions, but appreciating their enthusiasm and enjoying the sparkle in Ricki's eyes as they talked. Her attention was pulled back to the chatter fully, though, when Ian said to Ricki, "It's great that Paps comes to so many games. You're lucky your family cares so much about the school and what you do. Hell, the only thing my wife likes about football is it gets me out of the house!"

Everyone laughed at that, but Kaya looked over at Ricki and tried unsuccessfully to catch her eye. *Is it just me, or is she suddenly avoiding eye contact?* Over the weeks they'd been dating, Kaya had noticed that Ricki had only good things to say about her family, and she had started to wonder when she might be able to meet them. She had assumed, though, that Ricki had just been too busy with school and football to think about something like that. But if her grandfather attended all the games, surely there would have been an opportunity for at least an introduction. *Maybe it's time I ask her.*

* * *

Jamie had been right—there were a lot of advantages to playing on Saturday afternoon instead of their usual Friday nights. They'd stayed at the Alumni quite a bit longer than they typically might, and afterward the night was still young enough for Kaya to hope for some time alone with Ricki. As they walked back to Ricki's house in the cold, early November dark, Kaya watched her breath mist the air in front of her, wondering at Ricki's silence. To a large extent, she'd grown accustomed to Ricki being a woman of few words, but tonight felt different.

Even from the moment they'd arrived at the pub, Kaya had sensed it. She'd slid into the booth expecting Ricki to sit next to her, but instead Ricki chose the other side. This marked the first time they'd been out with friends since they'd really started dating, and Kaya knew she shouldn't be surprised that Ricki was apparently not one for public affection. Now, though, they were the only people in sight on the street and still Ricki maintained a space between them as they walked.

Once they reached the house, Kaya paused, unsure whether she should head for the front door or her car. Ricki stopped beside her but didn't turn to talk. Instead she looked up at the stars. Kaya followed her gaze but then looked at her companion. Ricki looked weary. Not just tired from a long day or even a long season, but a sort of run-down weary, tinged with a hint of sadness. *Is she still thinking of Bre?* Kaya understood that Bre was never far from Ricki's mind, and no doubt the earlier conversation had stirred that up. But maybe there was something else.

Kaya started to ask, "Is everything—"

"I'm sorry—" Ricki spoke at the same time, then stopped and turned from the stars to Kaya.

Kaya hitched her chin. "You first."

Ricki nodded and sighed. "I'm sorry about earlier. I didn't mean to be so cold in the restaurant. It's just...being out with the guys...but that's no excuse."

Kaya listened quietly. *You weren't cold. Just...distracted, I thought.* When Ricki didn't go on, she reached down and took her hand. "What is it about being with the guys that was uncomfortable?"

Ricki looked at their joined hands and then back up to Kaya's eyes. "It wasn't you. I mean, in a way, it was. About us, anyway, but not anything you did." Ricki shook her head, but Kaya didn't think the motion was meant for her.

"Us." Kaya repeated what Ricki had said, rolling the word around in her mind. Somehow, she had imagined the first time hearing Ricki refer to them as *us*—as a couple—would be more satisfying. "What is it about *us* that troubles you?"

Ricki shook her head. "No, it's not like that. I'm not troubled. Well, I probably am, but not about that. It's been so long…since I was with anyone…I guess I just forgot how to mix worlds. You and I, we're feeling things out, seeing what we might have. It doesn't seem like that's anyone else's business."

"It's not," Kaya agreed uncertainly. "But that doesn't mean we need to hide what might be developing. If we're going to have a healthy relationship with each other, the *us* part needs to be compatible with the everything else part." Ricki didn't say anything, and Kaya started to get a bad feeling. "Right?"

"Yes, but still, I just wonder if we couldn't…I don't know." Ricki again fell silent.

What the hell? Ricki was talking like someone still in… "Wait a minute." The idea seemed absolutely ridiculous. *It can't be.* "Are you…You're out, right?" Kaya could hardly believe she was even asking that. Anyone with eyes could see Ricki was gay, and when she'd talked about college, she'd bluntly said she'd been a player. *You can't be a player and be in the closet.*

Ricki's continued hesitation bewildered Kaya. "How? I mean, I know we're in the rural Midwest, but surely you're out."

Ricki pulled her hand from Kaya's and ran it through her hair. "It's not that I'm closeted. Well, not really. I mean, not intentionally."

What the hell does that mean?

"Like I said, it's been a long time and I just haven't had a reason to talk about it with anyone."

Kaya shook her head. "You can't be telling me that the guys don't know. They've known you for years!"

"You're right, they probably know. I mean, Ian at least does, but it's not…that's not what I'm trying to say. I don't care about that."

"Don't care about what, Ricki?" Kaya was having a hard time understanding and her frustration was beginning to come through in her voice.

"Don't care what the guys think. I mean, I do, but not about that. They love you, and they'd be cool with us." There it was again, the *us* that lacked any gratification. "You said it yourself, we're in the Midwest. Public affection isn't really done, gay or straight."

In this day and age? "That's bullshit." Kaya wasn't sure if she was angry or just in disbelief. She hadn't been in the closet or dated someone in that position in a decade, and she'd completely forgotten what a mess it could turn into. Her frustration drained from her, though, when she caught the hurt look in Ricki's eyes. Somehow, a space had sprouted between them, physically and communicatively. Ricki took another step back, and Kaya recognized a retreat when she saw one.

"Hey. I didn't mean that. I'm sorry." She stepped forward, wanting to close the gap before it could get any wider. "You've taken me by surprise is all."

Ricki nodded, but she didn't meet Kaya's eyes.

"Look, maybe we should just—"

"Don't." The command in Kaya's tone stopped Ricki from finishing her thought, but it wasn't enough to get Ricki to look at her. There were three feet of air and a wall of silence between them. *She's running again. Why does she always do that?* Kaya saw that Ricki had caught her bottom lip in her teeth, uncertainty washing over her face. Where was the confidence and cockiness she had on the football field? *Or when she kisses me?*

"Ricki?" Kaya wasn't sure if waiting would do any good this time, but Ricki finally looked up. "Can we back up a second?"

Ricki nodded.

"Look, can we just forget about the outside? You talk about us, so let's focus on us. Are you happy with me?"

"Yes." To Kaya's relief, Ricki stepped forward, emphasizing her reply. "I am."

"Then why do you run at the first hint of difficulty?"

Ricki dropped her eyes again. After a moment, she released a deep sigh. "I don't want anyone to get hurt."

Kaya furrowed her brow. "Who's getting hurt? It's been a month."

"I know." Ricki chewed at her lip again, apparently trying to find the words. "I've gotten ahead of myself, haven't I?"

Kaya smiled, her best warm, understanding smile that she hoped invited Ricki to match it. "I think maybe we're both guilty of that." Kaya reached up and brushed her hand along Ricki's jaw. "You didn't ask, but I'm happy with you, too. If you're not comfortable with public affection or with telling your friends about us, that's something I have to accept. I won't lie, I haven't known anyone in the closet in a long time, let alone dated. I'm out. Completely. Are you okay with that?"

Ricki offered a timid half smile in return and leaned into Kaya's palm. "Yes. And you're right, I'm not exactly in the closet. I'd bet the guys know. There are other people who don't, but it's probably more because I haven't had anyone to tell them about more than actively hiding anything. It's just been a long time, you know?"

You keep saying that. Kaya nodded. "I know, baby. You asked for time, and I'm okay with that. I was surprised, and I overreacted, but I can give you the time you need." She paused, wanting to be sure she worded her next thought clearly. "As long as you tell me you want me, and you're happy with me, we can work things out. I'm a naturally affectionate person—" She pulled her hand away from Ricki's face, and waved her fingers between them. "But I'll try to rein myself in if you are willing to open up with me. I need to know what you're thinking, if we're ever going to stand a chance."

Ricki caught the hand in both of her own. "I'll try. I guess I'm just better in private." She tried a grin, and Kaya chuckled.

"Is that a promise?"

CHAPTER TWENTY

Kaya pulled the phone out of her pocket and glanced at the screen. Toni had always been early to rise, and once she'd learned of Kaya's new morning ritual, she occasionally texted around that time. *Maybe I should be grateful that Rynn likes to sleep in.* She smiled, thinking of her friends. Sure, she teased Toni for being so thoroughly whipped, but Toni always had time for her, no matter what.

You're coming up tomorrow night, right?

It was hard to believe it was Thanksgiving week already. It seemed like just last week that Kaya had piled up her car and left the city. She sent a short confirmation and let her mind wander through the past few months as her eyes found Ricki circling the track. It was amazing, in some ways, how much and how quickly life could change.

Her pocket buzzed again as another text came in. *Are you bringing your cutie?*

This time, Kaya stared at the phone. How had she completely spaced on the idea of spending the holiday together?

She realized immediately that she certainly wanted to share the short break with Ricki, but she had no idea what Ricki might have planned. *Only one way to find out.*

By that time, Ricki was approaching after her cooldown lap, so Kaya rose and climbed the bleachers down to the track. She loved the way Ricki's hot breath steamed the air between them and the faintest beads of sweat made her hair sparkle in the artificial lights of the stadium. It was late enough in the year that they couldn't watch the sunrise together, but the track lights were easy to turn on if you had the keys to the breaker box, which Ricki did.

"Hey." Kaya smiled her greeting and stole a kiss.

"Mornin'." Ricki pulled on the sweatshirt that she had tossed on the ground earlier. It was cool, almost cold, and Kaya was glad that Ricki layered up. By the afternoon, it would still get into the fifties, but before the sun warmed things, the grass wore a thick coat of frost and the air held a sharp bite. "You know," Ricki said, "you don't have to come sit in this cold. I know you're not going anywhere."

Kaya smiled. "I probably won't keep it up all winter, but I think I can hold out till the first snow, at least." They walked slowly toward the locker room. "Speaking of going anywhere, though, I am going to be out of town for a few days."

Ricki glanced sideways at her but said nothing, so Kaya continued. "I'm going to Toni's for Thanksgiving. I'll leave after school tomorrow and come back Sunday night." She turned to Ricki, wanting to gauge her reaction since she was expectedly quiet. Kaya was surprised to see—*was that relief?*—flicker across her face. Suddenly uncertain, she went on. "I was...well, I know it's terribly short notice, but I was wondering if you wanted to come with me."

They stopped walking just outside the locker room door. Any unusual reaction she thought she might have seen was gone, replaced by only frustration. If anything else had been there at all.

"I can't." Ricki glanced away. "I'm sorry. That sounds like fun."

Kaya tried not to let her disappointment show. Having not even considered the possibility before, she now found that she really wanted Ricki to come with her. "I don't know why I didn't ask sooner. I've been going to Toni's for Thanksgiving for a few years now—ever since she and Rynn got together. It's kind of their thing to host a big, family Thanksgiving. I guess I've only ever gone alone, but it would have been…" She fell quiet for a moment, before asking, "Are you sure you can't come?"

Ricki sighed. "I'm sorry, Ky. I've already promised my mom I'd do Thanksgiving with her and Paps. She's expecting me to help cook and all."

Kaya nodded. "I understand." She reached for Ricki's hand and gave it a small squeeze before Ricki disappeared into the locker room. As they parted, Kaya left unsaid the thought that popped into her mind. *Maybe next year.*

As she sat behind the wheel the next night, Kaya's mind wandered. On a normal day, the drive to Chicago was roughly four hours. On the day before Thanksgiving, she was happy to only hit one hour's extra drive time in traffic. The ride had given her time to think, and it was no surprise that her thoughts had mostly been occupied with Ricki. She realized she missed her already, although that felt a little silly, and found her thoughts returning to the idea that, for the first time in nearly two months, she wouldn't be able to keep Ricki company during her morning run tomorrow. The thought saddened her, and she wondered if Ricki would miss having her there.

Kaya tried to reassure herself that Ricki wouldn't be alone. After all, she'd probably be at her mother's all day. The idea that Ricki had plans and hadn't mentioned them to Kaya at all seemed a little odd, until she realized that was exactly what she herself had done. Perhaps the craziness around the holidays just made everyone a little scatterbrained.

As the miles wore on, she reflected back over their time together. They hadn't really gone out on any dates, but between seeing each other at school and eating together at one of their homes a few times a week, Kaya was satisfied with their time.

Admittedly, taking it slow as Ricki had requested was murder on Kaya's rampaging libido, but she knew Ricki was worth the wait. The bigger challenge might be coming up, knowing that Toni would demand details and likely give her a hard time. She sighed to herself in the car. Toni was her best friend, and she knew how to handle her. *I hope.*

Having only left after school let out, it was late by the time she arrived at her friends' house. She wasn't surprised, though, that they had waited up for her. Rynn greeted her with a big hug and pulled her into the house. "Toni's buried in the kitchen," she reported as they walked through the living room. "Don't be surprised if you end up covered in flour from hugs."

Kaya smiled, and her grin grew even wider when Rynn got a fistful of flour tossed at her as soon as she pushed through the kitchen door. Kaya delicately stepped around Rynn, who feigned a glare at her wife as she dusted off the fine powder. "I'm calling 'not it' on cleaning duties, if this is the way you're going to cook," Kaya said.

Toni laughed and embraced her. "Rynn gets cleanup duty for mocking me. But I'm sure I'll find things for you to help with tomorrow." She clapped Kaya on the back before releasing her from the hug, and Kaya didn't need to look to know that she now had a floury handprint marking her as a guest.

Rynn, still bearing signs of her ambush but no longer bothering to clean, muttered playfully, "Told you so." When Toni threateningly grabbed her mixing bowl, Rynn ducked to the other side of the room. Kaya just laughed. It was good to be among friends.

The following afternoon, she was assigned to door duty. Answering the bell, Kaya found herself swept into a giant bear hug. "Kaya! So good to see you again!" Steve returned her to her feet, while behind him, David was maneuvering through the front door carrying another case of wine to add the one Steve had just set down. "Are you boys planning on getting everyone drunk?" Kaya joked.

David laughed and greeted her with a quick kiss on her cheek. "Honey, Steve was so embarrassed that we ran out last year, I think he almost wept."

Steve blushed, despite his immediate protest, "I did not!"

David nodding knowingly, "He wasn't about to let you all down again this year. But that's why we love him. So sweet."

Steve started to object again but gave up with a sigh at his boyfriend's gentle teasing. Kaya shook her head at the happy couple and led the way into the living room to join the rest of their friends. People milled around, passing back and forth between rooms as they chatted. Toni was finishing some last-minute touches in the kitchen, and Rynn was trying to make space in the dining room for all the additional side dishes that their guests had contributed. Kaya felt so much at home, it was hard to believe she hadn't seen most of these people in months. She found she had missed them more than she realized. The house was bursting with the warm energy of friendships, old and new. Over the course of dinner and into the afternoon, Kaya found herself in deep discussions, even with the newcomers she hadn't met before.

In a moment between conversations, Kaya wandered to the edge of the room to refill her wineglass. Turning back, she looked around the room, just taking in the joy of the holiday. Despite the attempt to downplay it, she couldn't help but notice that part of what made the gathering so comfortable was the total ease with which people mingled. Gay and straight, couples and singles, women and men. None of that mattered here. As it turned out, that was something she had missed in her new home as well. But before Kaya could dwell on that too long, she bumped into the human brick wall that was Daniel Rocker.

"Daniel!" Kaya, hardly short, had to stretch to place a kiss on his cheek. "I'm so glad to see you here. No game this week?"

"Oh, yeah. We're at Oakland Sunday, but we won't leave till tomorrow. Since the season's been going pretty well so far, Coach rewarded us by giving us the day to be with family."

Kaya smiled, understanding completely that both of them were with family at Toni and Rynn's.

"But I don't want to talk about me. You, little lady, had my hopes up and then *crash*—" he clapped his enormous hands together, startling more than a few of the people nearby— "Just shattered my dreams and left me deflated."

Over the years, Kaya had come to know Daniel well, understanding most of his moods and emotions. But here, she could do nothing more than look blankly back at him, at a loss as to what he was talking about.

Fortunately, Toni joined the chat and stepped to Kaya's rescue. "I may have mentioned that you might be bringing someone this year." *Crap. Some rescue.*

Daniel pretended not to notice the glare Kaya shot at her best friend and eagerly pumped for details. "Toni tells me you've got a special someone. And she knows football!" Any frustration Kaya might have felt at having her love life brought the center of attention melted away immediately at Daniel's enthusiasm. *What is it about that ridiculous sport that everyone I love loves so much?* Then again, she shouldn't be surprised that an NFL player and his agent would have gossiped about her budding romance with a football coach.

It didn't hurt that the thought of Ricki instantly brought a smile to her face. That reaction merely provided something further for Daniel to pounce on. "Looks like someone's been happy lately. Come on, girl, spill."

Kaya faked a sigh. "I don't know, Dan, you might not like her." She paused dramatically. "After all, she is a Colts fan."

Daniel gasped and grabbed his chest as if he'd been shot. "No! Say it ain't so. The Colts?" He wiped a fake tear from his cheek. "And all this time, I thought you had good taste."

Kaya grinned. "I do. I'm not dating a Packers fan, am I?"

Daniel laughed so hard, the tear he wiped from his cheek this time was real. "You have certainly got me there. Well, I'm sorry she couldn't make it this weekend. It would have been nice to meet her. You just give me a call if she ever wants to come watch a real football team sometime."

Kaya couldn't resist, "Oh, you know someone who could get us Patriots tickets?"

Daniel glared at her, and Kaya jabbed a finger at his washboard abs. "Relax. I was once a Boston girl. You gotta let me hold some allegiance."

He pouted a moment, before rolling his eyes and letting the conversation move on to other topics. There were, despite popular belief, things beyond football to chat about.

* * *

Ricki sat alone on a bleacher, the morning still dark around her. The lights on the track had clicked off a few minutes earlier, their timer having run out with no one else to reset them. Ricki hadn't been able to sleep, so she'd arrived at the track earlier than usual. Getting started was no problem, but as the laps added up, the emptiness of the stadium weighed heavier and heavier. Ricki knew Kaya wouldn't be there, knew she was in Chicago, but knowing it and feeling it were two different things.

She had slowed, her energy level just not what it should be. Her run became a jog, which in turn shifted to a walk. After a few more laps, she gave up and took a seat in the bleachers. When Kaya first told her about her Thanksgiving plans, she'd been relieved. She'd been struggling for days, trying to figure out what to do about the holiday. When it turned out Kaya had plans, at first Ricki felt as if she'd been given a reprieve. She wouldn't have to make up an excuse not to invite Kaya to meet her mom and Paps. She wouldn't have to dodge any questions or tell any half-truths.

Now, though, the feeling of reprieve gave way to feelings of guilt. Was she hiding? Was she ashamed of her relationship with Kaya? No. And yet, she couldn't face telling her mother and grandfather the truth.

She also didn't want to ignite Kaya's temper again with the idea that she wasn't out to her family. College and co-workers were one thing. Kaya was right, the guys surely knew even if they'd never talked about it. But Mom? Paps? Not only did they not know, but Ricki was sure they would not take it well.

All of which just left her in a mess, sitting alone in the dark trying to figure it out. For the longest time, it didn't matter that she couldn't tell them because she had no one to tell them about. But Kaya? Ky made her feel things that she hadn't felt since college. Things she hadn't really expected to ever feel again. But not just attraction and arousal—though there was no shortage of that—but peace and even pride that had been long buried.

She sighed into the softening predawn light and rose from the bleachers. There was a turkey dinner waiting for her assistance. Besides, acknowledging that she missed Kaya wouldn't bring her home any faster. Although denying it didn't ease the ache, either.

CHAPTER TWENTY-ONE

"So what's really the story with you coming here alone?" Toni sat down onto the couch next to Kaya and curled her long, slender legs beneath her.

Kaya looked up from the book she'd brought with her. She had been waiting for Toni to corner her on this. It was inevitable, but at the same time, Kaya appreciated that Toni had waited a couple of days. The extra time hadn't really helped her think of an answer though, despite how much Ricki had been on her mind.

"Come on, surely you knew I would notice the way you dodged out of telling Daniel anything yesterday."

"Yes, I knew. But I really don't know what to tell you."

Toni sipped from her glass of wine. "Why isn't Ricki here?"

"Because I forgot to invite her, and by the time I did, she already had plans."

Toni gave her an incredulous look, but then shrugged.

"Really?" Kaya asked. "You're going to let me off that easy?"

Toni shrugged. "I know you well enough to actually believe that."

Kaya narrowed her eyes. "I think maybe I should be offended by that."

"Am I wrong?" Toni asked.

"No." Kaya considered saying more, but again, she wasn't really sure what to say.

"I can see that's not all there is to it, though," Toni added.

Kaya drew in a deep breath. "You're probably right, but I'm not really sure what to think about the whole thing. I think I know what's going on, but I'm not sure how to handle it."

"Why don't you back up and lay it out for me?" Toni asked.

"It's not that complicated." Kaya paused. "And yet, it is. Ricki spent yesterday with her family. Her mom and grandfather. Whom I haven't yet met."

She felt her friend's studying gaze, but she was nearly talking to herself, hashing out loud the thoughts that swirled in her mind. "She's still closeted. Or at least partially."

Kaya looked up at Toni. "She's afraid to introduce me to her family. And I have no idea what to do about that. God, I came out in high school. I can't imagine living like that anymore. But at the same time, I know it's a personal choice, and she has to make her own decisions."

"We all do. But that doesn't mean we make them alone."

"No, of course not. Albeit, alone does seem to be her modus operandi. In fact, that's the primary reason she gave me the one time we talked about this. She said she just hasn't had anyone to tell people about, so she never told them she was gay, either."

"That sounds a little odd."

Kaya shook her head, suddenly feeling a need to defend Ricki even though she knew Toni meant no harm. "It's not as simple as I'm summarizing for you now. It's not at all odd to me that she's been alone, but at the same time, I don't know how we can have a healthy relationship if she's afraid to claim *us*."

Kaya thoughtfully chewed her bottom lip, having now gotten as far aloud as she had been able to process mentally. "I really care for her. You know better than anyone else that I haven't been this mixed up over a girl...well, ever, really. But I have no idea what to do about this."

Toni reached across the space between them and patted her friend's knee. "I think maybe you just answered your own dilemma. You really care for her. Isn't that all you need to know right now?"

"But what about—"

"Just slow down. Be there for her. If she cares about you too, you'll figure things out together. If whatever she's told you about her past makes it understandable that she might still be closeted, then isn't it also understandable that she'll need time to break away from that seemingly safe space she's known?"

"I get why she was alone. It's still a little bizarre to me that she's clinging to the closet. I mean, you've seen her. She's the prototypical gorgeous, slightly butch lesbian. I mean, she's got it all. The tight, strong body. The short, thick hair that just begs me to run my fingers—"

"Woah, okay Hotshot, I don't need to hear your inner erotica novel," Toni laughed.

Kaya blushed. "Well, it does."

Toni just shook her head. "Yeah, yeah. I think you may be getting off topic, though."

Kaya shrugged but smiled. There was a time when they had shared the physical details of dates with each other, but Toni wasn't interested in those conversations anymore. *And really, I don't need to share those thoughts either.* The way Ricki made her feel, physically and emotionally, was just between them. Perhaps that was another key difference between mature relationships and the flings and short-term romances she'd had before.

Refocusing on the conversation, Kaya spoke again. "So you don't think I have to do anything about this?"

Toni considered her for a moment, and Kaya appreciated that she took the time to give her a thoughtful and deliberate answer. "It's not that you don't have to do anything about this, exactly. It's more that this doesn't have to be a make-or-break issue—yet. So far, you've shown your feelings by being there when she needs you, even if she doesn't want to admit she needs you. So if that's what your heart is telling you, then that's what you should keep doing. Is your relationship suffering because she's afraid to come out to her family?"

Kaya reflected on her feelings. "It bothers me. I'd like to know her, to know the people who are important to her. I want to be part of her life, and if she's closeted, then I never fully can be."

"Do you need to be that part, right now?"

Kaya sighed. "She did ask that we take it slow. I think she'll get to a point where she can be comfortable with me meeting her family, even if it's not at the pace I'd go."

"So then," Toni concluded, "you just need to be a little patient."

"Yeah, but we both know how good I am at that."

Toni rose from the couch. "You spent ten years teaching in a world that chews faculty up and spits them out daily. And now you've been getting up before dawn to keep the school bleachers company. I think you're far more patient than you care to admit."

Kaya smiled, warmed by Toni's compliment. "Maybe. But if I admit it, you'll start to expect it."

Toni chuckled and leaned down to hug her before heading up to bed. "And we certainly wouldn't want that, now would we?"

CHAPTER TWENTY-TWO

As she drove home Sunday afternoon, Kaya thought for the umpteenth time about her conversation with Toni and her fledgling relationship with Ricki. She had never been one to sit back and see where something led, particularly not when there was an apparent issue, but she certainly couldn't think of anything better to do.

She missed Ricki. After having only been gone for four days, she wanted to see her. Wasn't that indicative of high potential? *Either that, or the impatience and desperation of high school romance are rubbing off on me.* She wanted to hear her voice, see her smile. Even if that smile could be a challenge to bring out. But then, maybe after a few days apart, it wouldn't be that hard.

Kaya glanced at the clock on the car center console. By the time she got back to her new, small-town home, it would be after nine o'clock. Was that too late to visit Ricki? Probably, but she couldn't resist at least asking and grabbed her cell phone.

Kaya assumed Ricki either saw the caller ID or would recognize her voice. "Hey. It's me."

"Hey. Are you on your way back?"

Maybe Kaya was imagining things, but she thought she heard a smile in Ricki's voice.

"Yeah. About halfway there."

Time seemed to pass a little easier as they chatted. They'd talked twice while Kaya had been gone, but those conversations were short as Kaya hadn't wanted to be rude to her hosts by disappearing for long periods of time. Now, though, with only the stripes on the road to keep her company otherwise, they had plenty of time.

When her phone battery beeped in protest some time later, Kaya realized she didn't want to say goodbye and remembered the reason for her call in the first place. "Hey, my phone's going to die soon. I was wondering…" She fell silent, suddenly a bit shy to invite herself over.

"Ky? You still there?"

"Yeah. Would it be crazy if I stopped by when I get back? I've missed you."

When Ricki didn't respond immediately, Kaya mentally smacked herself. *How dumb am I? I'll see her at work tomorrow. Am I really so love-struck that I can't wait another twelve hours?*

"Yeah, I'd like that."

"Wait, what?" Having just internally chewed herself out, Kaya was now surprised by the response.

Ricki must heard her confusion and found it amusing. "I said I'd like that. Unless you changed your mind in the three seconds it took me to spit out an answer."

"Oh! No. I still want to see you. But yeah, I thought maybe…"

"That it was silly to want to see me tonight when we'll be at school tomorrow? Yeah, I feel that. It's why I didn't respond right away. But I missed you, too."

Kaya smiled in the dark. She'd get to see Ricki tonight, and she couldn't think of any way she'd rather be welcomed home.

* * *

While Ricki waited for Kaya to arrive, she did more of what she'd been doing since Kaya left. She sat alone and thought.

Okay, sometimes she'd gone for a run and thought. So much thinking wasn't unusual for her—she'd been a thoughtful loner for years. But so much thinking about a girl was different. She'd embraced being alone, certain she deserved nothing more.

Kaya obviously disagreed with that and after spending time with her, it was almost becoming possible to believe that she might be right. Or at least partly right. Ricki deserved hell for the sins of her past, but she was thrown for a loop by the thought that her being alone might cause others grief. It had never before occurred to her that maybe Kaya deserved to be happy. And if Kaya wanted her, wasn't her self-imposed solitude causing problems?

Then again, that sounded awfully egotistic. Plenty of fish, someone better out there for Kaya, blah, blah, blah. Thoughts swirled in her brain, ebbed and flowed and often got caught in little eddies, but Ricki could feel their overall trajectory. She was being pulled inexorably toward Kaya.

The unexpected part was the peace that came with the relentless current. Kaya calmed her in a way she hadn't truly felt since before Bre had died. Even being able to think about Bre without the crushing despair was something still so new it surprised her. She was able to remember, and not feel hopeless.

Hope for the future had been so foreign for so long, but Ricki found now that maybe she did want a future. And just maybe, she wanted to explore the possibility of Kaya being a part of that. There were still fringes of guilt at the edges of her consciousness, but that they were at the edges was significant.

Ricki could logically separate Bre's memory from Kaya's present. She knew they weren't the same. Knew they would never face the same threats or risks. It was not possible for Ricki to cause Kaya the suffering she was responsible for at the end of Bre's life. But even knowing that, she still feared that someone would get hurt because of her selfishness.

She didn't think that agreeing to Kaya's visit tonight could lead to anyone getting hurt. Well, it might open the door to further their relationship, and with deeper commitment came greater risk. But that kind of hurt was easier to see coming, wasn't it? It wasn't like anyone was in physical danger. Not this time.

Kaya should arrive soon. Ricki knew she had to make a decision. They could visit, kiss—hell, probably make out—and say good night. Or she could invite Kaya to stay. Would it be selfish to follow her heart and her body this time?

She still hadn't come to a decision when she heard the soft knock. As she walked toward the door, she determined she was simply thinking too much. Perhaps she should just ride the flow and see where it ended up taking her.

She was greeted by Kaya's warm smile. Ricki grasped her hand, pulling her into the house and into a welcoming embrace. The few seconds in Kaya's arms felt like home, and Ricki released a long sigh.

"That doesn't sound good. Is everything okay?" Kaya pulled back enough to catch Ricki's eyes. Ricki offered a small smile, and leaned close again, this time for a short kiss.

"Yes. Actually, things are pretty good. I just missed you, I guess." Admitting to Kaya the truths she used to deny even to herself was getting to be almost instinctive.

Kaya smiled softly. "Good."

Ricki moved closer, slipping her hand inside Kaya's open coat and claiming her mouth in a much stronger kiss.

She loved the way Kaya kissed. The heat and the hunger that were so easy to feel, so easy to match. Without breaking the kiss, pinning Kaya back against the front door, she felt Kaya's hands in her hair. She hesitated, wanting to cup Kaya's breasts but needing to respect Kaya's wishes. Her doubt was chased away by the soft moan of need and the way Kaya leaned into her.

Taking Kaya's breasts in her hands, she rubbed the pads of her thumbs over her nipples, hard through the thin fabric of her T-shirt. When Ricki realized Kaya wasn't wearing a bra, her desire magnified, and she moved her mouth down to Kaya's neck, needing to taste skin.

"Oh God." Kaya whispered the words as she let her head fall back against the door. Her fingers were still tangled in Ricki's hair. Ricki chuckled, overjoyed to be sharing this need with this wonderful woman.

"Don't laugh. And don't stop." Ricki felt a gentle slap to the side of her head, and pulled back just enough to see the smile in Kaya's half-closed eyes.

She kissed her, met her tongue again, as she walked her fingers up to the neck of Kaya's shirt. She tugged on it, wanting more, but this time it was Kaya who laughed before shoving her away.

Ricki stepped back, dazed. Kaya was ripping her coat off, her face flushed with heat and desire.

"I need to go out of town more often, if this is how you're going to greet me."

Ricki grinned. "It wasn't planned. But you feel so good." She moved toward Kaya again, but again Kaya pushed her back. Ricki loved that she could now see Kaya fully. Her slightly messy auburn hair, the blush on her face that spread till it disappeared under her T-shirt. The way her chest rose and fell as she breathed hard, air stolen by their contact. The curve of her breasts, her hips. The way her jeans both clung tight and hung loose in the just the right places.

"Why am I over here, when you're over there?" Ricki tracked her gaze back up Kaya's stunning body and landed again on her hazel eyes. "Did I do something wrong?"

"No. Exactly the opposite. You did something so right, I need a minute for my head to catch up with my body." Kaya closed the gap between them.

"I want you to kiss me again," she said, her voice barely a murmur.

Ricki kept her hands to herself, a level of control she was surprised she possessed at the moment. "And?"

"And I don't want to leave after."

Ricki never looked away, her eyes locked with Kaya's. "Then don't." She reached between them and took Kaya's hand.

She could hear her heart pounding in her ears, drowning out the last echoes of the doubts and questions that had plagued her for weeks and lain dormant for years. She wanted Kaya. Needed this connection. It was right in a way she had never felt before.

She stepped backward, still holding Kaya's hand. "Stay with me tonight."

CHAPTER TWENTY-THREE

Ricki pulled Kaya with her into the bedroom.

"Take your shirt off for me, baby," Ricki asked. Instead, Kaya reached for Ricki's shirt. She craved the skin that lay underneath.

"Ah, ah. I've got this. I want yours off." Ricki leaned back but popped loose another button. Kaya swallowed, taking in that teasing movement. Ricki wore a sports bra, but she could see the skin of her flat abs, and she wanted badly to feel that skin against hers.

Kaya yanked her shirt over her head and tossed it aside. *Enough teasing.* She grabbed the tails of Ricki's shirt and dragged Ricki down to take her mouth in a hard kiss. The urgency from downstairs overtook her again and she fell back on the bed, pulling Ricki with her, her mouth hungry on Ricki's skin.

Ricki tugged desperately at her own shirt, her wrists caught in the sleeves, and Kaya took advantage of the momentary bind. She pushed her bra up and sucked her nipple into her mouth. Ricki groaned and pushed harder into Kaya. She yanked free of her shirt and ripped off her bra.

Kaya explored Ricki's body with her mouth and her hands, touching, tasting all over. Ricki was doing the same to her, her hot mouth at her neck and her hands at her breasts. Together—Kaya couldn't tell who was leading and who following.

Ricki pushed Kaya's pants roughly down her hips, her hands sliding up to grab her ass and pull Kaya against her. Kaya kicked frantically at her pants, freeing her legs so she could wrap herself around Ricki's hard stomach. She moved her hands from her hair, fumbling for the waist of Ricki's jeans.

"Naked, God, I need you naked," Kaya gasped. With the last of their clothing gone, they crashed back together, Ricki on top of Kaya, hands and limbs hopelessly entangled. Kaya felt Ricki, skin to skin, her hands holding and stroking her everywhere. All Kaya could do was hang on for dear life. When Ricki slid her hand between Kaya's thighs, Kaya opened for her, needing her inside.

Ricki entered her, fingers sliding deep, and Kaya arched her body and threw her head back. She tried to hold onto the scream as Ricki pumped inside her, clung desperately to her, mindless of the scratches she was carving into Ricki's back. Ricki's mouth was at her breast, her other arm wrapped tightly around Kaya's waist, holding them together and setting a frenetic pace.

Kaya felt Ricki's wetness as she rode her thigh, thrusting into her again and again. She was losing control rapidly, her orgasm threatening to overtake her too quickly. She tried to hold on, but she couldn't, surrendering then to Ricki's demanding touch. Every muscle in her body contracted, strung tight as the scream ripped from her throat. She clung mindlessly to Ricki as pleasure washed through her, her orgasm stealing every coherent thought from her being. It lasted, lasted longer than she had ever known, until her body gave out and she collapsed back into the bed.

As awareness returned through the lingering tendrils of her orgasm, she felt Ricki on top of her and held on to her with what strength she had left. She could feel Ricki's hot breath on her chest, could follow the rise and fall of Ricki's labored breathing against her body. She was barely able to catch her own breath, and they lay together in silence for a moment until she could find the air required to speak.

"You destroy me. I'm going to make you feel the same just as soon as I—"

"I'm already there."

Kaya opened her eyes, needing senses other than touch to make sense of what Ricki had said.

"What? I haven't even touched you."

"You don't have to. You're so beautiful, so incredible. Just the feel of you under me, the look of you giving yourself to me like that. I came with you."

Kaya stared at her, not quite comprehending. "You...with me?"

"Yes." Ricki lifted slightly, bracing herself with the arm still wrapped tightly around Kaya. "Is that okay?"

"I...I still want to touch you."

Ricki smiled. "I sure hope so. But I think I might be wrecked enough for one night." She shifted again, and Kaya felt her withdraw her fingers. Although infinitely gentle, the sensation still made Kaya gasp and close her eyes again. She was minutely aware of every place their bodies touched as Ricki pulled herself up to kiss her.

"You're sure you're satisfied?" Kaya whispered.

"Satisfied?" Ricki sounded genuinely incredulous and Kaya trusted the truth between them. "Baby, satisfied doesn't begin to describe what you do to me. I've never felt so incredible."

Kaya snuggled against her, safe and content in her arms and losing the fight against her body's need for rest. *Me either.*

CHAPTER TWENTY-FOUR

Ricki leaned over as gently as she could. She didn't want to wake Kaya, but she didn't want to leave her either. She settled on kissing her brow as she lay sleeping peacefully, and left a note on the bed stand.

"Baby?" Kaya's half-asleep question called her back to the bedside.

"You leaving?" Kaya was adorable in her semiconsciousness, not quite capable of forming full thoughts, but managing to relay her concern.

"I'm just going out for my run. I'll be back soon." Ricki whispered and kissed her gently.

"Run? It's dark out," Kaya mumbled.

Ricki just barely managed not to laugh. "Yes. It's been dark for my run for the past few weeks. Don't you remember? You've been there."

Kaya reached for her weakly. "Still dark. Come back to bed."

"I'll be back soon. Go back to sleep."

Kaya mumbled something else. Ricki smiled and stroked her cheek, peaceful again in sleep.

Leaving was hard, but running was grounding. The past few days, running alone while Kaya was away, had been rough. She'd missed Kaya, missed her constant presence watching from the stands. Today was completely different because Kaya wasn't really absent. She was home.

Thinking of the amazing night they'd shared—and the promise of more—gave Ricki an energy she hadn't felt in a long time. The laps fell rapidly and before she really realized it, the track lights shut off. Since she'd put them on an hour timer, she knew she'd stayed longer than planned. She'd have to run home now to fit in her shower and see Kaya before heading to school.

Opening the front door, Ricki was immediately attuned to the presence of another, a sensation jarringly foreign to her. She'd never had an overnight guest in this house. Not even so much as a friend.

In the kitchen she found Kaya leaning against the counter, sipping a cup of coffee, hair wet from her shower.

She was gorgeous.

"Good morning," Ricki said softly, and walked over to her.

"Good morning," Kaya replied and set her coffee aside. "I had this crazy dream last night. This absolutely amazing woman made love to me until I couldn't move, but when I woke up in the morning, she was gone. Now, why do you think I might have dreamed something like that?"

Ricki smiled. "Is that what happened? A dream?" She moved closer and slipped into Kaya's arms, a completely natural fit.

Kaya wrapped her arms around her waist. "Must have been. I can't think of any other explanation for waking up alone this morning."

"Ah." Ricki nodded knowingly. "But, if that's the case and it was just a dream, why did you wake up in my bed instead of yours?"

Kaya looked past her, as if she were considering a serious inquiry. "See, that's the part I haven't worked out yet. It just doesn't make sense."

"And besides that," Ricki added. "If it was a dream, how do you explain talking to me before I left?"

At that, Kaya appeared genuinely confused. "I did?"

Ricki laughed. "Yes." She relayed their earlier conversation and Kaya laughed too.

"I don't remember that at all. But at least I can rest assured that I make more sense asleep than you do awake. Leaving our bed to go running? Clearly I didn't do a good enough job last night."

Ricki felt her body kick into gear. She remembered exactly what Kaya had done last night. Every sigh, every scream and thrust. But damn if they didn't have to go to school. Really, she should have been in the shower ten minutes ago.

"Do you think anyone would notice if we both took subs today?" Kaya murmured. "I want nothing more than to take you back to bed and do to you what you did to me last night."

Hearing her say that, Ricki felt her knees buckle. "We can't do that, but now thanks to you, that's all I'll be able to think about all day."

"Good." Kaya kissed her. "Now go shower. Homeroom starts in an hour, and it seems we need to be there when it does."

* * *

Kaya sat at the front of her class, watching the kids work through the problem sets she'd given them in groups. In another moment, she'd convince herself to get up and walk around, observing more closely and offering more hands-on guidance. But for now, she was taking a moment to daydream.

Ricki never left her mind, but sitting in front of a room full of teenagers made it a little easier to tone down her body and just think. *I wonder if the kids notice any difference in me.* The thought almost made her blush. She'd never thought about her own teachers that way when she was in high school, but in college and later in life, she could always see it on her friends' faces when their relationships moved to the next level.

She knew if Toni could see her now, the heckling would never end. She shifted in her chair, and took a moment to savor the sensations in her body. She was just a little sore, in that delicious way that only happened after the most incredible nights. She smiled to herself and imagined many more days like this to come.

Walking around the classroom, she was pleased to see that for the most part her students were doing well with this work set. They had done well all year, and she enjoyed the enthusiasm in their eager young faces. *I've been a teacher too long if I'm starting to see "eager young faces."* Again she smiled to herself but knew her students only enhanced her good mood. Nothing could upset her today.

The next bell would bring with it lunchtime.

That she wanted to be with Ricki was a given, but while the kids might not notice that look in their teachers' eyes, her co-workers might be more perceptive. She had a feeling that Ricki would not be too pleased by the idea that anyone here might know about them. Last night might have changed their relationship, but Kaya doubted that it had suddenly made Ricki want to shout anything from the rooftops.

Kaya was okay with that. For now. She liked the idea of having Ricki all to herself, their romance a secret. That took her to the alternative: eating lunch privately with Ricki in the math lab, as they had on several occasions before. The problem with that was Kaya was fairly certain she wouldn't be able to be alone with Ricki for that long and not jump her. Completely inappropriate on school grounds with students in the building.

Does that mean on school grounds without students here would be okay? She shook herself mentally for that impulsive thought. No, no it wouldn't. But at the same time the rebel in her couldn't help imagining some colorful scenarios.

With ten minutes to go in the period, she called her students' attention to the front and they went over their work sets. Having to act from a position of authority, and about physics no less, was enough to chase Kaya's fantasies back to the recesses of her mind. She finished up her teacherly duties and assigned her students the evening's homework before they escaped to the cafeteria.

She swung by Ricki's classroom and the math lab on her way, but Ricki wasn't in either. Kaya acknowledged her slight twist of disappointment.

Entering into the faculty lounge with her tray, she glanced around. Instead of finding Ricki, she was flagged over by Ian. The expressive, large man waving for her attention was impossible to miss. Why not sit with the guys? Besides, if Ricki did show, that's where she would be sitting anyway.

"Hey, guys." She took the empty chair next to Ian and across from Jamie. "How was everyone's Thanksgiving?"

"Thanksgiving was great. An entire holiday revolved around eating? It's my favorite time of year." Ian's voice was always jovial and booming. Everything about him was big and loud, and Kaya suddenly found herself thankful that they'd become friends. In another life, she probably wouldn't have had much reason to associate with men like Ian at school, but it was just one more great thing Ricki had brought to her world.

They chatted away the period, and although she enjoyed the company, Kaya wondered where Ricki might be. The smallest doubt seeped into her mind. *Surely she wants to see me as much as I do her.* She tried to shrug off the doubt. Their relationship was stronger now, solidified by the night they'd just shared and the promise of more. She didn't have to doubt Ricki anymore, and couldn't doubt her if—

"Hey, guys. You'll never believe what I've had to deal with this morning." Ricki flopped down into the chair next to Jamie and launched into a story about how she'd caught some sophomores with a flask in the locker room during her off period.

Ian in particular thought the whole incident was hilarious, and with the conversation briefly centered on Ian, Kaya looked at Ricki. When they locked eyes for a brief second, she caught her smile and the sparkle in her gaze. Ricki even gave her a wink before turning back to the last minute of storytelling with Ian.

Kaya kicked herself for ever doubting her.

CHAPTER TWENTY-FIVE

The week flew by. Ricki was happier than she could ever remember, thriving on newfound energy. She'd spent a few more nights with Kaya, each one more amazing than the last, but they'd agreed to take a sanity break the night before. So when she rounded the track on Friday morning and saw Kaya sitting in the stands again, she couldn't keep from smiling broadly.

She didn't slow her pace as she went past, but held up four fingers to let Kaya know she only had one mile, four laps, left to go. Kaya hadn't been there in the morning since before Thanksgiving, between her trip and then their shared nights, but knowing she was now going home to Kaya after her run, Ricki didn't feel alone even when the stands were bare.

Finished with her laps, Ricki slowed, still breathing heavily, and waited for Kaya to join her.

"I can't believe I'm saying this," Kaya spoke softly as she approached, "but since you now know my natural sleeping habits, I suppose it doesn't hurt to admit I missed this."

Ricki smiled and darted away when Kaya reached for a hug. "No touching. I'm all sweaty."

Kaya laughed and reached for her again, and this time Ricki let herself be caught. "True, but I don't mind. I think we've managed to work up a pretty good sweat a couple times this week."

Ricki kissed her, and her heart pounded just as much as it had when she'd been running.

After they separated, Kaya turned to walk to the locker room with her. "Since I had some time to myself last night, I did a little thinking."

Ricki glanced at her. That sort of comment in a relationship was often foreboding, but she didn't sense anything to fear now. Instead, she felt calm as she waited for Kaya to go on.

"I still feel a bit like I screwed up with Thanksgiving, not asking you to come with me until the day before I left."

Ricki wanted immediately to clear that regret away. "It wouldn't have mattered. I'd committed to going to Mom's weeks before. So, please, you didn't screw anything up."

"If we'd talked about it sooner, could I have spent the day with you?"

The sense of foreboding that had not been present a mere moment before suddenly buzzed in Ricki's mind. "Uh, no. I don't think that would have worked."

To Ricki's surprise, Kaya just nodded in acceptance. "Yeah, that's what I thought."

"It's not about you, or us. I just...my mom and Paps and I just do something small. Just the three of us. It's been that way for years, and they kind of like their routine. I don't want to disrupt things."

Kaya shook her head, and wouldn't look to Ricki when Ricki tried to meet her eyes. "So small that one more...never mind. That's not why I brought this up."

"Kaya, it's not like that."

Kaya did turn to face her now. "It's okay, Ricki. I understand. I won't pretend it doesn't make me sad, but I get that you don't want me to meet the family. I hope that will change someday, but it's your family and you need to be comfortable with it all."

"Ky—"

"Listen, Ricki, can we just skip this part?" Kaya reached for her hands. "I don't want to argue."

Ricki certainly didn't want to argue either, and she was afraid to admit that deep down she knew Kaya had a good point. She would need more time to work that out though, and if Kaya was going to let things go for now, that was probably best.

"No, no arguments," Ricki agreed.

"Good. Because, as I said, that's not what this is about. What I'm trying to get at is I want you to be part of my holidays. I want to share that with you, and since you're not comfortable with the idea of me meeting your family, I..." She paused and took a breath. "I was wondering if you wanted to meet mine."

Ricki looked at her, shocked. She had never really considered that possibility, knowing that Kaya's parents lived in San Diego. "I...how?"

"I was looking at flights last night. I'm sure this will shock you, but I'm a bit of a procrastinator." Kaya smiled, and her self-deprecating comment helped to calm Ricki.

"No, I never would have guessed that."

"Yeah, yeah." Kaya pushed her lightly away and they started walking again toward the locker room. "Anyway, as I was looking at flights and talking to my mom, I realized how much I want you there with me."

"For the holidays? I don't know, I mean, my mom and—"

"Hold on a second. Let me finish. My mom and dad are going to spend a few days before Christmas and Christmas Day at my brother's in LA."

"You have a brother?" The new information surprised Ricki. Kaya talked about her parents all the time, even her grandparents, but had never mentioned siblings.

"Yeah. And your reaction is probably an indication it's no surprise that I have no desire to join them."

Ricki tilted her head, silently asking for more. Kaya sighed. "It's a long and frustrating story. Suffice it to say we're no longer close. I'm getting off-topic again, though."

She obviously didn't want to talk about her brother right now, and it hurt Ricki to see Kaya's sadness. She hoped eventually Kaya would fill her in.

"I'm probably going out to San Diego on December twenty-seventh. I thought that maybe that would work out well for you, too, since it would allow you to spend Christmas Day with your mom and Paps, then we could celebrate later."

Ricki quickly she realized she wanted to go. She wanted to spend the time with Kaya, meet her family, share the holidays. "Okay."

CHAPTER TWENTY-SIX

Christmas arrived before Ricki was ready. It was normally a relaxed holiday in their house, with a small gift exchange before Midnight Mass on Christmas Eve, and then more gift giving in front of the tree the next morning. Now, she was curled up on the couch in the home her mom and grandfather shared, staring blankly at the book Paps had given her. It was one she'd been wanting to read for a while, a compelling argument on the complexities of the economics of football, but now she couldn't concentrate long enough to get through the introduction.

She could hear her mother puttering around in the kitchen, preparing their Christmas feast. She wasn't sure where Paps was, but she felt a little pride knowing that odds were he was in the garage playing with the new tools she'd given him.

For years now the holiday manifested itself as simply spending time relaxing in one another's company. They'd share and eat and talk, comfortable in the routine. It was a good way to spend the time, especially since their family was so small.

Something was missing this year, though. Or rather, someone. Ricki couldn't imagine having Kaya here with her today, but she longed for it nonetheless. Kaya had opted to visit Toni and Rynn, and the plan was for Ricki to drive over in two days in time to have lunch with her friends before the two of them headed to the airport.

She'd been worrying on her decision to go with Kaya like a dog with a new rawhide. Her emotions boomeranged between excitement and fear. She gave up on her new book, got up and headed for the kitchen. Maybe she could find a distraction in food or her mother or both.

Once in the kitchen, she smiled at seeing the extent of the food prep chaos. She stood quietly and watched her mother, surprised to recognize again that she was getting older. Her hair, once as black as Ricki's, was now streaked with gray, tied back in a tight bun. Her strong hands kneaded the dough, and Ricki could see the power stored in her shoulders from a lifetime of hard work and hard knocks. Her stout frame led people to wonder if Ricki got her height from her father, a question that Ricki would never know the answer to. Still, none of that past had stunted her mother's generosity, as evidenced by the amount of food filling the kitchen.

"Did you invite the whole church over last night and not tell me?" Ricki joked.

Her mother glanced up from the pie crust she was just beginning to roll out. "Well, some of the ladies from the choir are rather jealous of these pies I'm making for you, so you best not tease me too much or I'll just give them away."

Ricki reached over to steal a cinnamon apple, but her mother swatted her hand away. "I wouldn't miss out on your holiday feast for anything. It's just three people, and you've got enough here to feed a small army."

Her mother went back to rolling the crust. "Well, until you get yourself in gear and get married and start giving me grandbabies, I guess I'm stuck with just you to keep stuffing fat."

Ricki flinched. It wasn't the first time her mother had mentioned grandchildren, but before she'd started seeing Kaya it was easy to blow off. She had assumed for years now she would just be alone for the rest of her life, so it didn't matter that her mom nagged her to get married.

Now, however, she felt like she was lying. She was definitely hiding something, but with her mother tossing out presumptive comments like that, how was she supposed to correct her? And on a holiday, no less. That would certainly be a great time to disrupt everything.

"I don't know why you think I'm ever getting married." Ricki paused, Kaya's smiling face suddenly flickering in her mind. "You never did, and this little family turned out just fine."

Her mother put down the roller and looked sharply up at her daughter. "We weren't talking about me getting married."

"Fine then." Ricki didn't try to hide her annoyance. "Let's not talk about me getting married either."

Her mother narrowed her eyes. "What's gotten into you? I've been asking for grandbabies for years."

Ricki sighed. "Nothing. I just don't feel like going there today. I mean, we're happy with the way things are, right? We've got a good thing going—you, me, and Paps. Do you really want to change things up?"

"There is nothing in life that isn't made better by grandbabies." Her mother gave a definitive nod, as if that settled the topic.

"So you want a bigger family? You'd be happy to have someone else join us on days like this?"

Her mother was back at work on the pies, gently laying the rolled dough into a glass pie plate. "Of course, I'd be happy if you had a family of your own to bring. Is that what you're asking me?"

Ricki shook her head. She knew her mother's vision of her future happy family involved a nice man and her large with child while another toddler ran at their feet. That was a vision Ricki herself had never had. She'd never seen herself as the barefoot and pregnant type, and she'd certainly never seen a man in the picture with her. Unbidden, an image of Kaya and her looking down on the face of a newborn child sprang into her mind. Startled, she physically shook the image from her thoughts.

"Don't you go shaking your head at me, young lady."

"What? I'm not shaking—"

"Don't close your heart to the idea. Being a mom is one of the best things I ever did, and I hope you get to experience that joy someday, too."

Ricki stared at her mother, who was deliberately not looking up from her baking. It seemed she wasn't the only one who was acting strangely today. But as she stared, she realized how much she loved her mother, this strong woman who had striven so hard to give her a good life.

She rose from her chair and went over to hug her.

Her mother held up flour-coated hands, a gesture of annoyance over being interrupted, but Ricki felt her lean into the hug. "Yes, well," her mother said. "I wouldn't want you to miss out on the years of stinky diapers and muddy blue jeans. It might be poetic justice, hearing you try to play dolls with a perfect little princess, after all those Barbies you decapitated."

"I love you, too, Mom." Ricki smiled. They weren't words often spoken in her family, and it made her feel good to say them now. Though it hurt that the topic that had brought them out was still something that her mother would never understand. Sadly, she knew that vision of grandchildren playing around the Christmas tree would never come true as her mother saw it.

CHAPTER TWENTY-SEVEN

"You've still got at least half an hour before you have to leave, so don't you try to rush off so quickly."

Kaya grinned at Toni's scolding. She didn't want her visit to end either, but if they waited much longer, she was afraid Ricki might have a heart attack.

It had come as quite a surprise when Ricki had confessed she hadn't flown anywhere in years. It was obvious that Ricki was anxious about flying, and during the holidays, it certainly wouldn't hurt to allow a little extra time at the airport.

"I'm not rushing anywhere, and you know it. I thought you'd be proud of me for not procrastinating to the point of sprinting through the terminal as I normally do."

Toni laughed, and Rynn chimed in, "She does use you as an example of the stresses of procrastinating any time I put off my honey-do list."

"See?" Kaya enjoyed it when Rynn took her side in these little mock arguments. She was glad her best friend had found a partner with a good sense of humor. Disregarding the fact that they worshipped each other.

"You know," Ricki spoke, and the others turned their attention to her immediately.

So I'm not the only one who's noticed how quiet she's been this morning.

"I'm beginning to think I should visit more often. This seems to be my best source for the inside scoop on the real Kaya." Ricki winked at her.

"Oh sure, we can certainly tell you everything you need to know." Toni steepled her fingers and tapped the tips against each other in a conspiratorial gesture. "I've got over a decade of dirt on her that I've just been waiting to spill, but if I get started now you two really will miss your flight."

Kaya stood in feigned abruptness. "Well, I guess that's really all we have time for now. Time to get going. Come on Ricki, let's hop."

* * *

Airport security wasn't quite like Ricki remembered it. She hadn't been exaggerating when she'd told Kaya she hadn't flown anywhere in almost ten years. She hadn't really wanted to go anywhere very far from home.

She was pretty sure she caught an amused glint in Kaya's eyes when she asked for the seat by the window. There was something mesmerizing—maybe because she'd experienced it so infrequently—about watching the city fall away, and the way the clouds looked soft and solid at a distance but faded to insubstantial mist as the plane cut effortlessly through them. She felt Kaya place a hand on her knee and turned to her. She knew Kaya had been watching her watch the outside world go by, but that didn't bother her. She was at peace, here with her.

"Is everything okay?" Kaya asked.

Ricki smiled. "Yes. Actually, I was just thinking about how happy I am to be here with you."

Kaya matched her smile and rubbed her thumb in gentle circles where it lay on her knee. "I'm happy, too. I can't tell you how excited I am that you're coming with me. My parents are looking forward to meeting you."

"Oh really?"

"Don't worry. I only told them good things. Honestly, I think they're more curious to see me with you. They were surprised."

"Why?" Ricki knew Kaya had been out for years, even to her family. "You're the first woman I've ever brought home with me."

It was Ricki's turn to be surprised. "Seriously? But you told me your parents have known about—"

"Oh, they've known for ages that I date women, and they've met a few of my girlfriends in the past when they've visited me. But I've never brought someone home with me for the holidays, I've never felt strongly enough to want to. So they're curious."

Ricki nodded. Kaya was special to her too, even though sometimes she knew she fell short in expressing that.

"So don't worry," Kaya continued, "I'm sure they'll love you just as much as I do. All you need to do is have fun and be your charming self."

Ricki placed her hand over Kaya's and laced their fingers together.

"You sound so close with your parents. What happened between you and your brother?"

Kaya looked away from her, sighed, and slumped back into her seat. "It's nothing exciting or even all that unusual. We just grew apart."

Ricki studied her. Surely Kaya didn't expect her to believe it was that simple. "You've never told me anything about him. Were you close as children?"

"Yes."

Ricki pushed a little further. "I don't even know if he's an older or younger brother."

"Younger." Kaya drew in a heavy breath, and Ricki waited for her to go on.

"Donny's only a year younger, and we were very close growing up. Maybe because I wasn't your typical little girl, but we had a tight bond. I think we drove my mom nuts with all our roughhousing, but it was a solid foundation for what should have been a life-long friendship.

"When I figured out I was gay, he was the first person I confided in. He was a lot bigger than I was by then, and I remember he wrapped me in a giant bear hug and made me feel safe. After that, he proceeded to check out the hot chicks with me, and it was like a childhood wrestling all over again. Banter and playfulness that always made me feel like that was exactly what family was all about."

She fell quiet, and Ricki spoke quietly. "That sounds really great. I always kind of wished for a brother when I was younger. I mean, the guys on the team were like brothers, but I wondered what it would be like to have a real one."

Kaya nodded. "He was great. I couldn't have asked for better. When my first girlfriend broke my teenage heart, he offered to beat her up, even if she was a girl. 'Nobody treats my sister like that.' That made me laugh so hard that I quickly got over her."

She smiled at the memory, but then her smile faded and Ricki knew her mind had jumped ahead in the story. "Sometimes, I wonder if we started to grow apart when I left for college. I went to Boston University. The family was living near D.C., and it was far enough away that visits were uncommon. My whole family helped me move into the dorm that first fall, but after that I didn't see my brother—except at Christmas—until the end of my freshman year.

"We talked by phone, but not much. Usually when I called, it was my parents who did all the talking. I wondered if maybe I wasn't the one changing, being the big college girl and all. When I went home for the summer, things felt like they were right back to normal.

"The following fall, I headed back to Boston and he headed south for college. I think that's where the Baptist preaching first started creeping in. My parents didn't raise us in a religious household, but they taught us love and tolerance. We were brought up to embrace differences. In the south, Donny witnessed another outlook on life."

There was religious animosity in Kaya's past? That was not good news.

"He still loved me and was happy for me whenever I'd met someone new. I can remember him mentioning once or twice some of the views he was now being exposed to, some of the beliefs people were sharing. I think now that he wanted to talk about them. Who knows, maybe he was looking for guidance from me, but I made the mistake of just blowing off what I considered—and still do, really—idiocy. Surely the idea of 'the homosexual lifestyle choice' was as ridiculous to him as it was to me. He'd known me all his life and obviously knew that there was no merit in that. Or at least I thought it was obvious."

Ricki wished they weren't belted in next to one another on the airplane. Kaya's voice was strong as she relayed her history, but Ricki longed to hold her.

"I didn't have those conversations with him, and I guess he started to listen to the people who did. He met a girl, a southern belle-type who wasn't shy about her opinions of 'those people.' Not just 'the gays' either. I'm not sure I've ever met anyone else quite so openly racist, homophobic and classist. I'll never understand why, but for some reason, Donny fell in love with her."

Kaya turned to Ricki with a wistful smile. "I mean, this chick is a royal bitch, but God help him, my brother is whipped. I know he doesn't believe the bunk he heard while he was in the south, and I was hoping when they moved to LA he might remember the world is a diverse and wonderful place. He still loves me, but he's a pushover when it comes to her. She doesn't like me—not that she's ever taken the time to get to know me. She actually tried to not invite me to the wedding, but my mother wasn't having any of that."

She paused. "My mother, not Donny. Donny didn't even fight for me then, didn't insist I be invited to his wedding. I think that was when things between us really broke. He didn't defend me, didn't stand up for me at all. I still can't comprehend what sort of love worth having makes you turn your back on family like that. But it's a fight I'm not willing to have anymore. He came to visit me a few times when I was living in Chicago, and he calls every now and then. But I just don't have it in me to reach out to him anymore. Not as long as he's still letting her call the shots."

Ricki ached for Kaya. She kissed her softly. "I'm sorry, sweetheart. I'm so sorry he did that to you."

Kaya reached for Ricki's hand and held on to her reassuring touch.

CHAPTER TWENTY-EIGHT

"My baby girl is home!" Kaya was engulfed in a hug before she even had a chance to respond.

Then, Kaya laughed at the expression on Ricki's face as she too was trapped in Talia Walsh's enormous bear hug. Kaya just stood to the side and waited until her mother let go.

"It's so wonderful to have you both here!" She fussed over them while her father brought their luggage in from the car.

Donovan Walsh was a quiet man, but his eyes sparkled with joy. Kaya gave him a big hug as well. "It's good to see you again, Dad."

"You too, baby girl." He turned to greet Ricki as well, and Kaya saw that she was relieved when he extended a hand instead of sweeping her into another unexpected hug. *Maybe I should have warned her that Mom would do that.* Then again, seeing her stunned reaction had been priceless.

Her mother managed to hug them both again at least once more as she ushered them into the house and peppered them with questions. "How was the flight, dear? Did you find your luggage all right? Sometimes they have trouble with the luggage and it takes forever to come out. But you're here pretty quickly, so it must have been all right. Unless your father was speeding again. Donovan, were you speeding again? Ever since he got that new car..."

Kaya smiled, the familiar feeling of home seeping back into her bones. The sun glittered in the open and airy hallway, the soft wood finish a welcoming sight. The large ranch-style home in Carlsbad was the perfect place for her parents to retire after a lifetime of military relocations. Her mother herded them into the bright kitchen, where she had a cheese platter waiting. "I've just put dinner in the oven, so we'll be eating in probably an hour or so."

Kaya pulled a stool out from under the center island and sat to munch on crackers and chat with her mother. Ricki followed her lead and took the seat next to her. Kaya sensed from her posture that she was a little overwhelmed by her mother's exuberance, but she knew she'd be okay once she got used to it. *She just has to survive the interrogation.*

"Ricki, dear, tell me more about yourself. It's so nice to finally meet you."

Kaya laughed. "Goodness, Mom, give her a chance to catch her bearings. I think you might be scaring her."

"Me? Scaring? Well, I never! I don't mean to overwhelm you, dear." She patted Ricki's hand, which was resting on the table in front of her. "Please, do make yourself at home. Can I get you a drink?"

She turned and pulled open the refrigerator and started listing off the options. Kaya took the opportunity to lean in and whisper in Ricki's ear. "Relax, babe. I know she can be a little overwhelming, but that's just because she wants you to like her."

"You could have warned me," Ricki mumbled back, and Kaya knew she would be just fine.

* * *

Ricki took a seat in one of the recliners in the living room, glad to have a moment of peace. She had not expected the whirlwind that was Kaya's mother, but she smiled as she thought about the past few hours.

"Welcome to the Walsh family. I'm glad to see you survived dinner." Kaya sat on the arm of her chair.

Ricki grinned. This was not what she had expected, but she was happy here. "I enjoyed dinner and talking with your parents."

"Good." Kaya leaned back and wrapped her arm around Ricki's shoulders. "I'm happy being here with you."

Ricki instinctively tensed and pulled out of her embrace. Her parents could walk in at any time.

"No."

She looked up when Kaya spoke.

"Sorry?"

"No," Kaya repeated. "You don't get to run away from me." She pulled Ricki closer, settled her arm around her shoulders again.

"Ky, your parents—"

"My parents know we're dating, and they like you. Besides, it's not like I'm trying to grope you or get you naked right here. You're allowed to show affection in this house. My parents have always been supportive of that.

"Ricki," she continued. "You don't have to worry about what my parents do or do not think of you. They trust me to make my own decisions, and they prove that trust and patience by continuing to tolerate the harpy that Donny married. If you treat me right—and you do—they will love you as much as I do. They're not going to freak out if they walk in and see me sitting with my arm around you. Hell, they probably won't even blink."

Ricki drew a deep breath. This fit perfectly with the stories she'd been hearing all evening. The resulting image was a loving, open connection between parents and daughter.

CHAPTER TWENTY-NINE

Two days later, Ricki was enjoying a quiet afternoon of football. Kaya was taking a nap and her parents had gone out for the afternoon. It was amazing how quickly Ricki had come to feel at home in this place. It was still louder and more talkative than she was used to, but it was a relaxed kind of chaos.

Things with this family were cozy and comfortable. She was seeing a side of Kaya that she hadn't before, with a little bit more childlike innocence and deference in her demeanor. She loved her parents, and they loved her.

Her own mother and Paps loved her, too, but they didn't share this openness. They didn't have the casual banter, and certainly not the jokes about romance and sex that had popped up once or twice. Talia and Donovan had welcomed her into their home without hesitation or doubt. Ricki just could not picture Mom and Paps doing the same for Kaya.

She was lost in her musings when a hand snaked over her shoulder and brushed down her chest.

She caught Kaya's hand and turned to look up at her, her heart pounding, and Kaya smiled down at her. She gave her arm a sharp tug, pulling her over the back of the couch and into her lap.

Kaya squealed and laughed, caught completely off balance. "Okay, you win."

Ricki kissed her, claiming her victory. The football game and her thoughts of home were quickly forgotten as their kiss deepened, but when Kaya's hand snaked under her shirt, she pulled back.

"Sorry, baby. I don't think that's a good idea today."

"What?"

"I love making out with you, but if you touch me, I'm going to need more than that."

"Who said I wasn't going to give you more?" Kaya asked.

"Babe, we're on your parents' couch."

"So? They're not home."

"I think that might cross a line."

Kaya blew out a sigh. "They went to dinner and a movie. They won't be home for hours."

"I still don't think it would be right to get it on on their couch."

"Look, I get that you're not the naughty type who ever fantasizes about fooling around in her parents' house." She stopped and shot Ricki a look.

"Ricki, how long have we been here?" Kaya blew out an exasperated breath.

What? Ricki didn't follow the jump in topic. "Three days."

"And how long was I in Chicago before that?" she asked.

"Five days."

"Right. So it's been eight days since I've had your hands on me. And you want me to wait another three until we get back to Indiana?"

Ricki hadn't been keeping track, but yes, that had been her assumption.

"Kaya, you know I want to, but I can't do that here."

"Oh please, why not?"

"It would be disrespectful."

"Okay, we won't do it on their couch." She grabbed Ricki's hand again and muttered under her breath. "Even if that has been a fantasy of mine for years."

A small yelp escaped Ricki's throat. What could she possibly say to that?

"But that doesn't mean I'm waiting till we go back. I need you so bad right now, I'm going to burst."

"Kaya, come on. That's not fair."

"What's not fair about it? Are you saying you don't want me?"

"No! The fact that I do want you is why it's not fair. You're teasing me."

"It's not teasing when I'm offering to deliver. You're the one clinging to some sort of old-fashioned chivalry." She tossed her hands up in frustration. "Really, Ricki. It's not disrespectful. My parents know I'm sexually active, and I'm sure they assume it's with you. I've been open with my parents about this since I was a teenager. Hell, my mom was the first person to buy me condoms. They left today to give us a chance to be alone."

"You can't know that."

"The hell I can't."

Ricki dragged her fingers through her hair. Somehow, in trying to be decent, she suddenly felt like the bad guy, and she had no idea how this had happened.

Kaya dropped to a squat in front of Ricki and took both of her hands. "Ricki, I understand this is foreign to you. And I understand that all you're trying to do is respect me and respect my parents. But you don't have to stay away from me to do that."

Ricki leaned forward, meeting her eyes.

"I know that you love and respect me. And I'm asking you now to show me. I want to connect with you. There's nothing disrespectful about that." She pressed forward, and Ricki welcomed her kiss.

"If you truly are uncomfortable, then of course I'll wait. I waited for you before, and I'll do it again if that's what you need." She rose and tugged on Ricki's hands.

She let Kaya help her to her feet. She couldn't deny the need in her expression. Why was Ricki denying them both?

After a moment, she nodded. Kaya smiled, not in a gloating way, but in a soft, sensuous way that told Ricki she'd made the right decision. She followed her, trusting that Kaya would never lead her wrong.

CHAPTER THIRTY

"So you and Dad are just staying in tonight?" Kaya asked.

"Yes. He bought a very nice bottle of champagne, and we like to watch the New York party on the television. That way, we can celebrate and still go to bed at a reasonable hour."

Kaya laughed. "The whole point of New Year's Eve is to stay up later than a 'reasonable hour,' Mom."

"Not when you're our age. It's better to welcome another year with your soul mate and get a good night's rest."

Soul mate. Kaya knew she was lucky to have grown up in a household where her parents were deeply committed to one another and never afraid to show their children an example of lifelong love. She'd always hoped she might be able to find that someday. It was far too early in her relationship with Ricki to be thinking along those lines, but the idea that it was possible warmed her heart.

"So what do you say, Ricki? A night on the town, or a nice bottle of champagne with these two old fogies?"

Ricki looked up from the floor, apparently grateful that the conversation had shifted. "We could stay in, if you don't mind."

Kaya truly wasn't sure what she wanted to do. In the past, she'd always gone out dancing and partying until the early morning hours. Now, she found she just wanted to be with Ricki. Although a night of dancing would be fun.

Ricki must have read her silence as a desire to go out. "I don't really like clubs, but I'll make it up to you," she offered.

"Yeah?" Kaya thought this could be an interesting offer. "What do you have in mind?"

Ricki grinned, and glanced over to Kaya's mom. *What is she thinking?*

"Well, since we were talking about school dances earlier, I was wondering if maybe you'd go to prom with me."

Kaya felt her mouth drop open in surprise, and her mother squealed with delight. "Oh, baby girl, prom!"

Kaya reminded herself to close her mouth and fought against the blush creeping over her face. *Leave it to Ricki to find a way to embarrass me with her chivalry.*

"Oh, Kaya, give her an answer. You can't just leave her standing there like that!" her mother scolded her. "Where are your manners?"

Ricki just stood there watching her, and Kaya shook her head. "Isn't it a little early to be thinking about prom?"

Ricki shrugged. "Not when you're asking the most beautiful girl in school." She winked at her, and Talia gushed again. "Oh, isn't she just a charmer?"

Kaya relented. "All right. I suppose a prom date is an okay exchange for a New Year's Eve dance." She set her potato down and hugged Ricki. "You had to do that in front of my mother, didn't you?" she whispered in her ear.

Ricki returned the hug and stepped back, a glint of pride in her eyes.

How can I resist that?

CHAPTER THIRTY-ONE

School was back in session during the first week of January. Ricki was engrossed in her computers when Kaya arrived at the math lab, and Kaya enjoyed just watching her work. She'd learned over the course of the fall just how much time and effort Ricki had put into getting the grants and permissions to upgrade the school's computers, and seeing her poring over her projects always brought a smile to Kaya's lips.

"I can hear you back there, you know." Ricki grinned as she turned away from her screen. "Are you going to come say hello?"

Kaya pushed off from the wall she'd been leaning against and crossed over to her. A quick glance back at the door confirmed that she had closed it behind her, so she bent down for a kiss.

She took the seat next to Ricki and they talked until lunch was almost over and she needed to get back to her classroom. Ricki caught her sleeve. "I've got to go talk to Ian about something. Let me walk with you?"

"Of course."

Walking through the school halls with Ricki was always interesting for Kaya. When they walked together anywhere else, they usually held hands, or at least walked fairly close. Here, with the exception of the teenage crowd bumping them into one another, they maintained a larger distance between them.

In the few minutes between lunch and classes, the halls were quite crowded. That didn't stop a group of boys from playing basketball in between the lockers though.

"Easton! Wesley! The hallway is not a basketball court!" Kaya hollered at them, and when they smirked as teenage troublemakers do, Ricki simply confiscated the ball. Kaya didn't miss a beat as they simply kept walking, listening to the surprised whines that some slow old teacher had snatched their ball. It was hard not to laugh at the boys' dismay.

"You know," Ricki said, quietly enough that the students around them probably wouldn't hear, "as nice as it would be to have a couple of six-foot-four athletes on my team, I think I'm glad the Paskril twins opted for basketball. They sure can be a handful."

Kaya just chuckled. "Don't lie. You know darn well that if they were on your team you would have molded them into fine young role models by now."

She considered that for a moment, so Kaya laid on one more layer of flattery. "I mean, if you could get Keenan, Stanford and Dillon to show some respect? Please, the Paskrils would have been a walk in the park for you."

Ricki smiled. "Thanks."

"Will I see you later?"

To her disappointment, Ricki shook her head. "I can't tonight. I've got dinner plans with Mom and Paps."

Kaya carefully blanked her face, although she knew even doing that would alert Ricki to her mood.

"Ky—"

"Don't worry about it. I'll see you tomorrow." She started to turn to go into her classroom, but she saw that Ricki wasn't moving. "Really, Ricki. Don't worry about it." She wanted to hug her, to reassure them both that it was okay, but she couldn't do that here. Instead she had no choice but to turn and walk away.

* * *

At dinner that night, Ricki was having a hard time paying attention to the conversation. Her mother had cooked a delicious meal, and Paps was excited to talk to her about the Colts' game from the previous weekend, but sitting here, it was terribly obvious to her the differences between her own family and the one she had just visited in California. It wasn't just the superficial characteristics of Kaya's family. In fact, maybe it wasn't the different families at all. *She* felt superficial, and she'd never felt that way in this house before. She loved talking football with Paps, and she truly appreciated her mother's wonderful dinner, but her mind kept playing back to the idea that Kaya talked to her mom about everything, including sex, love and relationships. This wall she'd built between herself and her family was beginning to feel like a lie.

Maybe Kaya had been right about that freedom and security that came with being out. What would it feel like to know, without doubt, that she was loved for who she was? Nothing more, nothing less?

That was all well and good, but what if she wasn't? Paps was religious, her mother more so. She understood that was a side effect of having a child out of wedlock, fathered by a loser of a man who just took off. Thirty-odd years later, it still defined her. She'd found the structure and absolution she needed in the church. But how would all that play out if Ricki were to be honest with them?

"Where are you at tonight, Sport?" Paps called her attention back to the conversation.

"Sorry. It was just a long day at school." Ricki offered the excuse automatically, but realized as she said it that maybe the blow-off answer shouldn't be quite so rote.

She forced herself to pay better attention, and Paps was willing to let the topic stay in the safe zone of football. As she walked home later that night, Ricki pondered the possibilities. Maybe she could work up the courage to tell them, but she had to give herself time. Something so big? She had no idea how to share that.

CHAPTER THIRTY-TWO

The next weekend, Kaya awoke in the night, warm and safe in Ricki's arms. She didn't know how long she'd slept, but she didn't think it was that late yet.

She didn't want to move, certainly didn't want to get up. There was no place she'd rather be than here, curled up against Ricki's side, her head pillowed on Ricki's shoulder. She started to draw little circles across Ricki's skin, a gentle caress dancing lazily over her stomach and chest. She felt Ricki press a kiss into her hair and squeeze gently with the arm wrapped around Kaya's back.

She continued her indolent exploration of Ricki's body, not trying to arouse her, although she saw that her nipples were hard. *She makes me feel so incredible.* Kaya realized that she wanted to touch Ricki as she had been touched, but she was also greatly enjoying her delicate journey.

Kaya widened the range of her movements, drifting her fingers to scratch lightly down Ricki's side to her hip and across the tender skin at her pelvis. When she grazed lower still, she felt Ricki shift slightly to spread her legs, allowing Kaya to draw her nails back up along her inner thigh. She felt and heard Ricki's breathing quicken, but Kaya avoided the sweet area at her apex, returning instead along the line of her hip and up to her stomach. She closed her eyes, focusing on her other sensory impressions.

When she began to drift lower, Ricki reached up and stopped her, holding her meandering hand in her own.

"Something wrong, sweetheart?"

Ricki didn't say anything, but Kaya felt her shake her head. *I was enjoying that.* She tried to move again, but Ricki held her hand still. Kaya opened her eyes again, drawing in a heavy breath.

Oh. She saw the blush of Ricki's skin and noted again the hardness of her nipples. *That's why she stopped me.* She hadn't realized she'd been torturing Ricki with her aimless perusal. Of course Ricki's body would react to her touch.

The knowledge that Ricki was so greatly aroused flipped a switch in Kaya's mind, and she wanted to explore her differently. She tried to move her hand once more, and bit back a chuckle when Ricki still held her tightly.

All right, then. Kaya resorted to her backup plan.

She nuzzled at her neck and began to kiss her. Ricki rolled her head up, baring her throat, and Kaya grazed her sensitive skin with her teeth. She was aware that Ricki had not released her hand. She raised her head so she could whisper in Ricki's ear.

"Trust me."

At that, Ricki let go, moving her hand instead to Kaya's hip and allowing her to do whatever she wanted. That permission was a powerful gift, and Kaya began her slow exploration once more, vowing with her touch to give Ricki her all. She moved her hand higher and squeezed Ricki's breast. She quickened the massaging movement of her hand, and listened as Ricki's breathing and heart rate responded in kind. When she flicked her finger across her nipple, Ricki gasped and pressed her chest into Kaya's touch.

After that, going slowly took more control than Kaya possessed. Kaya dragged her hand down the center of Ricki's stomach and over her mons, dipping her fingers into her heat. *God, she's wet.*

She looked up then and found Ricki's eyes, those crystal blue eyes that drove her mad with desire, now barely open as Ricki fought to keep her control. Kaya worked her hand against Ricki's center until she could see that Ricki was at the edge. Then she whispered, "I love you," and entered her in a long, hard stroke.

Ricki groaned and her body bowed, rigid under Kaya's thrusts. Her head fell back, and Kaya quickened her pace until Ricki cried out her orgasm, her breath held and her body taut. When she'd taken all she could, she collapsed back to the bed and Kaya slowed her motion. She had learned if she gave Ricki a few minutes to catch her breath, she'd be able to take her over the edge again.

She kept up a persistent stroke, rubbing against her clit with the heel of her hand. Sure enough, it wasn't long before she felt Ricki's inner muscles pulsing against her fingers. Kaya shifted again, moving her leg over Ricki's body to straddle her hips and position herself to ride Ricki harder this time.

She was so focused on Ricki's body, on Ricki's responses, that she didn't even realize how hot, how close to the edge she was herself, until she felt one of Ricki's hands grip her ass. Ricki drove into her and she screamed, her orgasm immediately upon her. Through the obliteration of pleasure, she knew Ricki was there with her, coming with her. *Oh God.*

She couldn't think, couldn't breathe after that. Time was forgotten until finally her body and mind were able to find themselves again. She lay on top of Ricki, her head on Ricki's chest, their limbs tangled. After a few more minutes as her senses began to work again, she realized that she could feel the beat of Ricki's heart against her cheek, and it matched the pounding of her own. *One beat.*

She tested her strength, not sure it had returned enough to support her weight, then moved up to kiss Ricki. Her hunger beyond sated, this kiss carried a different message, one of lasting intention and devotion. When they parted, Kaya curled into Ricki's side, letting the peace of sleep overtake her.

CHAPTER THIRTY-THREE

When Kaya woke the next morning, she wasn't surprised that Ricki wasn't in the bed beside her. As much as she'd like to lie curled up with her for a little longer on these weekend mornings, she'd accepted that Ricki was seemingly incapable of skipping her morning run. *One of these days, I'll find a way to convince her to linger.*

She was starting to drift off to sleep again, at peace with her thoughts, when she heard movement across the room. She jumped and instinctively pulled the sheet up. Ricki was sitting there, not out somewhere on a run.

"God, you startled me."

"Sorry."

Something was wrong, which didn't seem possible after the night they'd just shared. "Ricki? What's going on?"

She rose from the desk chair and crossed over to her, then sat on the edge of the bed and brushed a strand of hair from Kaya's face. "Did you sleep well?"

"Yes, but…" She was confused. Ricki seemed remote, but her touch was warm and tender.

Ricki looked away, staring toward the sunlit window. "I'm a little all over the place this morning. Why don't you pull on jeans and a sweatshirt and come downstairs."

With that, she stood up and walked out.

What the hell?

She sat in the bed, trying to understand what had just happened.

Had something gone wrong last night? Thinking back, she remembered exactly what had gone on, but there wasn't anything wrong about it. She couldn't think of one possible link between their unbelievable passion and Ricki's baffling behavior. In fact, thoughts of last night kicked her body into overdrive, and that was the last place she needed it to be. *I need to think.*

She threw back the covers, walked nude to the bathroom and took a cool shower.

Afterward, she found Ricki in the kitchen, seated at the table with two cups of coffee in front of her. She watched as Kaya entered the room, and Kaya felt her gaze follow her as she slowly moved over and took the chair across from her. Ricki pushed one of the mugs over to her.

"Sorry."

Kaya reached forward and picked up the mug, just to have something to do with her hands. She studied Ricki. "You keep saying that, but I still don't have any idea why."

"I love you."

Kaya's breath caught. She loved hearing Ricki say that. Every time, it made her heart stutter. This was the first time it was laced with uncertainty.

"Why do I hear a 'but' at the end of that?"

Ricki scrunched her face in surprise. "What? No!" She stood suddenly and looped around to Kaya's side of the table. She knelt beside her and took both Kaya's hands in her own. "No. No 'but.' I didn't mean for you to think that."

Kaya's chest pounded with relief while her head ached again with confusion.

"I'm making a mess of things. I'm just nervous, that's all. And doing a terrible job communicating."

Kaya just watched her. Ricki looked behind her. When Kaya followed her gaze, she saw the clock. What in the world could make her care about the time right now?

"It's a beautiful morning. Come outside with me?" Ricki asked.

"What? Ricki, it's February. There's snow out there."

"There's sunshine and most of the snow has melted since the last storm."

Ricki pulled her to her feet. Kaya tried to voice her confusion "Ricki, wait. What is going on?"

Ricki led her to a sunny spot across the deck. She looked out over the park behind her house.

"I really enjoyed meeting your parents over the holidays. It was...Your family seems so different compared to mine."

Kaya at least now had some idea of a topic. *Well, sort of. What is prompting this?*

"My dad took off right after I was born. I think I told you that. I was raised by my mom, Gram and Paps, and then Gram died when I was still little. Mom and Paps are the only family I've had for my entire life. I know you think I'm ashamed of us and afraid to let you meet them. That's not true. Well, not the ashamed part. I am afraid. But it's not just of what they'll think of us, of me. I'm also a little afraid of what you'll think of them."

Kaya was trying to make sense of what she was hearing in conjunction with Ricki's unusual behavior since she'd awakened. "They mean so much to you. I'm sure I'll love them."

Ricki paced before her, a blizzard of nervous energy. "You might want to wait until after you meet them to say that."

Seeing the anxiety painted over Ricki's features Kaya reached for her.

Ricki jerked back, then looked at her, an apology in her eyes. "Sorry. Just...wait."

"What am I waiting for, Ricki?"

"You said you wanted to meet my Paps. I'm trying not to go crazy right now, because I don't know how this is going to go, but here's your chance."

"What?" Kaya exclaimed. *Surely she doesn't mean right now!*

Ricki took another step back, quirking her head as if she'd heard something. She looked over to the far end of the deck. A man, lean and fit despite the gray in his short-cropped hair and the deep age lines on his face, rounded the corner. He had on a worn, brown leather jacket, open to reveal a neatly pressed shirt tucked into his black trousers. He called over to Ricki with a big grin, "Hey, Sport! Haven't seen you in so long, I figured I'd come to make sure you hadn't fallen and broken a hip or something."

Ricki laughed, and even with her own thoughts a jumbled mess, Kaya heard the effort behind it that she tried to hide. Ricki had clearly been expecting him to show up, even arranging for them to be outside waiting. "Hey, old man, you know you're in way more danger of breaking a hip than I am. You're not as young as you used to be." She shook her head. "Besides, it's only been two or three weeks since I last saw you."

"Yeah, well, when you only live half a mile away, you should visit your mother and Paps more often."

Kaya saw the deep breath Ricki sucked in before she crossed the deck and hugged him. With the two of them standing next to each other, she noted that he had several inches of height on Ricki, who was herself fairly tall. After their brief embrace, he turned to Kaya. "This one's never been any good at introductions."

Kaya stepped forward, almost on autopilot as the craziness of the situation was only starting to sink in. He offered her a hand, and Kaya noted the rough warmth of his touch. His palm had the calluses of a man who had worked hard his entire life, and his eyes shown with pride and confidence.

Ricki took her cue. "Kaya, my grandfather, Patrick McGlinn. Paps, this is Kaya Walsh, one of the other teachers at Glenwood."

Kaya could see the family resemblance in their tight, fit bodies as they said their hellos. She had been introduced in a professional capacity, with no mention of their relationship, and although she had always expected that would be how she first met Ricki's family, it bothered her.

"You're not one of those crazy early morning runners like my granddaughter here, are you?" He laughed and Kaya just shook her head with a smile. "No? There aren't too many other reasons she'd have you up this early on the Day of Rest."

Kaya felt his appraising look, and wondered if he had any idea who she really was to his granddaughter. Kaya's eyes flicked over to Ricki.

"Maybe you can talk some sense in to her for me."

Kaya wasn't sure what he was talking about, knowing only that it was no longer early workouts.

Ricki groaned. "Paps, not now. It's not polite."

Patrick laughed again. "Polite? Polite ain't gonna matter much when you're standing in front of St. Peter's gates." He turned to Kaya. "I come by as often as she'll let me." He jerked his thumb at Ricki. "Trying to talk my wayward offspring into getting her butt in the pew where it belongs. I'd come every week, but she started locking me out completely last time I did that, so we had to compromise." He sighed, sadness tinting his features. "She used to be such a good little girl, listening to whatever I told her. Now she's all grown up and not interested in what I have to say. But I won't give up. Not on my girl."

Kaya quirked an eyebrow as Ricki flushed bright red. Paps jabbed pointedly at his watch. "So? You coming?" Without waiting for an answer, he turned back to Kaya. "You're welcome to come to. Are you a faithful woman?"

"Paps!" Ricki saved Kaya from having to come up with a reply.

He just looked at his granddaughter expectantly. "Well?"

"Paps, come on. You know I don't join you. And you can't just go interrogating my friends like that. Now, go on, you're going to be late. You know Mom hates being late."

"Yeah, yeah." He gestured to Kaya as he turned to leave. "See if you can't talk some sense into her."

And then he was gone, leaving Kaya staring and speechless behind him. She hadn't said two words.

They stood in silence for a moment, Kaya still playing catch-up, trying to understand what had just happened, before

Ricki spoke. "Well, you wanted to meet him." She turned away and crossed the deck to lean on the railing, her back to Kaya.

Ricki had never mentioned before that her grandfather was religious. On the surface, that might explain some of her fear, her resistance to stepping out of the closet. Still, the whole encounter—hell, the whole morning—was just bizarre.

Kaya took a few tentative, uncertain steps toward Ricki. "How long have you known he'd be coming over?" she asked. The timing and setting of this awkward first meeting seemed to be the easiest thing to clear up.

"He stops over the first Sunday of every month, trying to get me to go to Mass with him."

Every month. So this was not unexpected, not the kind of thing where she'd had an hour's notice. *Every month? Then why hasn't she told me, why hasn't this meeting happened before?*

As if reading her mind, Ricki added, "I probably should have mentioned this whole ritual to you sooner, but it just seemed easier to casually suggest we stay at your apartment the past two months. I'd been kind of planning on doing it again last night, but…"

Kaya felt foolish, having been a pawn in Ricki's sidestepping game without even realizing it. "Would you rather have just avoided the whole thing? Left me in the dark indefinitely?"

Ricki turned to her. "I wasn't trying to keep you out of it. I was trying to keep it away from us."

It. Us. *What does any of that mean?* "What exactly were you trying to keep away, Ricki? Your Paps? His preaching? I don't understand."

"Yes. To both. And more."

"Then why didn't you just leave me up in the bedroom?"

Ricki shrugged. "And if you hadn't lingered? If you'd come down for breakfast in a bathrobe? Paps doesn't believe in front doors or in knocking. He always comes around the back, and if I'm not out here waiting for him, he lets himself in. Better you meet him in jeans and a sweatshirt."

She had a good point. Still, the whole situation didn't sit well with Kaya. "You could have given me a little more warning."

"I know. I didn't mean to toss you to the wolves like that. I didn't know what to do."

Ricki's face was partially hidden in the shadows cast by the surrounding trees, but nonetheless Kaya could read her guilt. She felt an impulse to go to her, but something stopped her. A big part of the problem this morning was lack of communication. *Is that the same as a lack of trust?* Ricki needed to know she could turn to her when she was struggling. No matter how much Kaya had done to earn it, Ricki was the one with the power to give her trust.

Kaya stayed where she was. But she held her arms open, inviting Ricki to come to her both literally and figuratively.

* * *

Ricki knew she'd dropped the ball big-time this morning. She'd led Kaya into an unexpected and uncomfortable situation, subjected her to Paps's overeager faith, just left her hanging altogether, all because she'd simply forgotten what day it was.

And after all of that, there Kaya stood, arms open and waiting for her. Ricki didn't hesitate. She moved quickly from her place in the shadows to Kaya, where even the sun seemed to be telling her that this was a better place to be.

"I'm sorry. I just didn't know what to do."

Kaya hugged her, and Ricki was grateful for her touch. "I guess I owe it to you to be honest after all this. I've been thinking for a while that I wanted you to meet him, but I just couldn't work out how to do it. This morning I panicked, but maybe a part of me saw an easy escape from the trapped feeling I've had."

Kaya pulled back enough to look at her. "You could have talked to me about this. Not just about this Sunday morning ritual, but about wanting to talk to them. I'm thrilled to finally meet Paps, but I'd hoped it might go a bit differently."

"I know."

"You could have trusted me."

"I do!"

"You don't act like it. I don't know what else I need to do to prove to you that you can trust me."

"I do." Ricki repeated. "It's me I don't trust. I'm terrified of messing things up." Ricki dropped her chin, disappointed in herself.

"Hey, none of that." Kaya immediately nudged her head up. "Do you really trust me? Because I'm not so sure."

"I do. I swear."

"Okay then. I noticed you introduced me as a co-worker, not your girlfriend, and I still haven't met your mom."

Ricki grimaced. She knew the co-worker introduction was a coward's move.

Kaya continued. "Maybe we can try this again, and I can meet them both for real."

Ricki saw the encouragement on her face, and it was hard not to hope that something like that could work. There were obstacles of course, but maybe Kaya could help her through that.

"I guess there are better ways than a seemingly random drop in."

Kaya laughed. "Yes. I should think so."

Ricki wondered for a moment how she'd been so lucky to find such an incredible and patient woman. "Maybe dinner sometime?"

"Yes." Kaya smiled. "That sounds a bit better."

Ricki felt some of the weight she'd carried for so long lift from her shoulders. This hadn't gone well, but it hadn't gone as poorly as it might have. And now with Kaya's help she could put together a plan to make things right. The idea made her feel optimistic in a way she hadn't in a long, long time.

CHAPTER THIRTY-FOUR

Ricki looked up as Kaya set down her red pen and pushed the stack of papers away. "Good enough for tonight," she said. She'd been working to catch up with grading papers, and Ricki knew she was exhausted.

"You ready for your massage, then?"

"God yes, but actually, I want to talk a bit first."

Ricki studied her, not sure what was on her mind.

"Dinner tonight was delicious," Kaya started.

"Thank you."

"You said it was a recipe of your mom's?"

"Yes." Ricki suddenly felt the familiar unease when the topic of her family was broached.

"Have you thought anymore about the four of us going to dinner?"

Ricki looked away. Yes, she'd thought about it, but no, she wasn't ready to do anything about it.

Kaya didn't need her to say anything to understand the truth. "Look, Ricki, I know you need time to plan things out, but I need to see that you're making an effort."

Ricki didn't know what to say, so she stayed quiet.

Kaya sighed. "After last week, don't you think you kind of owe me that?"

She looked at her, surprised she would bring that up again. "I thought we were okay after that. I know I screwed up, but I said I was sorry."

"Yes. And I forgave you. But that doesn't mean it didn't happen. You also said you wanted me to meet them properly."

"I do." She wasn't lying, but the idea still terrified her. "I'm just not ready."

"Do you have any idea when you might be ready?"

Ricki felt cornered. "I don't know. I said I was sorry for the way you met Paps last week. I panicked. I thought you understood that. I didn't mean for you to be caught unprepared."

Kaya stood up and paced across the kitchen. "I'm not accusing you of anything. I understand what happened last week. I just don't want it to happen again. You mention your mom's recipe, and that leaves me in the dark again because I've never met her. They apparently live right down the street, and you won't introduce me."

"I did introduce you to Paps," Ricki countered.

"Oh please, that doesn't count. You blindsided me with Paps."

"That's not fair."

"Fair?" Kaya was suddenly fired up, her exhaustion apparently forgotten. "It's not fair that you don't trust me enough to introduce me to your family."

"I do trust you."

"Do you trust *us*?"

Ricki held her gaze for a moment before looking away. The silence that followed was far from the tranquility she'd been savoring just a few minutes earlier.

"Ricki…" Kaya spoke quietly, and Ricki heard that the fire had left her voice.

She saw the hurt in her eyes.

"Yes, Kaya. I trust in us." She stood to go to her, but Kaya stepped back. Kaya had never stepped back from her before.

"I don't know how to do this, Ricki." Kaya's voice was so quiet, Ricki had to strain to hear her. "I understand that you need to come out on your terms, in your time. But it kills me that you don't trust in what we have enough to confide in me about your fears, enough to want to tell your family about us."

"I do want to. I'm just scared."

"You don't have to be scared alone. You don't have to run away from me, or avoid your family. You can't just pretend that these worlds are not on a collision course."

"I know that, Kaya."

"Do you? Do you understand how much I love you? How much it guts me that you doubt everything? You doubt us, you doubt your family, you doubt yourself. I don't know how much of that I can take."

"Ky, what are you saying?" Ricki felt panic rising in her chest.

"I don't know, Ricki." She shook her head. "I don't know."

"Where did this come from? I thought we were just having a pleasant evening. I promised you a massage, even. How did we end up fighting?" Ricki tried not to beg, but she wasn't sure what was happening, and it all felt wrong.

"I know you did. And dinner was great. Maybe I'm just exhausted and stressed and picking a fight," Kaya responded.

"Kaya, please don't leave me."

"I'm not planning on going anywhere. Not for the long term. But maybe it's better tonight if I just go home. This really bothers me, Ricki. I'm trying to give you the time you need, but I need to see you're trying."

Ricki didn't respond right away. She'd always heard that you should never go to bed angry with your lover, and now that's exactly what Kaya was suggesting. She wanted to go home, when Ricki had just begun to see her as at home *here*.

What could she say to that?

Kaya walked over to her, leaned in and kissed Ricki gently on the cheek. "You need time to sort out what you want. And I'm more stressed than I should be for a conversation like this. Think about everything, Ricki, and I'll see you in a few days."

Ricki didn't have anything more to say. She felt frozen, unable to understand what was happening.

Kaya turned, grabbed her coat from the closet and walked out the door.

CHAPTER THIRTY-FIVE

The next week was hell. Kaya wanted to go find Ricki, apologize for her outburst. She'd picked a fight that night, when all Ricki had done was cook her dinner and offer her relief from her hard day at work.

Yes, I picked a fight, but it was one we needed to have. She knew that if their relationship was going to grow, Ricki needed to do a better job with communication. Not just with her. She needed to communicate with Paps and her mother, too. Kaya hadn't meant to force the issue, but now that she had, she couldn't take it back.

The only good that had come from their fight was that Kaya had had the entire weekend alone to catch up on life. Now sitting alone on a Tuesday night, she looked around her clean apartment and the stack of graded papers sitting neatly on the table. *Well, fuck.*

This wasn't what she wanted, and she didn't know what to do with herself. She toyed with her cell phone, punching in Ricki's number only to cancel it. She'd been sitting there doing nothing else for a while before she finally dragged her thumb across the screen and hit the "Call" button for the "Favorite" contact.

"Hey. It's me." Kaya sighed into the phone.

"Kaya? What wrong, hon? I haven't heard from you in ages." Toni picked up on her mood instantly.

"Nothing much. School's just been hectic, and you know how I tend to get behind."

"Yes, I know you, but you don't sound overstressed, you sound sad."

It took a bit of prodding on Toni's part, but eventually Kaya relayed the details of her argument with Ricki. "I don't know what to do about it now. I forced an issue that didn't need forced, but now that I have, I can't go back. If I just let it go and run back to her, our relationship will never have the foundation it needs. But that leaves any future we have up to her."

"Maybe. Maybe you could talk things out again without losing that footing."

Kaya sensed more was coming. Instead of rushing to speak, she just waited for Toni to continue. Maybe she'd spent too much time with Ricki after all, if she was willing to be patient until someone else to spit out what they were trying to say.

"Or maybe it is in her hands."

There it is.

Kaya sighed. "I feel like I've been here before. I'm doing all I can, but I can't be the only one to do something, can I?"

"No. That's not how relationships are supposed to work."

"I'm in love with her, Toni."

"Have you told her that?"

"Yes." Kaya felt tears beginning to well. "And I know she loves me, too. We've only been dating for four months, but there's something big here. I'm afraid I pushed her too hard though."

"You said yourself you can't be the only one keeping this relationship strong. If this is pushing too hard, then maybe she's not right for you."

"Don't say that to me." Kaya didn't want to consider that possibility.

"Kaya, I love you, and I mean this in the best possible way, but you can be a handful."

She laughed. "Just a handful? I'll have to try harder." She could just imagine the way Toni would shake her head and roll her eyes if she were here with her.

"My point is, you need and deserve a strong woman to balance you. If Ricki isn't that woman, then you need to accept that."

"That's just it, Toni. She is so much stronger than she gives herself credit for. I see so much power in her, if only she could see it herself."

"But until she does, she's not right for you."

"You keep saying that, but I can't accept it."

"Maybe you just need to talk to her again. But you need to think about what it means for your relationship if you're the only one trying to bridge this gap."

Toni wasn't pulling any punches tonight, and for once, Kaya didn't think that was what she needed to hear from her best friend.

They talked a little longer, but Kaya didn't have the energy for chitchat. Afterward, she stared blankly at the wall. Everything Toni said was true. From the day they'd met, it seemed, Kaya had been chasing Ricki, waiting for Ricki, hell, practically stalking Ricki. It broke her heart, but she didn't think she could do it again. She needed Ricki to come back to her.

Kaya retreated to her bedroom and readied for sleep. Yes, she believed they could work through it, but Ricki had better contact her soon. She wasn't sure how much longer she could wait.

She stripped and crawled between the cold sheets. She had been having trouble sleeping since she no longer had Ricki's hot body next to her. She missed her more than she could ever remember missing another person.

Please, Ricki. Please let me know we can make this work.

Her phone buzzed on the nightstand next to her bed. She reached for it and checked the incoming text message.

Will you meet me tomorrow morning? At the track.

She stared at it for a long time. Sleep would not be coming easily tonight.

CHAPTER THIRTY-SIX

Ricki didn't know if Kaya was coming. She'd never received a response to her text. She'd learned over the years that there were two situations when she overexerted herself during her morning runs. Either she was in a groove, feeling good about life and just got lost in the rhythm, or she was trying to outrun some looming trouble. With each lap around that track that Kaya wasn't there, she wondered if she could ever run far enough to escape this.

There was a small part of her that wanted to be angry with Kaya for pressing her into coming out when she wasn't ready. But she knew that wasn't Kaya's intention. How could she fault her for wanting to be part of her life? For wanting to know the people she loved?

Then there were the other questions. Did Mom and Paps really love her if they didn't accept her feelings for Kaya? Was Kaya's love worth losing if that's what it took to stay right in her family's eyes? On the other hand, could they really love her if she never let them see who she really was?

Maybe it had taken longer than it should have, but Ricki finally had to admit that Kaya was right. Now she just prayed that Kaya would hear her out and let her make amends.

* * *

Kaya walked slowly over to where Ricki sat on the bleachers.

"I don't believe that words do much good when actions don't back them up," Ricki began softly.

As she spoke, Kaya watched the steam from her breath rise between them in the still morning air.

"I know my actions have fallen far short of my words. But still, I hope you'll believe me when I say I love you, and I want to do right by you."

"How?"

"Well, for starters, I have dinner reservations at the St. Edward Inn on Saturday night. I already talked to Mom and Paps. They don't know the reservation is for four yet, but I'm hoping you'll give me a reason to tell them it is."

Kaya drew in a deep breath. *That's a good start.* "Are you planning to tell them about me before we meet? Or just have them share an awkward meal with your co-worker?" She hadn't meant to speak so sharply, but she needed to know if Ricki was sincere.

"No. If you'll agree to come, I'll talk to them before that night and tell them exactly who you are." She stepped closer again, nearly closing the gap between them, before adding, "And exactly how much you mean to me."

Kaya hesitated, afraid of getting burned again. *But isn't this exactly what I've been asking for?* Accepting Ricki's plan, she leaned forward and kissed her softly. "I love you," she whispered, but added, "don't do this to me again."

"I love you, too. I'll make this up to you, I swear."

Ricki kissed her again, and Kaya's heart melted at the touch of her cold lips. Before she let herself go too far, she stepped back. "We both have about ten minutes to get to our classrooms."

"Shit! I need to shower!"

Kaya laughed at the oddity of the moment. "Go. I'll see you later."

Ricki turned but spun back and kissed her one more time. "Thank you. I love you." Then she bolted for the locker room.

"I love you," Kaya said softly, smiling as she headed into school.

CHAPTER THIRTY-SEVEN

Kaya tested the knob of Ricki's front door, and finding it unlocked, let herself into the house. "Ricki?" she called. *Maybe she's already upstairs.* Kaya's libido had been out of control ever since she'd seen her at the track that morning. She wandered into the kitchen, and was confused when Ricki didn't appear to be there.

Then a movement outside caught her eye. She walked over to the deck door and stepped outside. "Ricki?"

"Hey, baby." Ricki was there, leaning on her elbows on the rail and looking out across the park.

"What are you doing?" Kaya crossed over to her. "It's freezing out here."

"That's exactly why I'm out here. It was too hot in there. *I* was too hot in there." She wrapped her arms around Kaya and kissed her. "I've been hot for you all day."

Kaya forgot the cold the second Ricki's lips found her neck. Ricki pulled her close, their bodies fitting together perfectly. It was amazing what a few days' absence could do to the hunger Kaya felt for her.

Ricki snaked a hand under the tail of Kaya's flannel shirt, and Kaya yelped and jumped back. "Your hands are ice, sweetheart." Ricki didn't seem to care though, and reached for her again. Kaya kissed her, and led her back toward the door. "Take me inside."

Ricki didn't seem interested in stopping long enough to go into the house, but Kaya managed to backtrack enough to get them there. Once into the kitchen, Ricki tried to slip her hands under Kaya's shirt again, but Kaya intercepted them. Holding Ricki's hands in her own, she rubbed heat into them, and Ricki continued to work her mouth along Kaya's neck.

In between kisses, Ricki managed to speak. "Let me touch you. I need you so much." She slipped one hand from Kaya's grasp and reached up to tug her shirt collar away. Kaya's knees buckled, and she was glad she had found a way to lean against the kitchen table. "Upstairs. Now."

Ricki nodded against her skin, sucking at the tender flesh along her collarbone. Ricki was undoing buttons, and Kaya matched her, pulling open Ricki's shirt with an equal urgency. Together, they managed to move through the kitchen, bumping into things in their distracted state. But they didn't make it any farther than the wall at the base of the stairs. Ricki pushed Kaya against the wall, her mouth working lower as her hands seized her breasts. *Thank God I didn't wear a bra.*

Kaya raised her head, baring her throat and soaking in Ricki's touch. Being without her this past week, wondering if they would ever touch like this again, had been horrible. Now that she had Ricki's hands on her once more, she couldn't get enough, fast enough.

"God baby, I missed you," she murmured, pressing herself into Ricki when she felt her hands squeeze her breasts, lightly pinch her nipples. Ricki's mouth was at her throat again. Kaya clung to her, her hands around Ricki's back, under her shirt, pulling her closer, needing her body hard against her.

Ricki had her pinned, lifted against the wall. Kaya was no longer even supporting her own weight, and she hooked a foot around the back of Ricki's calf, opening her legs to invite Ricki's touch. When she felt one of her hands leave her breast to open the fly of her jeans, Kaya was grateful that Ricki supported her, because she could not have held herself up anymore.

Ricki shoved her hand into Kaya's jeans, under her panties and dipped into her wetness. *Oh God.*

"Jesus, Mary and Joseph."

Ricki ripped her hands from Kaya's hot skin, leaving Kaya stunned and dazed. She could barely comprehend what she was seeing as a wide-eyed Paps retreated through the kitchen door through which he'd just come.

"Oh fuck." Ricki stepped back from Kaya, panic in her eyes, and Kaya barely had enough warning to get her feet back under her.

"I apologize," Paps said, just before he hurried out.

"Oh fuck, oh fuck," Ricki repeated, though Kaya's brain was still having trouble processing what she was seeing. She had been seconds away from orgasm, and now Ricki stood before her, clumsily trying to button her own shirt to go after her grandfather.

"Ricki, wait." He was gone, so Kaya didn't see the need to cover her own exposed body. "Ricki, look at me."

Ricki turned to leave, but Kaya caught her by the arm and spun her back. "Don't leave me here, Ricki. Not like this. Not right now."

"Kaya, do you not understand what just happened?" Ricki was hysterical. "I was practically fucking you and my grandfather walked in on us!"

Her words felt like a slap across Kaya's face. *Fucking me? Is that all that was?* But she knew Ricki wasn't thinking. "Yes, I understand what just happened. What good is going after him going to do?"

"I need to explain. It's not—"

"Don't you dare say 'It's not what he thinks.' We were doing exactly what he thinks he saw, and if you deny it, we'll never do it again."

"Kaya, that was my grandfather."

"I know that, Ricki!" she shouted. "And nothing you say can make him unsee what he just saw. You can go talk to him later, but if you walk away from me like this, you're walking away from us. Do you understand me?"

Ricki stopped and looked at her. Still Kaya didn't try to hide her body. She wanted Ricki to see her, shirt open and chest bare, her pants pushed low on her hips. She had offered Ricki her body—and her heart—and she wanted Ricki to see how close she was to losing both.

"You have to make a choice, Ricki. What do you want?"

Choose me. Please choose me.

Each second that passed thundered in Kaya's ears. She could feel her heart racing, though whether from their interrupted passion or from the enormity of this confrontation, she didn't know.

When Ricki finally reached a decision, Kaya saw it flash in hers eyes a second before she stepped back into her arms and claimed a kiss. It wasn't the hard erotic kiss that they'd been consumed by just a few minutes earlier, but she had never felt so much power in a kiss before.

"I'm sorry. I need you. I love you. I don't want to lose you." Ricki took a step back, but not so far as to leave space between them. "I panicked again."

"You need to stop doing that."

"I think I'm at least justified this time, but will you forgive me?" she asked.

"Yes." Kaya kissed her lips again briefly, and ran her fingers through the short hair at the back of Ricki's head. "I need you, too." She held her tight for a moment, wanting to forget what was happening, but hiding from the truth didn't make it go away. "Do you want to go find him now?"

"I don't need to find him. I know where he is, and he's out of my reach for the moment."

"What?" Kaya didn't understand. "What do you mean?"

"I forgot what day it is. I've been so messed up over you this week that it all completely slipped my mind. He only comes here unannounced when he's inviting me to go to Mass with him—"

"But I thought you said that was the first Sunday. It's Wednesday, for Christ's sake. What Mass is there on Wednesday?"

"Exactly. It's Wednesday. Ash Wednesday. If I know my grandfather at all, after what he just saw, he beelined it to the church. I'll talk to him later."

She paused. "You gave me a chance I didn't deserve. Thank you, for forcing me to follow my heart instead of my fears."

Kaya felt Ricki's strong fingers guide her chin back. "Thank you. I love you. I'm so grateful I still have you." She kissed her again, and Kaya soaked in her conviction as she returned the kiss.

"What will you do about Paps?" she asked when they parted.

"Mass will last an hour. Maybe a little longer tonight, since they've got some extra stuff going on. I want to spend that time here with you, but then I'll go over to their house and have the conversation I should have had a long time ago."

Ricki brushed her fingers along Kaya's jaw. "Is that okay? I'm sorry the night I had planned for you has been ruined."

"No, it's all right. I think my body is too much in shock at the moment to pick up where we left off. I know how important this is. You take care of your family. I'll be okay for the night."

"Thank you."

Ricki put a little more space between them and carefully rebuttoned Kaya's shirt. She left the pants to Kaya, which made her smile. "I'm sorry I scandalized your grandfather," she offered wryly.

Ricki quirked her brow. "Oh, I'm sure you did much more than that. I have no idea what I'm going to say to him, but it's time I figure it out." She moved away from Kaya, back over to sit on the edge of the couch. "Fuck, what *am* I going to say to him?"

Kaya joined her and put an arm around her. "We'll figure it out together. We've got a little time now. Let me help you."

Ricki leaned into her embrace. "Together? All right."

CHAPTER THIRTY-EIGHT

The next morning, Kaya stopped by the track to talk to Ricki after her run, since Ricki hadn't called the night before after she'd gone to talk to Paps. Kaya had hoped to hear how things went, at the same time understanding that Ricki was probably preoccupied with it all.

When she got to the track, though, it was dark and there was no sign of Ricki.

Pulling her cell phone from her pocket, she hit the button for Ricki. It went to voice mail. She left a short message, then slipped the phone back into her pocket.

Maybe she finished up early and is already in her classroom.

She might just have time to swing by there after she signed in at the office.

Entering through the large glass double doors, she waved hello to Trish. The secretary popped her gum with the same indifference Kaya had seen the first time she entered the office looking for Ricki all those months ago, but by now, Kaya was used to that bored expression on her face.

"Good morning, Trish." Kaya offered a polite greeting, as she did every morning. Trish popped a bubble and nodded in her direction. *Who chews gum before eight in the morning, anyway?*

After she signed the log book, Kaya drew her finger up the sign-in roster to see just how early Ricki had arrived. Instead, she was alarmed to find that someone—probably Trish—had scribbled "Substitute" next to Ricki's name.

"Hey, Trish? Did you take the call for Ms. McGlinn for a sub?"

"Mmhmm."

"Is she sick?"

"Nope."

Kaya waited, and Trish gave an exasperated sigh. "Said something about her grandfather in the hospital. I don't know what for."

Kaya turned and left the office abruptly.

She walked quickly through the halls to her classroom, not knowing what to do next. *Paps is in the hospital?* She unlocked the door of her classroom and let the kids in, but instead of entering herself, she turned into the room across from hers.

"Mrs. Badden?"

The older teacher sitting at her desk looked over. "Yes?"

"Hi. Can you keep an eye on my class for a few minutes? I need to run and check on something." The doors of the room were close enough that she'd be able to hear if things got too unruly.

"Of course, dear."

Hopefully, Ian was in his office near the gym. She got lucky, and he was at his desk.

She asked breathlessly, "Ian, have you talked to Ricki?"

"You mean about Paps?"

"Yeah. I haven't talked to her since last night, and I only just heard from Trish that's he's in the hospital."

"Ricki called me this morning. Paps had a heart attack last night while he and her mom were at church, but that's all I know."

It's more than I know. "Thanks, man. Did Ricki sound all right?"

"She didn't call you? I'd have thought you'd be the first person she would call."

Kaya didn't know what to say. No, Ricki hadn't called her, but right now she had more important things to think about.

When she didn't answer, Ian shrugged and went on. "She was upset, understandably. But she'll be okay as long as Paps is. And Paps is a fighter. He'll pull through just fine, I'm sure."

"I need to get back to my classroom. Hopefully it hasn't gone *Lord of the Flies* in there yet. Will you let me know if you hear anything else from her?"

"Yeah, sure."

Kaya thanked him and hurried back to her classroom. Fortunately, her kids were behaving, most of them just chatting in small groups around the room. Three were asleep at their desks. Perhaps it was too early in the morning for them to cause too much havoc.

She found it nearly impossible to concentrate and by lunch she felt like a frazzled mess, worried sick for Ricki and not knowing what—if anything—she should do about it. As soon as the students had cleared out of her room, she pulled out her cell phone and tried Ricki again. When it went to voice mail, she almost hung up out of frustration. Instead, she managed to leave a message nearly begging Ricki to call her back.

She realized she didn't even know which hospital Paps had gone to. She picked up her phone again and pulled up a directory page for the local hospitals. On the second call, she found out that Paps was at Memorial, and after some pleading with the receptionist, she even managed to talk with a nurse who told her that his condition was stable.

She slumped back into her seat with relief. At least that was one question answered, even if there were still a dozen others.

Why hasn't she called me? Is she okay? What do I do?

CHAPTER THIRTY-NINE

Kaya had to remind herself not to speed as she drove across town to Memorial, where Patrick McGlinn was in room 820. On her way up to that part of the hospital, she stopped to look at a directory, locating the visitors' lounge nearest to Paps's room.

Ricki was there, staring out the window with her arms wrapped protectively around herself.

Kaya didn't hesitate, entering quietly and pulling the lounge door closed behind her.

"Sweetheart?" She walked over to Ricki, who turned at the sound of her entrance.

"Kaya? What are you doing here?"

"I came as soon as I could. Is he okay?" She reached forward to hug Ricki, but Ricki turned back to the window. Kaya let her arms fall to her sides, stung by Ricki's rejection but knowing this wasn't about her.

"He's stable," Ricki said, but offered nothing more.

They stood together in silence. Ricki was distant, her face calm and expressionless as she stared out the window, but Kaya could see the torment in her eyes. Her posture was rigid, her arms folded around herself.

"Are you okay?" she asked softly, thinking that Ricki might be in shock.

Ricki didn't reply.

Kaya waited a beat then tried something else. "Is your mom here, too?"

That seemed to shake Ricki from her silence, and she turned to face Kaya, shaking off her touch in the process. "Yes. She's in with Paps. He's sleeping, but she wanted to stay with him."

"Why aren't you in there with them?"

"I needed to get some air."

"Inside?" Kaya questioned automatically.

Ricki met her gaze. "Don't criticize me, Kaya. Not right now."

"I wasn't...I didn't mean to." She was surprised by the venom in Ricki's quiet voice, and before she recovered, Ricki turned her back again.

"Sweetheart, talk to me." Kaya reached for her, determined to give the support she seemed unwilling to accept.

"Go home, Kaya." Ricki spoke without looking at her. "You don't belong here."

Kaya froze, her hand in midair between them.

"What do you mean?'"

"You don't know him. You don't know Mom. What are you even doing here?"

Ricki's words were so harsh, Kaya felt a defensive flame lick at the corners of her consciousness. *She's hurting. Be patient.*

"I might not know them, but I know you. I'm here for you." She squeezed her fingers into a fist before forcing herself to relax and extending her arm to brush a tender touch along Ricki's back.

Ricki spun on her.

"Don't touch me." She stepped back, and Kaya sensed the storm about to break. "The fact that you know me is the whole reason Paps is in the hospital. If I hadn't been so selfish, if I hadn't let myself want you, he wouldn't even be here right now."

"You can't believe that."

"Believe it? I know it. His heart gave out because of what he walked in on last night. Because of my selfishness."

"Ricki, sweetheart, that can't be true."

"It is! He got as far as the church, and then collapsed ten minutes into the Mass. How can you say that's anything other than my fault?"

"It's certainly not your fault. Even if the shock somehow triggered his heart attack—which I don't believe—then it's our fault. Both of us. So don't you blame yourself and push me away."

"Is that supposed to make me feel better?" Ricki stared her down, and Kaya struggled for an answer.

"No. That's not what I meant. My point is that it's not anyone's fault."

"You don't understand." She turned and crossed to the other side of the room, seemingly wanting to get as far away from Kaya as she could.

"Then explain it to me." Kaya let her go. She didn't try to close the gap but didn't plan to go anywhere either.

"Kaya. Go home."

"No."

"Kaya, please. Just leave me. I can't do this, and I don't want you here."

Kaya managed to sit in one of the stiff waiting room chairs before her knees gave out. "What are you saying?"

"I'm saying, I can't keep pretending like I'm not hurting anyone by giving in to my selfish desires. I love you, Kaya, but I can't do this anymore. People keep getting hurt because of me."

Kaya went to her, seized her face in both hands. "Look at me. If you're going to do this, at least look me in the eye."

Finally Ricki did so, and the agony on her face only made Kaya angrier. "Tell me I've misunderstood you. Tell me you're not really breaking up with me because you think our relationship is somehow responsible for your grandfather's health."

Ricki didn't respond.

Kaya felt hot tears rising in her eyes. "Ricki, how can you do this? Just last night, you said you needed me, you said—"

"I know what I said, Kaya. I was wrong."

"Wrong? No, you're wrong now. I love you, Ricki. What's wrong is your constant need to run from that. From us."

"I shouldn't have let *us* happen in the first place. I knew it couldn't work. I knew someone would get hurt. And now Paps—"

"This isn't about Paps! It's about you and me, Ricki. You want to know who's getting hurt? You and me. You're hurting both of us with your foolish guilt. Doesn't that matter?"

"You're better off without me," Ricki insisted. "You would have been better off never knowing me."

"But I do know you, Ricki," Kaya whispered, the ache in her chest growing sharper. "I do know you, and I do love you. Stop running from me. Stop using every difficult situation you encounter as an excuse to run from life. Why can't you see you don't have to be alone?"

"Because every time I give in to my own selfish needs, someone gets hurt."

Kaya looked at her. Ricki wasn't talking about Paps anymore. The misery in her voice was coming from somewhere deeper than that.

"Ricki? What are you talking about?"

Ricki shook her head. "It's my fault Paps is here. Just like it was my fault he killed her."

CHAPTER FORTY

Ricki had been sitting in the common room of their house, trying to pick through her latest education assignment. When Bre crashed into the house and bolted up the stairs, Ricki followed her. Bre was sitting in her room, on the edge of her bed, her back to Ricki. It took Ricki a second to realize she was crying.

"Hey, hey." Ricki pulled Bre into a hug. "What is it? What's wrong?"

Bre pulled away from Ricki's tight embrace, and Ricki saw immediately what had happened. "That fucking bastard." The bruise on Bre's face was already discoloring her perfect skin from her eyebrow to her jaw. "I'll kill him. He'll never hit you again, I swear it."

Ricki moved to stand up, but Bre grabbed her. "Don't."

"Bre, he beat you! Don't you understand that? That fucker deserves to die."

"Don't, Ricki. Just leave it," she begged.

Ricki nearly punched a hole through the wall, envisioning what she wanted to do to Bobby Dean Carroll, but the fear in Bre's voice stopped her. "Bre, he hit you. Again."

"It's not what it looks like."

"How is it not? How can this—" She reached her hand up to brush delicately just beyond the edge of Bre's bruised face, "—be anything other than what it looks like? He's hurt you for the last time."

"No, Ricki, stay out of it."

"How can you ask me to do that?"

"It was my fault this time. I shouldn't have provoked him like I did."

"Bre," Ricki whispered, her voice cracking with the sorrow and confusion of hearing Bre take the blame for Bobby Dean's barbaric behavior. "This is not your fault. He abuses you. That is his fault. No one else's. Can't you see you deserve to be treated better than that?"

Ricki pulled her hand down, realizing suddenly how much she longed to kiss Bre, and not for the first time. She wanted to say, "I would never hurt you like this," but she had always known those thoughts were doomed. Instead, she said, "You deserve a real man, someone who would only ever touch you with kindness and love."

When Bre leaned forward and kissed her, she was so startled she jumped up from the bed. "What the fuck? What are you doing?" she exclaimed.

"You love me, don't you Ricki?" Bre asked.

Maybe she should have denied it. Maybe she should have called Bre crazy or just left the room. But all she could do, looking into those green eyes that had haunted her dreams since the day they'd met, was tell the truth. "Yes."

"You've loved me for years." This time, Bre's words were a statement, not a question.

"You knew?"

"Yes." Bre reached for her, and Ricki let her pull her back down to sit beside her.

"I never told you. Never told anyone." She was shocked, not knowing how else to respond.

Bre laughed, the sweet tone of her amusement like water to Ricki's parched soul. "You aren't really very good at hiding how you feel. You've always been here for me. You're the one here for me now."

Now, the words she had stifled earlier came out before she could stop them. "I would never hurt you. Not like this." She reached again to touch Bre's face, careful to avoid her bruise. "And not here either." She moved her hand down, to hover over Bre's heart.

She was too entranced to move when Bre pulled off her sweater, caught Ricki's hand and drew it to her chest. "No one has ever looked at me like you do."

"Bre, what are you doing? You know how I feel. Please, don't mess with me."

"I'm not, Ricki. I need what you give me. You make me feel like I'm worthy of love. You make me feel beautiful."

Ricki couldn't resist what was being offered, what she had always dreamed of. She took Bre's mouth in a hungry kiss, then moved her lips down Bre's throat, whispering between kisses, "You *are* beautiful."

She moved her mouth and fingers over Bre's body. As she shifted, tasting her skin in new places, she found more bruises and scrapes, in various stages of healing. Every time, she pulled back, met Bre's eyes, and vowed never to let anyone hurt her again.

She had caressed every exposed inch of Bre's skin before her brain caught up to her body and heart. She pulled back abruptly. "I shouldn't be doing this. God Bre, I want you, but you don't—"

Bre silenced her with a kiss. "Make me feel loved," she whispered when she pulled away. Ricki hesitated, her body at war with her head. She knew. She knew Bre was straight, knew Bre didn't understand what she was doing. But when Bre opened Ricki's shirt and touched her for the first time, any hope of control she had was gone.

College had been exciting and full of new experiences for Ricki. She was no stranger to the girls around campus, and she knew how to please them. But this night, holding Bre, was nothing like she had ever even imagined. She worshipped Bre's perfect skin, touching her and caressing her until Bre clung to her with need. When she brought Bre to orgasm, she knew she had never seen someone so beautiful, someone so stunning in all her life. Her heart overflowed as she held Bre afterward, never having dreamed this could ever be real.

She kept Bre wrapped tightly in her arms as she slept, exhausted from their passion. All of the fantasies she'd tried to ignore over the past three years came rushing back to her mind in vivid color. She lay there, imagining the life they would share, her one true love suddenly having recognized their perfect fit.

A little while later, Bre stirred and mumbled something incoherent. Even though it was barely after midnight, Ricki kissed her and whispered "Good morning, beautiful."

Bre smiled, a hazy look in her eyes. "I never knew it could be like that."

"Neither did I."

Bre's brow furrowed in half-asleep confusion. "But you… you've been with other girls."

Ricki chuckled softly. "None of them hold a candle to you." She kissed her again. "I love you."

Bre nuzzled her face closer against Ricki's neck. She never heard anyone approaching. When the bedroom door slammed open, Ricki protectively tightened her hold and pulled the sheet higher to cover them both. Bobby Dean stood in the doorway, his hard, angry eyes taking in the sight before him. He snarled and clenched his fists, and Ricki felt a deep fear, not for herself but for the woman she held close.

They stared each other down, then after a moment, he sneered—almost smiled—and left. Ricki felt her heart racing, felt Bre's shiver of fear against her body. Neither of them moved for a minute, then Bre tried to get up. Ricki didn't want to let her go.

"Ricki. The door."

Ricki had to release her so Bre could close the bedroom door. It didn't matter that their other roommate probably wasn't home. She understood that they needed privacy right now.

She didn't understand, though, when Bre began to dress herself. "Bre? What are you doing?"

"I'm getting dressed, Ricki."

"Why?"

"Why?" Bre echoed her question. "Because I just cheated on my boyfriend. Because he walked in on us. Because I'm straight. Because this was a mistake."

Her words were hot barbs lodging themselves deep in Ricki's chest. "But Bre…"

Bre didn't even slow her movements as she pulled clothes over her body. "Bre, I love you."

She did pause then, her back to Ricki. But her hesitation lasted only a moment. "I know you do, Ricki. But we both know I could never give you what you need." She turned to face her. "I love you, too, but I'll never love you like that. Surely you understand that."

Ricki didn't want to understand that, and hearing the words after what they had just done was acid poured on an open wound. But she did know. She knew Bre could never reciprocate her love. "Then what was it we just did?"

"You comforted me when I needed it."

"Comforted you? That's what that was?"

"Yes." She finished pulling the sweater over her head, now again completely covered from Ricki's sight. "Please, Ricki. Don't make this harder than it already is."

"Fine. I get that you can't love me, but please…please don't go back to him. He doesn't love you. He hurts you. Maybe I can't be the one to give you what you need, but you deserve better than him."

Bre shook her head sadly. "I'm sorry, Ricki."

CHAPTER FORTY-ONE

"She walked out. I never saw her conscious again."

Ricki had kept most of the details in her memory, but now Kaya at least knew the whole story. She had slept with Bre, and that had triggered Bobby Dean's violent rage that ultimately killed her.

"Maybe I should have gone after her. Maybe I should have gone after him. He might have killed me instead, and her life was so much more valuable than mine. She was so good, Kaya, and I killed her."

Ricki didn't really want to look up, didn't want to see the judgment she deserved reflected in Kaya's eyes. Now that Kaya knew the truth, she'd understand why Ricki was poison. Always had been. When she finally did meet her gaze, she was surprised by the tears she saw streaking Kaya's cheeks and the overwhelming sadness in her eyes.

"Ricki..." She stepped toward her, and Ricki didn't know what to do. She didn't merit consolation or compassion, but leave it to Kaya to offer that anyway. "Ricki, it was not your fault he killed her."

"Did you not hear what I just told you?" Ricki couldn't believe she could say that to her, now that she knew what had really happened.

"Yes, I heard every word, and I can see your remorse. But it's not your fault he killed her any more than it was ever her fault that he beat her. Bobby Dean was a horrible, evil person and only he is responsible for his crimes."

"I suppose you're going to try to tell me again that it's not my fault Paps had a heart attack, either."

"It's not!" Kaya exclaimed.

Ricki just shook her head sadly. It was, and she knew it. Kaya was blinded by her feelings for her, feelings that she never should have let get this far.

"If I had been stronger—"

"Ricki, you are strong. You were strong then, and you're strong now. So strong, in fact, that you insist on taking the blame for things far beyond your control."

She wasn't surprised by Kaya's response. Everything about Kaya was passionate, so to expect anything less was ridiculous. She would never understand though. Ricki knew that now. She knew she wouldn't—couldn't—make the same mistake with Kaya that she'd made before. It wasn't the same, she knew, with Paps being the one in the bed down the hall, fighting for his life just as Bre had fought for hers. The doctors expected him to survive, but Bre hadn't been so lucky. Still, it was her fault and the guilt choked her soul just the same.

Ricki hadn't wanted to think they were making a mistake, but to deny it now was the epitome of selfishness.

"People get hurt when I lose control. It happened to Bre and now it's happened to Paps. Maybe you can't see that, but I do."

"Ricki, that's not what happened. You love me. Love doesn't cause this kind of pain. It's the fear and the hate and the isolation that hurt you. Let me help you through this. Let me love you, let me show you that this thing between us is stronger than the regrets you've been carrying for too long."

She wanted to give in and let Kaya hold her. But her demons would haunt her for the rest of her life, and Kaya couldn't take her burden from her.

"Kaya, I'm sorry. But this is my only choice. I can't see you anymore." The words burned her throat as she said them, but Ricki knew that she was doing the right thing. The only thing.

"Ricki, please. You're scared and hurt by Paps's sudden condition. Please, don't cut me out. Don't run from me, or do something you can't take back."

"I won't take it back, Kaya. I can't. It's already gone further than it ever should have, and I need to end things now before you get hurt, too."

"Before I get hurt? It's too late for that. Don't you see you're the one hurting me? You're pushing me away again, and after what you said last night, I thought we were finally past this."

"I already told you, I made a mistake last night. Don't throw that back in my face."

Ricki could see she was hurting Kaya, knew Kaya couldn't understand what had to be done. Lingering any longer wouldn't help them.

"Go home, Kaya. Go home, and don't try to visit again. I'm sorry I've hurt you, but this is for the best."

"Ricki, please."

Ricki hadn't expected Kaya to beg. She knew how badly her own soul hurt at the prospect of losing Kaya, but she was doing this for Kaya's own good. She had hoped that Kaya would understand that and not make this so damn difficult. Or at least that she would respond with the fiery temper Ricki had come to know, since anger was so much easier to handle than tears.

"Leave."

"You don't know what you're doing."

"Yes. I do. Go away, Kaya."

"If you run from me this time, this really is this end. I won't chase after you. I won't just sit around and wait for you to come running back."

"You shouldn't." Ricki knew if she was making that threat, her anger was starting to get the better of her hurt. Good. It would make it easier for Kaya in the end.

"Ricki, please," she repeated.

"Kaya. I don't want you. Just go." Ricki uttered the words she knew would finally drive Kaya away.

And to her severe anguish, she was right. Kaya turned and walked away.

Ricki lasted about three seconds before she collapsed onto a hard waiting room chair and sobbed into her hands.

CHAPTER FORTY-TWO

"What are you doing tonight and this weekend?" Kaya had made it out to her car and cried alone for a full fifteen minutes before she pulled herself together enough to call Toni.

"Nothing, really. Why?"

"Good. I'm coming to visit."

"What? Now?"

"Yes now. I'll be there in a few hours and I'll explain everything then. I just need to get away from here."

"Are you all right?"

"Just have a bottle of wine ready by the time I get there."

"Kaya, wait. You're upset. Are you sure you should be driving?"

"I'm not driving yet. I'll explain everything when I get there," she repeated. "I'll be fine, but I do need to concentrate on the road right now. I'll see you soon."

"All right, hon, but be careful."

Kaya could hear the concern in her friend's voice as she hung up the phone. It made her take a few more calming breaths before she put the key in the ignition and left the hospital. School would have to make do with substitutes for both her and Ricki tomorrow, as there was simply no way she could stay in this town if Ricki really was ending things between them.

Kaya knew this time there was no going back. She couldn't believe Ricki could be so blinded by her unwarranted guilt to end what they had, but that was her decision and it seemed there was nothing Kaya could do about that.

Toni did better than requested and had a bottle for each of them by the time Kaya arrived. After Kaya downed the first glass, she hugged her friend.

Toni walked over to the couch and patted the cushion next to her. "So are you going to tell me what Ricki did this time?"

"Is it that obvious?"

"Only because I know you."

She sighed and took another deep swallow of wine.

"Well, you know we've been fighting..." she began.

* * *

Ricki sat in the dark near Paps's hospital bed. She had run out of tears some time after Kaya had walked out, but the emptiness was still there in full force. Kaya was gone. Her mother was in the chapel, more willing to talk to God than to Ricki at the moment. Paps looked so frail, sleeping there in the sterile setting. Everyone she loved knew now how weak she was.

She hated hospitals. The last time she'd been in one, she'd lost her first love. Now she'd lost the only other woman who had ever claimed a piece of her heart. The only good news she'd had since rushing here the night before was the doctors' expectations that Paps would be okay. Still, sitting here next to him, holding his hand, she carried the bitter aftertaste of fear and shame.

"Well, Sport, if I look half as bad as you do right now, it's no wonder they've got me laid up in this here bed."

Ricki looked up, surprised to hear Paps's raspy voice, and worried that it sounded so weak. "Hey. How are you feeling?"

"I've been better, no doubt. But I'm still breathing, so that's a blessing enough to thank the Good Lord for." He paused, his breathing slow and ragged. "Those frown lines on your face tell me you've been doing more worrying than praying. I'm still here, and you and me both best be thanking God that was His will."

Ricki had gotten used to the frequent references to prayer and God in everything Paps said. With the despair and fear heavy in her heart, she felt utterly abandoned by the God that Paps trusted so much.

"That's all right, Sport. You don't have to believe. I'm got faith for the both of us, and God's got faith in us right back."

She felt tears build again, and wanted desperately not to cry in front of her grandfather. When she felt his hand gently squeeze hers, she risked a glance toward him and saw that his eyes were again closed and his breathing deep. That was a relief at least, as she couldn't stop a single tear from escaping down her cheek.

She assumed he was asleep, but after a few minutes of silence, he added in a low, drowsy voice. "I hope your girl wasn't too upset. This foolish old man certainly learned his lesson about knocking, and I do hope she'll forgive my intrusion."

Ricki stared at him, dumbfounded. Then she found her voice. "What?"

Paps didn't respond, and Ricki couldn't believe he'd fallen asleep after saying what she thought she'd heard. "What did you just say?" she whispered incredulously. She wanted to shake him awake, make him repeat his words. She must have misheard, or maybe she'd only imagined he'd spoken at all. Paps wore his faith on his sleeve. Religious men didn't react like that to what he'd seen.

CHAPTER FORTY-THREE

Ricki was going crazy, not being able to talk to Paps again about his mumbled comment as he drifted to sleep, but she hadn't found herself alone with him in the past two days. There was always a doctor or nurse or her mother, if he was awake at all. He'd been sleeping a lot, which the doctors assured them was normal. He was sleeping again, and then he was scheduled to be discharged that afternoon after one final check. It would be such a relief to have him back home. Maybe then she'd finally have the chance to talk to him.

In the meantime, she was anxious and agitated, pacing around the waiting room. For the hundredth time, she tried to play out the conversation she needed to have in her mind, tried to imagine what he'd say and how he'd react. She also struggled to hear again exactly what he'd muttered two days earlier. But what she'd thought she heard couldn't have been correct.

As she imagined that pending conversation, she realized there was another that she needed to have, and one that she probably could have sooner rather than later. She'd not yet talked to her mom about anything, either, and she knew exactly where she could find her. The question was simply whether Ricki was ready for that chat.

But then, did it really matter whether she was ready or not? It was long overdue, and she had to gather her courage and just get it over. Turning resolutely from the waiting room, she headed toward the small chapel in the hospital. Her mother was undoubtedly there now as she had been so often the past few days.

She placed her hand on the simple wooden door and drew in a deep breath before pushing through. The chapel was dim, but sure enough, her mother sat alone in one of the front pews. As defeated and powerless as Ricki felt, she was surprised to see her mother's calm expression as she gazed toward the nondenominational symbols adorning the front wall of the small room. Her mother displayed a peace and strength that were so foreign to Ricki in this time of pain.

She paused, gathering her nerve. Then she finally walked softly to the front, and waited a moment for her mother to sense her presence.

"Oh, Ricki." She turned to see her daughter. "I didn't expect to see you in here."

"Ah, no." Ricki looked down at her hands. This wasn't a place she'd come to before, and she couldn't say she was here willingly now, but she couldn't put things off any longer. "I was wondering if we might talk."

Her mother patted the pew next to her, but Ricki hesitated. "Maybe somewhere else?"

"God listens to your concerns just as I do. Why not talk here in His place?"

Ricki felt her discomfort grow, but there was no point making this harder than it already was. She sat down next to her mother.

Where to begin? "This place…I'm glad it gives you peace. I can't blame you for preferring to talk to God instead of me…" She felt silent. She hadn't meant to say that. This was already off to a poor start.

"Why would you say such a thing? I'm always willing to talk to you." Her mother's tone was incredulous, and there was a trace of hurt there, too.

"I'm sorry." Ricki tried once again to gather her thoughts. "It's just…I don't know if Paps talked to you. I never meant for him to get hurt, and I'm so sorry to have caused all this. I just wanted to finally get things out there." She struggled with what to say, then simply repeated, "I'm sorry."

Her mother was looking at her, a frown furrowing her brow. "What are you talking about? What did you cause?"

"It was all my fault. I caused Paps's heart attack."

"What? How could you have done that? The doctors explained about the blockages they found. What does that have to do with you?"

"It was the shock of seeing us…Did he say anything to you the other night before Mass?"

"Ricki, dear, you're not making any sense."

She sighed. "I know. I guess I should back up. He came over to see if I'd go to Ash Wednesday Mass with you. Did he say anything to you about what happened then?"

"No. Just that you weren't coming, which I expected. Although I do wish you would come."

Ricki ignored the admonition. "He didn't mention what he saw?"

Her mother just shook her head, still obviously confused.

"Was he upset? He must have been upset."

"He, well, I suppose he seemed a little flustered, but nothing I worried about. We got right in the car and drove to the church. We prayed and the choir sang a beautiful prelude, and then just into the First Reading, he leaned forward and clutched his chest, like he was having trouble breathing. Thank God for the young woman in the pew next to us. She knew just what to do and the ambulance arrived very quickly."

Much of that recap Ricki had already heard when her mother had spoken with the doctors. "But he didn't say anything else about coming over to see me?"

"No." Her mother looked at her critically. "Why? Should he have?"

"It was my fault he had a heart attack. When he came to see me, he walked in on...a compromising situation. The shock—that's what caused this. I'm the reason he's here."

Her mother just looked at her, and Ricki could see the curiosity in her expression. But she said, "I have no idea what he could have seen that has you thinking such silly things. The doctors clearly explained his condition, and nothing you could have said or done would have caused this."

Ricki knew she was only saying that because the truth was so far from her mind. She had to tell her. She owed her that. "What he saw...it did cause this. I was..." Why was telling her the truth so difficult? She took a deep breath. "Mom, I was with someone. We were...in an intimate position, and he walked in. He saw me. With another woman."

Ricki was afraid to look at her mother. After what felt like hours, Ricki finally raised her eyes. She was shocked, disconcerted by the studying look her mother was giving her. "Mom? Do you understand what I'm saying?"

"Oh, of course. Really, I'm trying to figure out how you think that could have caused his heart attack. I suppose that would be a bit shocking, depending how intimate you mean. But then, your grandfather does understand how young romance works."

"I...what?"

"That would explain why he seemed a bit flustered. I'm sure he was embarrassed."

"Did you hear what I said? I was with another woman."

"Yes dear. You already said that."

Ricki couldn't believe what she was hearing. Her mother seemed completely nonchalant about the whole thing. She wasn't shocked or upset, still appearing to puzzle over the whole situation and sitting there as if Ricki had just told her that the sky was blue.

Maybe her mother just didn't understand. The stress of the last few days must be getting to her. "Mom. I'm gay."

"I know that, dear."

Ricki stared at her, completely astonished.

"Did you think I didn't know?" her mother asked. "You're my little girl. I know you."

"But I never told you." Ricki didn't know how to respond to any of this.

"No. But you never told me you were right-handed, either. I'm not stupid."

Ricki shook her head. None of this made sense.

"You said you wanted me to get married and have grandbabies."

"Well, yes. I do."

"But I'm gay."

"So? I hear about these things on the news. All sorts of people are getting married nowadays, and unless there's something else you're not telling me, you can still give me grandbabies."

"I...what about your faith?"

"Oh Ricki. Have you been afraid to talk about this? I always just assumed you were embarrassed by the topic, talking about romance with your mother. Goodness knows I never wanted my mother to know about my love life." Her mother pulled her into a hug. "My faith tells me to love. You are my daughter. I love you."

Ricki couldn't wrap her mind around anything she was hearing, but she felt the warmth and strength of her mother's arms wrapped around her. She didn't realize she needed to cry until her tears flowed freely. Her mother just held her close and rocked her gently.

CHAPTER FORTY-FOUR

Kaya picked up her buzzing phone from the coffee table and glanced at the screen. At the sight of Ricki's name, she drew in a sharp breath. They hadn't spoken since the hospital and she didn't know how to handle this call. Her thumb hovered then shifted to hit Decline.

She didn't set the phone back down, though, staring at the screen even though it no longer showed Ricki's name.

"That was her, wasn't it?" Toni asked. Kaya had been reading a book while Toni tapped away at her laptop, enjoying the quiet presence of a close friend. *I've also been putting off going home*, she admitted to herself.

"Yeah." Kaya didn't have anything else to say.

Then she asked, "You think I should have answered it?"

"I don't know. That has to be your decision. What if she wanted to apologize?"

"I can't do this again. I need to distance myself until I can see her or hear her voice without this ache building in my chest." She didn't need to explain to Toni the pain she felt every time she thought about Ricki. Toni had been with her the past three days. Kaya knew she understood.

"You're sure it's over?"

"I don't see any other option. I can't..." She felt her throat tighten again and fell silent.

Toni waited for her to find her voice again.

"There is a huge hole in our relationship. As long as she's in the closet, I don't think I can be part of that. It hurts too much. For both of us."

"And if she came out? Given what you said happened on Wednesday, it sounds like she's out whether or not she wants to be."

"I know. But that's not enough. Not anymore. I've been fighting for this to work from the beginning, and I need her to fight for me, too. I need her to believe that we're worth it."

"What do you mean?" Toni questioned.

What do I mean? Who do I even expect her to fight against for me? She needed Ricki to fight her own demons, her own fears. "Rynn stared down the barrel of a gun for you. I want someone who will fight for me, too. Someone who's not afraid to want me. Having her grandfather walk in on us is a far cry from her looking at herself in the mirror—and looking the others in her life in the eye—and embracing who she is and who she loves."

Kaya looked back to her friend. "No. I can't do this anymore."

Toni reached across the table between them and took Kaya's hand. "I'm sorry. I wish you weren't going through this, but you know I'm here for you."

"I know. That's why I'm here." Kaya forced a smile, reassuring herself and Toni that she would be okay.

* * *

Ricki swallowed around the lump that had formed in her throat when Kaya's phone went to voice mail. She waited for the tone, and then found herself unable to get any words out for a message so she'd just hung up.

"Hey, Sport. Your mama tells me that we should talk."

She looked up to see Paps entering the room. They'd been home now for a full day, and she was glad to see him moving around pretty well.

"Hi, Paps," she greeted him and watched as he took a seat on the recliner next to her. After they'd come home, she had had a few opportunities to finally talk with him, but the conversation with her mother had so surprised her that she was still processing that.

It seemed now Paps was starting the conversation for her.

"You've got something eating at you, so you might as well spit it out," Paps stated.

"I guess first I need to say I'm sorry. I never meant for you to end up in the hospital, and the shock of walking in on me like you did surely landed you there."

"Don't be ridiculous. My clogged up body landed me there, but the docs fixed me right up."

"Paps—"

"Sport, I'm not gonna lie and say it wasn't a shock to see you and your lady-friend like that, but it wasn't your fault my ticker threw a fit. You don't get to take credit for that adventure."

"Adventure?" Ricki couldn't believe he was so casual about the whole thing. He'd nearly died!

"Yes, adventure. I'm okay now, ain't I?"

"Yes, but—"

"No 'buts,' Sport. I pulled through it, and now the doctors have taught me what I need to watch out for to make sure I don't have to go through that again. So quit acting like this was about you."

Ricki needed a moment.

Paps spoke again, "Ricki, bad things happen. When I lost your grandmother, it nearly killed me. But I had you and your mom to help me through. If I'd allowed myself to believe for a second that her death was in any way my fault, it would have destroyed me. But the cancer wasn't my fault any more than this here heart attack was yours."

"It's not the same, Paps. The shock—"

"No, Ricki. You gotta trust me that this was not your fault."

Ricki dropped her gaze to her lap. Could it be true?

Maybe it was best Kaya hadn't answered. Ricki still didn't have any idea what she would have said.

She could feel Paps watching her, waiting for her to accept his words. She had always trusted his judgment, and she wanted to believe him now, but still the guilt and grief she felt were strong. After some time, she finally felt calm enough to raise her head.

Paps studied her a moment longer, than nodded as if he were satisfied with what he saw. "Now that we've cleared that up, there's another topic to tackle."

She looked at him, not sure she could handle any more right now.

"You've always been a bit… different. I've watched you grow from a little girl, Sport, and I've loved you every moment along the way. You know that, right?"

She blinked back the tears that threatened to fall. How could she have misjudged her own family for so long? How could she have feared so much? And how had she been so lucky to have them?

"I saw more than I ever needed to the other night, but I tried not to see too much. Was that the same girl you had over a few weeks back?"

Ricki drew in a deep breath. She still couldn't quite believe that she was having this conversation, and that Paps was so calm about it. After a moment, she nodded.

"What's her name again?"

Ricki felt a lump in her throat form just below the thoughts of Kaya washing through her brain. She was afraid for a moment that she might not be able to speak, but she managed to squeeze out one word. "Kaya."

"I guess I need to be apologizing to her for barging in. When do you think I might be able to do that?"

Ricki closed her eyes, the regret of her argument with Kaya rising to the surface. "I don't know, Paps." She opened her eyes and met his eyes. "We sort of had a fight, and I don't know where we stand now."

"Hmph. Well, the woman is always right, so you best make it up to her quick."

She blinked, one more surprise piled on top of everything else that had happened. "You don't even know what happened. Why would you assume she's right? And besides," Ricki felt a smile tug at her lips for the first time in days. "I'm a woman, too."

"Oh, you know what I mean." Paps brushed some imaginary lint off his pants, and Ricki couldn't believe that was the thing that might make him feel awkward. But he straightened up, the strong gentleman she'd always known sitting proudly before her.

"Do you have something to make up for?" he asked.

Ricki didn't need to look deep inside to know that every problem between them was her fault. "Yes."

"Then fix it."

Ricki shook her head. If only things could be that easy.

"Look, Sport, I don't know this girl—excuse me, woman— but I get the feeling she's someone special to you. Am I right?"

"Yes." Ricki hesitated, then admitted to herself and to Paps something she'd always been afraid to say. "I'm in love with her."

"Then go make things right."

CHAPTER FORTY-FIVE

Kaya had stayed at Toni's much longer than she should have, and it was quite late by the time she got home. She trudged into her apartment, longing for the oblivion of sleep and dreading that she'd have to get up early to be back in her classroom tomorrow morning.

When she'd pulled her phone from her jacket pocket to text Toni and let her know she'd made it home, she'd been surprised to find three more missed calls from Ricki.

After that, she hadn't been able to sleep much anyway.

It was a struggle to get herself to school the next morning. She made it through the morning mostly on autopilot, and she suspected the students were probably happy to have an easy day in class.

At lunch, she decided she'd rather eat a granola bar from a vending machine than risk bumping into Ricki in the cafeteria.

She grabbed the meager snack and a bottle of juice and headed back to her classroom. As she rounded the corner, she stopped in her tracks. Ricki was leaning casually against the wall next to her classroom door. *Fuck*.

The hallway was empty, but if she needed to face Ricki, better to do it in her classroom with no chance of an audience. She drew in a deep breath and gathered her courage.

Ricki looked up at the sound of Kaya's footsteps. Kaya forced herself to meet Ricki's eyes. Then she walked a step past her and unlocked her classroom without saying a word.

"Hello," Ricki offered quietly, but Kaya didn't respond.

"Can we talk?" Ricki's voice was low, and Kaya could hear the begging desperation there.

Kaya pushed the door open. If she was going to lose it, she had twenty minutes in her private classroom before students poured back in.

She entered the room and left the door open behind her. Placing the juice and granola bar on her desk, she kept walking across to the window.

She heard the door click closed and Ricki's quiet voice from across the room. "Kaya?"

Kaya took a steadying breath.

"What do you want from me, Ricki?"

Ricki stopped halfway across the classroom. "I'm sorry, Ky. I know how badly I've hurt you. I was a fool."

Yes. You were. "That doesn't answer my question. What do you want?"

Ricki took another tentative step closer. "I want to make things right with you. I want to make up for what I did."

Ricki moved closer still.

"I want you back, Kaya."

She wanted to give in. She wanted to let the tears out and let Ricki take her in her arms and tell her they would be okay. But it was too late for that. Ricki had hurt her too many times.

"I'm sorry, Ricki. I think you should leave."

"Please, Ky. Give me another chance." She was only a few feet away now.

"I can't do that, Ricki." She looked up at her, and immediately realized her mistake when she couldn't hold back her tears. "I can't keep doing this. You've been running from me all along, and I foolishly fell in love with you anyway. I don't have it in me to fight your fears anymore. It hurts too much."

"You don't have to. I won't hurt you again," Ricki pleaded. "I'm out now. I talked to Paps and Mom. They know about me. Turns out they knew all along. They want to meet you. In fact, Paps wants to apologize for the other night. He's embarrassed by the whole thing."

Kaya couldn't stop the short, cynical laugh that burst out. "*He's* embarrassed? He should try being on the other side of that scenario."

"I'm sorry, Kaya," Ricki apologized again. "How can I make it right?"

"You can't." Kaya shook her head. "You can't this time, Ricki." She turned her back, looking out the window again. "Please. Leave."

"Kaya—"

"Please Ricki."

She heard Ricki's footsteps leave the room, and needed every second left in the period to let her tears fall and then get herself back into shape to teach.

CHAPTER FORTY-SIX

It wasn't any easier to get up and go to school the next day. Kaya made it to her classroom later than usual, and a few kids were already waiting outside the door when she unlocked it.

"Ooo, Ms. Walsh has an admirer!" Two or three of the kids catcalled and heckled at the sight of the single yellow rose lying on Kaya's desk.

She marched over to her desk and picked up the rose. Next to it was a simple card, with the words "I'm sorry" penciled across it. She looked at the flower, vaguely aware that the crowd of students was growing and watching her closely. *I have to be strong.*

She dropped the rose into the trash can and sat stiffly in her chair. A few of the kids moaned in disappointment and one even tried to ask who gave her the flower. She ignored them and resolutely pulled her papers from her satchel. It was going to be a long day.

* * *

Ricki didn't really expect a response from Kaya the first day, but she was surprised to overhear students gossiping about it. She realized that, knowing Kaya sometimes ran late, perhaps bribing the janitor to let her leave the rose for Kaya wasn't the best plan. But she planned to do it again tomorrow.

"And every day until she'll give me another chance," she muttered to herself.

"What was that, Sport?"

Ricki had almost forgotten where she was, thinking again about Kaya. College basketball had never been her thing, but Paps liked to watch sports of any kind, and she couldn't turn down his invitation when he'd invited her over. He was excited about the conference tournaments getting started and the drama over who would qualify for March Madness.

"Nothing. Just talking to myself over here."

"Yeah, I noticed you haven't been paying attention to the game." He pointed the remote control at the screen and turned off the television. "What's eating you?"

It was still strange to even consider telling Paps what was really on her mind. She'd spent a lot of time at their house since he'd been released from the hospital, not really going anywhere except there and school. They'd had deeper conversations in the past few days then she could ever remember having before.

This, though, was very hard. She didn't know if she could talk about it just yet.

"Something with your girl, isn't it? That's the only thing I've ever known to put a look like that on a person's face."

Maybe she'd have to talk about it after all.

"She's not my girl anymore, and I don't know how to change that."

"I thought I told you to fix things. You always were a stubborn kid. Why don't you just listen to your old grandpaps?"

She was surprised by the compassion she heard in his heckling, and inwardly berated herself again for wasting so many years fearful of what he might say.

"I tried, Paps, but she won't have me. I fucked up bad." When she realized what she'd said, and who she'd said it to, she glanced up, flushed with embarrassment. Paps did not abide cussing, but this time, his look was more studying than stern.

"You told me you loved her. Were you lying?"

"No!" Ricki had never said a truer word.

"And does she love you?"

"Yes. But I've hurt her badly and she doesn't trust me not to do it again. I can't blame her, either."

"Well, if it's real love, she'll forgive you eventually. Just keep at it." He nodded and raised the remote to turn the game back on.

Ricki didn't have any other plan, and hearing Paps tell her to stick with it brought an encouragement she'd never expected to find in this house. She only hoped that he was right about Kaya's forgiveness.

CHAPTER FORTY-SEVEN

Kaya entered her classroom, picked up the rose, and dropped it into the vase with the others. After a week of throwing them away, some of the girls in her homeroom had complained about such beautiful flowers being wasted. When one of them brought in a vase and pulled the flower out of the trash, Kaya was too stunned to do anything about it. After that, the flowers stayed on the corner of her desk, and she only threw them away as they died.

It had gone on like this for over a month. Kaya didn't want to admit she liked the flowers, and she wouldn't permit herself to smile about them except when she was alone. Ricki hadn't really tried to talk to her, which Kaya realized was completely consistent with her stoic and quiet personality. But the roses were there, one every morning, and Kaya had begun to look forward to seeing them, despite herself.

She wasn't blind to the irony of their role reversal. When once she had sat silently on the bleachers waiting for Ricki to talk to her, she now had a daily reminder of Ricki's patience in waiting for her.

Just waiting isn't enough, though. I can't trust her not to run again, and if I can't trust that, I'll never really trust her.

The days had more or less returned to their routine. She taught, she worked a little late grading papers, she attended the kids' sporting events or concerts or plays. She went home to her solitary apartment. So far, no one had noticed she went to just about everything except the track meets. Or if they had, they hadn't said anything. She imagined some of them understood, Ian and Jamie to name a few. But she wasn't ready to see Ricki in action as an assistant coach. She wasn't healed enough for that.

On an afternoon almost identical to every other, she sat in her classroom an hour after the halls had cleared out, entering grades into the computer. A soft knock at her door startled her, and for a moment, she feared it was Ricki.

She turned and took a moment to orient her mind to the gentleman entering the room.

"Hello, Miss Walsh. I was just walking past and I saw your classroom lights still on. How is everything?"

"I'm doing well, Mr. Fisher. Just catching up on grading papers."

"Good, good. It's always a challenge to keep up as the school year progresses."

He paused, and Kaya got a sinking sense of déjà vu.

"Miss Walsh, I'm glad I caught you. I've been meaning to ask you about something for a few days now."

Oh no.

"As you know, the prom is next month. Since you were so kind as to help with Homecoming, I wondered if you might—"

"I'm sorry, Mr. Fisher, I can't."

He appeared startled that she had interrupted him, and she almost felt sheepish. Cutting off her boss wasn't a great way to keep her job. But the thought of going to prom, when Ricki had asked her, ripped a fresh wound in her heart. There was no way she could do that.

Mr. Fisher took a moment to speak again, the patrician manner slipping slightly from his tone. "Miss Walsh, I'm sure you understand our newer faculty always chaperone the dances. This has been our policy for quite some time."

"I do know that, Mr. Fisher, but I simply can't chaperone the prom." She heard the angst seeping into her voice, and cleared her throat to hide it. "I'm not available."

She saw the annoyance in his expression, and didn't want to upset her good standing at the school. "I'd be happy to help in some other capacity. Maybe with ticket sales or something else."

Mr. Fisher let out an exasperated sigh. "Well, the student council typically handles sales in the cafeteria before school and at lunch, but we do like to have a staff member supervising. The kids have been good in recent years, but we did have a problem some time ago with students refusing some of their peers equal admission through bullying during ticket sales."

"Great. I'll help with that. Just give me the details of what I need to do." *Fuck. I want nothing to do with the damn prom.*

He described her task, still evidently annoyed that he'd have to find someone else to chaperone, and then left. Somehow, Kaya had just let herself be conned into spending every morning and lunch in the cafeteria for a week, starting ten days from now. *But at least I won't have to go to the event itself.*

* * *

Ricki laid the rose and card on Kaya's desk, and walked to her own classroom. Since she'd not had a reason to linger at the track after her morning runs, she'd reverted to her old habit of getting to school very early. The stillness in the hallways helped her find enough peace and strength to tackle another day.

Suddenly, Ian crashed into her room. "Did you hear what your girlfriend went and did yesterday? Fisher is up in arms and the school board is demanding action."

She almost punched him over his callous reference to Kaya as her "girlfriend." He knew they'd broken up and he knew she was broken up over it.

"What the hell are you talking about?"

"She sold prom tickets to a gay couple. A pair of senior boys. Well, the student body president working the sales table next to her went home and told daddy, who happens to be on the board, and now people are in an uproar."

"She what? Oh fuck. That's not going to fly in this town."

"I know, right? Fisher's gonna chew her ass out when she gets here."

But Ricki barely heard his reply. As soon as the words had left her mouth she couldn't believe she'd said them. Why shouldn't that fly in this town? Why shouldn't those boys be allowed to enjoy their prom? God knows she understood what homophobia had cost her. Wasn't it her responsibility as a teacher to make the world a better place for her students?

"Ricki? Did you hear what I just said?"

"What?" She looked up at him. "No, sorry, I missed it."

"I said, they had an emergency meeting last night. The board wants Fisher to refuse the boys tickets and reprimand Kaya for selling to them in the first place. She's got a meeting with him in ten minutes, to resolve the issue before school even starts today."

"Shit. Does she know what it's about? If Fisher blindsides her with this, she's not going to take it well."

"I don't know. I'm only telling you what the teacher rumor-mill is churning out."

Ricki stood up. "I've got to make sure she at least knows the storm she's walking into."

Ian followed her from the classroom. "What are you going to do?"

"I don't know. But I have to do something."

She hurried through the building to Principal Fisher's office. Through the windows of his office she could see that Kaya wasn't yet meeting with him. She could also see just how agitated the situation was, since Fisher was pacing around his desk, occasionally yelling into the phone.

The phone. Ricki pulled hers from her pocket and flicked through the menus for Kaya's name. She walked a few feet down the hall, clear of the sightlines from Fisher's office, and prayed that Kaya might actually pick up.

"Hello?"

"Hey." Hearing Kaya's voice was such a shock to Ricki's system that she lost her train of thought. Honestly, she hadn't expected her to answer.

"Ricki?"

"Hey. Sorry. I just…" Now was not the time to say how good it was to hear her voice. "I heard some rumors this morning and I wanted to check if you were okay."

"Yeah, I'm fine. What kind of rumors?"

"That you've got a meeting with Fisher any minute. Where are you?"

"Walking across the parking lot. How do you know about that?"

The slight edge of suspicion in her tone caused a stab of pain in Ricki's chest. "I told you. Rumors around school. Do you know what it's about?"

"No. Why, do you?"

"Shit," Ricki mumbled, away from the phone, but Kaya must have heard her. "Ricki, tell me what you heard. All I know is Fisher called me last night and asked me to come by for a short talk before class. I get the feeling you know a lot more than I do."

Ricki glanced at her watch. If Ian had been right about the time of their meeting, and Kaya really was on her way into the building, then they might have a minute to talk before she went in to see Fisher. Ricki rounded the corner and saw Kaya just entering the building.

"Look up. I'm right down the hall from you."

Kaya hesitated as Ricki approached, then walked toward and past her. "I've got to get to Fisher's office. Are you going to tell me what you heard?"

The coldness in her voice stung. "I know you still don't want to talk to me, but wait just a moment okay? You'd be better off late than going in there clueless."

Kaya glared at her, but stopped walking. "Talk fast."

When Ricki relayed what she heard, she got exactly the reaction from Kaya that she expected. "Are you fucking kidding me?" Kaya nearly shouted.

"Just take a minute. Breathe. Think for a second and try not to get yourself fired."

"No, I'm not going to breathe. This is ridiculous, and I'm going to tell him as much."

"You're right, but you need to approach this carefully. It won't do anyone any good if you lose your job."

Ricki didn't think when she reached forward and caught Kaya's arm.

Kaya jerked back as if Ricki's touch had burned her. "Don't."

She stared at Ricki a second longer before pivoting and marching away.

Ricki let her go. What else could she do?

CHAPTER FORTY-EIGHT

"I mean, how does something like this turn into such a circus so damn quickly?" Kaya paced by the window of her classroom and vented her frustrations over the phone.

"I don't know, hon," Toni replied. "I'm having a hard time believing this is happening, too."

"I almost quit on the spot. It's insane! He even told me when he conned me into helping that the faculty volunteer was supposed to make sure *the kids* didn't bully their peers through ticketing. He told me that! And now I'm officially on probation and not permitted to speak to anyone about this. I wanted to quit, but I realized that wouldn't really do anyone any good. I've got to stay here and fight this somehow. The boys are going to be refunded their money—they're not permitted to attend the prom unless they take female dates, and they've been warned that they'll be asked to leave immediately if they so much as look at each other at the dance."

She glanced out the window at the commotion in the parking lot. "This whole thing is just sickening. Everyone's in an uproar, there's a fucking media van parked outside and five—*five*—local reporters are interviewing any teacher or student they can get their hands on."

"You're kidding me."

"I wish I was. One of the idiots somehow even got my private cell number and called to ask me if I'd give a statement or interview. I managed to hang up on him before I cussed him out, which is probably for the best since I'm sure he was recording the call."

"I'm actually impressed that you managed that level of control."

"Hey!" Kaya protested, but she realized Toni was teasing her, trying to lighten the mood. She felt so helpless with this whole situation. She'd never even considered that it might be an issue when she'd sold the tickets to the boys at lunch the day before. Now, after a school day of nothing but drama and bickering and absolute lunacy, she was almost afraid to leave her classroom, knowing that she would never make it to her car without being assaulted by reporters or people in the lynch mob that seemed to be gathering in the parking lot.

The only encouraging thing was that hers wasn't the only voice defending the boys. *Well, not that my voice has been part of this at all.* She was so upset over the whole thing that she knew she'd get herself fired—if not arrested—if she joined the fight immediately. Understanding that, so far she'd been avoiding the fray. For now. *I need to figure out how to help those boys.*

"Toni, I don't know how to handle all this. It's just so ridiculous that I can't even comprehend the magnitude of reaction. Why does anybody care? It's a stupid high school prom. The only people who should give a damn are the two boys going, and their biggest worry should be whether their corsages match. I can't believe—"

A sharp knock at her door interrupted her conversation. She turned and saw Mr. Fisher standing in the doorway, looking none too happy.

"I've got to go. I'll call you again later." She disconnected.

"Mr. Fisher." She acknowledged him, and realized there was a second man standing behind him, rigidly observing as if he were at attention.

"Miss Walsh. I'm glad to see you've at least had the sense to avoid the commotion out in the courtyard."

She bristled at his blunt rudeness but managed to hold her tongue.

"Obviously, I recommend you do not speak to the press. Should you feel the need to disregard my advice, understand that you will no longer be a part of Glenwood High. Am I clear?"

Her jaw worked as she fought back the desire to tell him to fuck off, because she quit. *That won't help the boys.* After a moment, she spoke. "Yes, sir."

"I am very disappointed in your disruptive actions. I thought you understood that we are a traditional community that values family and high moral standards. Your liberal city politics are not welcome here, and I am now forced into the unenviable position of cleaning up your mess."

Kaya wasn't quite sure how she managed not to cross the room and punch him, but she held her ground and her silence.

Fisher seemed to be expecting her to argue, almost as if he was waiting for an excuse to fire her. She wondered if the other man was here as a witness to any reaction he might provoke from her. When she refused to speak, he gestured to the man behind him. "This is Officer O'Neill. He'll escort you to your car, to avoid any problems with the media."

"Officer?" Kaya questioned. The man wasn't dressed in uniform.

"Yes." Fisher apparently didn't deem Kaya worthy of any further explanation. He held her gaze a moment longer before leaving without so much as a goodbye.

Officer O'Neill remained in the doorway, watching her as if she were some criminal. *How is this possibly happening right now?* Kaya took a moment to think then grabbed her satchel and shoved in a stack of papers that she knew she wouldn't actually grade tonight. Pulling on her coat, she followed her silent escort from the school building.

CHAPTER FORTY-NINE

Ricki wove her way through the crowd, surprised that the mass wasn't triggering any second thoughts. She had a plan, and she was confident about what she would do. Although her football-playing days had been a lifetime ago, perhaps they had prepared her to perform against all odds in front of a hostile crowd.

Not that she intended this to be a performance. When Kaya had walked away from her that morning, she had been left alone to wonder what else she could do. It didn't take long to figure out there was plenty she could do. At first, her concern had been Kaya, and while part of her hoped her plan might finally sway her to reconsider their relationship, she knew that even if Kaya never looked at her again, this was something she had to do.

Ricki wanted to think it was shocking how the school had reacted to the juicy gossip but in truth, she wasn't surprised. What perhaps had been most amazing to her was actually how many people supported the boys. She had lived so long in a place of internalized homophobia, she'd never realized how many allies there were right here in their community. Of course, they weren't enough to silence those who would have the boys punished.

The crowd was milling restlessly around the school courtyard, and it was easy to overhear more than one ongoing argument. The local media seemed to bask in the sudden uproar as they awaited the official school statement that Fisher was scheduled to make in about fifteen minutes. Rumor was that he would be joined by the chair of the school board. Jack had even set up a podium on the front steps for this hurriedly assembled press conference.

Ricki took a deep breath and closed her eyes, concentrating her energy and visualizing the stack of papers in her hand. It was time to punch the ball into the end zone.

She walked up to the podium and pulled out her coach's whistle. One long sharp blast commanded everyone's attention very quickly.

"Hello." She paused and waited for a few lingering voices to quiet. She was also cognizant of the local news cameras training on her.

"As you may have heard, there's been a bit of excitement here at Glenwood over the past day or so." She waited for a few chuckles to calm down, glad that her public speaking skills weren't as rusty as they felt.

"Well, I know you're all waiting for the important folks to issue a statement in a few minutes, but in the meantime, I'm going to share a few reactions that I've encountered today. For the record, I'm Ricki McGlinn. I'm a math teacher here, as well as an assistant football and track coach and Glenwood High alumna. When I heard that a conflict was brewing over whether or not a young gay couple here at our school should be able to attend the prom, I was at first disheartened that this should be an issue at all. I suspect few here will be surprised that I fully support the boys, and I will do whatever I can to see that all of our students here are able to enjoy what is perhaps the greatest of high school traditions."

A few murmurs bubbled up in the crowd before her, and she waited for them to settle. "It should be a simple and straightforward thing, buying tickets to the prom. But for these two boys and likely others in their class, it was a profound act of courage. They have demonstrated a bravery that many adults, myself included, have lacked. In my past, I haven't had the strength of character that these two have shown, and it cost me the most important person in my life. Their openness and strength in embracing themselves and each other should be applauded and supported, as should all young romance. The fear and anger directed toward them by those who would silence their authenticity are not easy to fight, but I'm here to let them know they are not alone. They are an equal and valued part of the Glenwood family."

She spoke over a rising crowd noise, a chaotic blend of cheers and jeers. "By speaking to you today, I am putting my own job on the line. That's a small risk to take to show these boys we've got their back, and to inform all of our students and the entire community that we are a school where everyone is welcome and accepted. But one voice isn't as strong as ten, or in this case," she held up the papers in her hand, "the seventy-three faculty and eight hundred twenty-six students who have signed my petition in support of these boys and all of our LGBT students, faculty and staff."

The cheers escalated into uproar, and it took several minutes for things to calm down at all. "And that's only counting those I was able to talk to today. I hope many more will speak out in support over the coming days."

With that, Ricki stepped away from the podium and moved into the crowd.

Immediately, she was surrounded. The jostle of people left her unable to really process much of anything, but the local reporters who had the most experience with this sort of chaos quickly found their ways to her, cameras and microphones at the ready.

Questions were hurled in her direction, but she was unable to hear any one clearly. She tried to work her way away from the podium, knowing the attention would be drawn back there when Fisher came out to make the school's official statement. A few shouts concerned her petition, so she turned and spoke to no one in particular. "I've put the originals in a safe place, but here are some copies." She then split the stack and passed them to the greedy hands that demanded the information.

Somehow she managed to push through the mob and eventually separate herself from the crowd. A few of the more persistent people followed her, but many stayed where they were, not wanting to miss the announcements yet to come. Ricki just kept walking until she was finally alone.

* * *

Kaya sat in stunned silence, staring at the television screen but not really paying attention to the continuing commotion. After she'd gotten home, she'd flipped on the television to see what those news vans that had been parked outside her classroom were able to dig up. This was the story of the day, and as she watched clips of interviews, she was amazed at the vehemence with which people expressed their opinions.

Every interviewee seemed to have a different vested interest. Here, a parent who was proud of her gay daughter and the boys who were breaking down doors for all their children. There, a student who thought "those two guys" were "always kind of weird, anyway."

Then in the middle of hearing an elderly man with a lifelong involvement in Glenwood High voicing his disgust at the corrupt and incorrigible kids that populated their town these days, the reporter's microphone had picked up a shrill whistle. Suddenly everyone's attention was on Ricki. Kaya couldn't believe what was happening.

Holy fuck. She just outed herself to the whole town. Not only that, but Ricki had said that Kaya was the most important person in her life. Kaya had never been one to get teary-eyed over those big public proposals and declarations of love that went viral on the Internet. It always seemed a little self-aggrandizing, with the emphasis on the publicity instead of the relationship.

But she knew Ricki was not one to seek attention. And this situation wasn't a safe, celebrated moment. If Kaya was on probation for selling the tickets, Ricki would surely be fired for what she'd just done. And while Kaya had no qualms about packing up and leaving this small, backward town in her rearview mirror, this place was all Ricki had ever known, all she'd ever wanted to know.

And she'd sacrificed it all for two students. *And for me.*

It took a few minutes, but when Kaya eventually got her mind running again, she grabbed her phone. She'd given Toni a continuing play-by-play of everything lately. Every frustration and ache over her breakup with Ricki, and today, every blurb of insanity about a silly high school prom.

"Hey, Toni."

"Hey, hon. Any more craziness to tell me?"

Kaya laughed. "Yeah, you could definitely say that." She smiled to herself as the idea took shape in her mind. "I think I've got a prom to crash."

CHAPTER FIFTY

Ricki couldn't remember a more exciting time in Glenwood history. Even her state title paled in comparison to the intensity of current events. It seemed that the school board was more divided than the teacher rumor mill had initially reported, and after Ricki's impromptu coup, their formal but vague statement that the school was working to determine what was in the best interests of its students had been met with little satisfaction from either camp.

By Monday morning, three board members had resigned, and Principal Fisher was furiously struggling for damage control. But most importantly, the boys were allowed to keep their tickets, and Ricki was allowed to keep her job. It seemed having the signatures of more than half the faculty had had some influence. Her own petition had been augmented by several hundred more students and a complementary list of parents and community members who took up the fight as well. The zoo of a few days prior in the courtyard had diminished, but quite a few people remained, now armed with picket signs.

Ricki was proud of the community's response, rallying to support the boys in a way she would never have imagined. Her fellow coaches, Ian, Jamie and Mike, had united at her side, and even Paps and her mother had wanted to help. She couldn't believe that, for so long, she had hidden a part of herself from these people for fear of rejection. They had her back in a fight she had never seen coming.

The one person who hadn't offered support was the one she had most wanted to see. Kaya hadn't contacted her, hadn't spoken to her. After all the attention crashed down on Ricki, most people seemed to forget that Kaya had been the one to sell the tickets in the first place. Ricki supposed that was a good thing. If Kaya wanted the spotlight, she was more than capable of taking it, but if not, Ricki was grateful to be able to be the distraction that gave her back her privacy.

She'd considered finding a replacement to chaperone for her on the big night, to avoid any further attention, but when she'd mentioned that idea to Ian, he scolded her.

"That'd be a chickenshit move," he declared. "You can't stir up trouble, even if you didn't start it, and then not be there to see it through."

She wasn't so sure, but he insisted. "No. You've got to be there to make sure those boys are okay. They're yours to protect, now." So she decided to stand by her commitment and hoped that things would settle down.

Overall, the two weeks between the eruption of The Great Prom Debate and the event itself were a blur, so much so that the short period every morning during her run and her rose-delivery ritual afterward were the only moments of calm she seemed able to achieve during the day.

The school held the prom at a local hotel, renting out its banquet space and letting the student decorations committee go wild. To Ricki, it didn't really look all that different from homecoming in the school gym, but the students always seemed to be much more excited for this event.

To her great relief, students arrived without any drama or unusual fanfare. A media van parked itself out front, but the reporter and cameraman kept a respectable distance and didn't cause any commotion. When the boys at the center of the storm arrived, stepping from a limo hand in hand, Ricki felt a small swell of pride to see that they seemed to have an entourage of fellow students protecting them and the news crew did nothing more than shoot some video for the nightly telecast.

Most years, she'd stood off to the side absently observing the sea of youth before her. Tonight, she did pay closer attention to the students, keeping particular watch over the boys. The joy on their faces was incredible, as they danced in matching tuxes. Perhaps the best part was that in this moment, they seemed just like any other young couple in love, enjoying the prom. Maybe people were sick of the drama. Or maybe once it came down to it, a dance really was just a dance. Either way, Ricki wasn't about to complain about an uneventful night.

* * *

Kaya waited until the dance was nearly over before entering the hotel. She didn't want to attract attention, and this event had certainly already had enough excitement. Putting on her best Teacher Face, she quickly crossed through the lobby to the ballroom. A few students who had drifted away from the dance to find slightly more private nooks in the hallways pulled apart when she walked past, and she resisted the urge to smile at their antics.

She slipped into the back of the ballroom and eased her way to a semihidden spot along the wall to give her eyes a chance to adjust to the dim lighting.

Ricki wasn't that hard to find. Along with several of the other chaperones, she was off to the side, watching the students enjoy their special night. Kaya followed Ricki's line of sight and when she saw the two boys who'd been at the center of the controversy enjoying a dance together, wide smiles on both their faces and surrounded by friends, Kaya mirrored their grins. *Maybe this town isn't so bad after all.*

Her attention quickly refocused on Ricki. Seeing her, knowing what she had done, Kaya knew she'd made the right decision in coming here tonight. She had never stopped loving Ricki, and it was time she let her know.

As she stepped away from her place against the wall, a voice stopped her. "You know, this seems awfully familiar to me."

She turned and found Ian standing next to her. She was a little surprised such a big man had snuck up on her, but then the music was loud and her attention was elsewhere.

"Hey, Ian," she greeted him. "What do you mean?"

"The last time I was stuck chaperoning one of these things, I remember Ricki watching you across the room, trying to work up the courage to talk to the pretty girl."

She smiled at his compliment. "Ah yes. I understand I have you to thank for her finally talking to me."

He shrugged. "I'm always right, and she knows it. Am I gonna have to twist your arm now, too?"

"No," she laughed. "I think this conversation is long overdue."

"Good. Because she's been a wreck without you. I was just about sick of all her moping."

Kaya appreciated that he was giving his support to their relationship. *Not to mention pointing out that I hurt her and better not do it again.* Kaya doubted that Ricki had told him—or anyone—why they had broken up.

"Well, I guess I should probably go get her out of her rut, then." She smiled at him and squeezed his arm to convey her gratitude, then turned and worked her way along the edge of the room to where Ricki stood.

She carefully ducked around behind her, so Ricki wouldn't see her approach. When she was close enough to be heard without shouting, which was *very* close given the volume of the music, she spoke. "The boys look happy."

Ricki spun around. "Kaya!"

Kaya just smiled.

"What are you doing here?"

Kaya was pleased at having caught her completely off guard, but waited, giving Ricki a moment to catch up.

"I mean," Ricki stammered, "it's not that I don't want you here! You weren't supposed to be chaperoning, and—"

Kaya silenced Ricki's rambling with a quick kiss. Ricki just stared at her.

"What you did for those boys was incredible," she said. "Looking out over that dance floor tonight, seeing how happy they are, how happy all the kids are, you made this possible."

Ricki didn't respond, and Kaya suppressed a grin. "You took a big risk, much bigger and much more calculated than anything I did to start the drama. And you won. You made tonight possible for them, and for us."

Kaya waited. Finally, Ricki opened her mouth and managed, "You kissed me."

Kaya laughed. "Yes."

"You kissed me," Ricki repeated, a smile beginning to dance in her ice-blue eyes.

"Yes. Would you like me to do it again?"

Ricki reached down and caught Kaya's hand. "Yes, but only if it's a sign of things to come."

"I certainly hope so." But Kaya held back, knowing this wasn't the time or the place.

The sparkle in Ricki's eyes turned serious. "Kaya, I'm sorry for what I did to you. I was a mess. I drove you away. I'm so sorry. Please, please forgive me."

Kaya brushed away the tear that threatened to fall down Ricki's cheek. *God, I want to hold you.* Ricki was exposed, letting herself be vulnerable in a way that she never would have before. Kaya loved her all the more for it.

"Ricki, I forgave you after the first dozen roses. But I was too afraid to give us another chance. I was too hurt, and scared that you would always run from me."

"I'm sor—"

"Shhh." Kaya quieted her with the gentlest touch of her finger to Ricki's lips. "You don't need to apologize. You've shown me, shown all of Glenwood, that this is behind us. So please, I want to look ahead now. I want to take on the future. With you."

Ricki's smile lit Kaya's world. "I love you, Ricki."

"I love you, Kaya. I can't believe I'm lucky enough to have you in my life."

The DJ's voice came over the speakers. "All right, all you young couples out there. I've got one more song for you tonight. Let's hear it for the last dance of prom."

As the ageless lyrics of "I Don't Want to Miss A Thing" began, Ricki reached up and caught Kaya's other hand where it now rested on her shoulder. Pulling her ahead, both hands in hers, she smiled. "Kaya, may I have this dance?"

Dedication

For all of us who have lost a loved one, especially those who have suffered sudden loss. May we always remember the good times, and never forget the love.

Bella Books, Inc.

Women. Books. Even Better Together.

P.O. Box 10543
Tallahassee, FL 32302

Phone: 800-729-4992
www.bellabooks.com